D0893626

The Ransom Game

By the same author:
The Suicide Murders

THE
RANSOM GAME

A Benny Cooperman Mystery

HOWARD ENGEL

Howard Engel (signature)

St. Martin's Press
New York

Library of Congress Cataloging in Publication Data

Engel, Howard, 1931—
    The ransom game.

    I. Title.
PR9199.3.E49R3   1984   813'.54   84-13281
ISBN 0-312-66383-8

First published in Canada by Clarke, Irwin and Co. Ltd.

First U.S. Edition

10 9 8 7 6 5 4 3 2 1

To my mother and father

ONE

The city was beginning to look deserted. Everybody who could afford to go to Florida was in Florida. My mother and father were in Florida, my brother Sam, the surgeon, was in Florida, my cousin Melvyn, the lawyer, was in Florida. Even the radio announcer who usually reads the local weather was in Florida. I can remember a time when Melvyn couldn't even read the time. I taught him. Now he was in Florida, sitting by a swimming pool getting a tan all over his hairy body while I, Benny Cooperman, was here in Grantham. No matter how I examined it, I couldn't make it come out looking fair. The coldest part of the winter, with starlings and sparrows falling stiff from the trees, frost creeping under my door and climbing the stairs two at a time, and I sat here, waiting for a client to read my sign: "Benjamin Cooperman, Licensed Private Investigator", and come in asking me to solve the sudden disappearance of a long-lost rich uncle. Nothing easier, in the middle of February: he's gone to Florida.

From the window I could look down on St. Andrew Street. The black pavement was chilled white, the frosty breath of the manholes rose straight up. Not a drop of snow as far as the eye could see; somehow that made it look even colder. I tried to find the evidence for cold without snow, just to kill the time until I could legitimately lock up the office and have some lunch. I gave myself points for the white salt stains on the cars, and the white lime on the brick wall of the bank. There was no colour anywhere, from the gray sky down to the gray and nearly deserted sidewalks.

I was occupied with these constructive thoughts, when I heard a knock on the frosted glass of the door. It was a feeble knock, and the knocker had obviously not seen the words "Come in," written in peeling gold-leaf at the bottom of the sign. I shouted the same message at the door and it opened an inch at a time.

"Are you Mr. Cooperman?" The question was asked by a good-looking blonde on the thirtyish side of twenty-five, and I didn't mind a bit. I nodded and heard my chair squeak behind me as I got up and came around the desk to help her off with her dusty blue Persian lamb coat. Her eyes were big and blue, and I guessed that under her expensive fur she was very nicely put together. She didn't quite come apart as she wriggled out of the sleeves. She was wearing a fuzzy white turtle-neck sweater and a light blue skirt with a slit up one side, so that when she sat down, smoothing her skirt under her, I got a glimpse of long lean legs that seemed to go on forever. She was wearing a couple of rings, which didn't match the coat. They were big, chunky pieces of costume jewelry, one with a heavy opaque green stone that drew attention to her small hands. These she folded in her lap.

"I saw your sign, and read your ad in the Yellow Pages?" she asked rather than told me. I was all at once gainfully employed, taking in every detail of her appearance and manner. What did she add up to? She was a cross between a burlesque queen, with her full figure and Betty Boop mouth, a mouth that cried out to be chewing gum, and a young middle-class matron with shopping list and golf scores at the bottom of her handbag. She caught me looking at her. There was an unembarrassed hitching up of an eyebrow, and we both grinned. I suddenly felt silly standing in front of her, when there was a whole uninhabited office for us to share, so I retreated around to my side of the bleached oak desk and settled into my squeaky chair in a manner that was supposed to inspire confidence. I tried to look grave. I didn't make a steeple with my fingers, but I considered it.

"I see," I said seriously about nothing whatever. "And how may I help you, Miss. . .?"

"Falkirk. Muriel Falkirk. Do you mind if I smoke?" I pushed my pack of Player's her way, but she frowned at them, taking a package of menthols from her purse. I leaned across the desk with its accumulation of overdue bills and lit her cigarette. She smelled of perfume of the middle range: something shy of Chanel Number 5, a little over-spiced and cloying for my taste. The scent made me wonder where she'd picked up the fur coat.

"Thank you," she said, taking another deep drag and holding on to the smoke like it wasn't just cigarette smoke before letting it go. "I don't know where to begin, Mr. Cooperman. I guess if I knew that, I wouldn't be sitting here." She stared at the big green ring on her right hand for a minute, then lifted her blue eyes level with mine.

"Do you know the name Johnny Rosa?" She opened her eyes astoundingly; I wanted to say, "Yes, yes" without thinking. I wanted to be able to solve all of her problems. When I unhooked my eyes from hers, I tried to think. The name was located, after a minute's reflection, swimming somewhere in the deep water out near the horizon of my memory. I tried to tow it home. It would have been harder if George Warren hadn't drowned in his pool before Christmas.

"Johnny Rosa," I repeated. "Wasn't he mixed up in the Warren kidnapping some years ago?" She nodded, while flicking an ash into my overcrowded ashtray. I pulled a Player's from my pack and lit it, watching the blue smoke rise from the spent match. Muriel Falkirk crossed her legs and I privately seconded the motion. I tried to turn the light on what I could remember of the case. I continued quickly: "Warren's daughter was snatched, held for a couple of days and released when the ransom was paid. The police traced Rosa and a couple of friends. . ."

"Three friends."

". . . and they all ended up sewing mailbags at Kingston. Rosa drew a fifteen-year sentence, I think, the others were hit less hard. The ransom money, I don't think that was ever recovered."

"That's right. I don't believe it ever was." She smiled at me as though we'd both accidentally stumbled over a crock of emeralds on the doorstep.

"Well, that exhausts me on the subject. If I'd known that was going to be one of your questions, I would have read up on the case. As I remember, the *Beacon* was full of it, and the out-of-town papers sent in their hot shots. One of the Toronto papers brought in an airplane. The hotels were full-up, the streets crowded. We don't attract notice like that too often in twenty years." I looked at her steadily, or as steadily as I could manage. "You knew Johnny Rosa?" She nodded.

"I first met him down in Florida about eight years ago." She took a puff with her head tilted. "He was running a numbers scam in Miami Beach, and he came to my place every month to do his arithmetic. I ran into him again in Kingston. I was visiting a friend and recognized Johnny in that rinky-dink railway station. He'd just gotten out on parole, and we talked all the way back on the train to Toronto. I gave him my number here, and was surprised when he looked me up. But then he was at loose ends and so was I. We went over the river to Buffalo for drinks and dinner, and. . ." She turned her head in the direction of the traffic on St. Andrew Street. "And . . . he moved in with me. That was about two months ago. Then, last month, still on parole, he disappeared. Vanished into thin air. I've had a parole board guy snooping around my place twice, and he thinks I know where Johnny's disappeared to. I'm worried, Mr. Cooperman. Johnny's a tough customer and all that, but he's been out of circulation for six years. And there are at least three guys who are sore at him because of that kidnapping."

"The Warren family aside, of course."

"Of course. You see, Mr. Cooperman, I sort of still like the ugly mug, and I'd like to find out whether he's just pushed off or whether he's come to grief of some kind. If he just took

4

a powder and ditched me, well, I'll get over that. It won't be the first time. But if some creep has scattered him, I want to know who did it and see to it that lots of *other* people know who did it."

"How did you happen to pick on me?" I asked. "This is a long way from most of Johnny Rosa's friends, isn't it?"

"He's got pals all over the map: Miami, Vegas, L.A., Toronto. You name it. He liked it here. It was quiet, but close to Buffalo and the track at Fort Erie."

"What I mean is, why don't you get a Toronto private investigator involved? Why pick on me? I generally concentrate on divorce work, you know, though I admit that's not exactly blooming as it once did. I can understand why you might not want to go to the police about Johnny, but why not let the parole board find him. They're pretty good at that. How did you say you got my name again?" I looked at her. It was hard not to, even while she was chewing on the corner of her mouth. On her it looked good. And so did the winter light coming through the window, illuminating her blonde hair. She opened her mouth as though she was going to speak, and then she shrugged and started again.

"My mother works as a cleaning lady. She's been going to Mrs. Chester Yates for the last fifteen years or so, ever since I can remember. She told me how you helped Mrs. Yates last year. Mom says that she was more than happy with the way you solved her husband's murder. She also said that you weren't all that expensive."

"Hold your horses. We're a long way from talking about money. Tell me first, what kind of checking you've done on your own."

"I've called a few friends down in Miami to see if Johnny'd turned up down there. They say he hasn't. He hasn't been in L.A. or Las Vegas either."

"And you believe them?"

"I guess I don't have any reason to believe they'd string me. They know me well enough to know that I'm not trying to sink my hooks into him. Unlike some other people I could mention."

"We'll get to them." My cigarette had gone out between my fingers. I abandoned it on top of the other butts in the ashtray. I paused. Usually, I've found, if you put a hole in a conversation, the other party fills it, often in a revealing way.

"Look, I know that Johnny's been in and out of the rackets since he was old enough to jimmy open gum machines, but I know him pretty good, and I don't think he would have lammed out on me without planting a goodbye kiss. He isn't that sort of guy, you know?"

"So you really think that he didn't disappear voluntarily?"

"I guess you could say that. I don't even want to think that he's come to grief. Sure he's made a lot of people sore at him one time and another, but what else is new?" She was relaxing a little and her native idiom returned. "If people settled all the scores they have against acquaintances of mine, I'd soon be surrounded by tombstones. Nobody takes things that seriously. And besides, he hasn't been out of the cooler long enough to get rid of his Kingston pallor, let alone get back into the rackets again. So you see, Mr. Cooperman . . ."

"Call me Benny, if it's easier." I smiled, but she didn't catch it. I rubbed my star sapphire ring against the lapel of my jacket, hoping that it would prove magical and give me another three inches of height at this the crucial stage in the interview.

"So you see, Benny, I'd like you to dig him up for me"—she winced at the expression—"and I hope it doesn't come to that."

"Is your interest in Johnny Rosa strictly sentimental, Miss Falkirk?" I watched her watching me back.

"If I understand what you are saying, sure it is. What's the matter with sentiment? You got something against it? Sure, I lent him some money to help get him on his feet again. But I don't care about the money, although I wouldn't mind seeing some of it again. It's really a matter of hunches. I had a hunch that Johnny Rosa was an okay guy, as guys go, so if Johnny skipped with my two grand, I want to know about it, because that means I made a big mistake in reading the bastard. And that would bother me more than the two gees, you know? If he's been plowed, I want to know about that too. I guess I owe him. What do you think?" She was coming at me again with those wide-open eyes of hers. I avoided contact.

"How should I know? Off the top of my head I'd say you'd be crazy to throw good money after bad. Johnny Rosa's no choirboy. Never was. Chances are he was using you until he found a spot in some organization where his talents are known. It doesn't mean anyone chose to shut him up permanently."

"I can think of five hundred thousand reasons why somebody might want to get to Johnny." She was leaning toward me across the desk. I could hear the stoplights changing from red to green outside in the street.

"That's a lot of reasons. You're talking about the ransom money?"

"Johnny was the last to see it. If Johnny doesn't know where it is, nobody does." It was time to get to work.

"If he was so well fixed, why did he take your money?"

"I can't figure that one either. Maybe that has something to do with why he took off so fast. He left for work and that's the last I saw of him. I've still got his razor and toothbrush. He even left the suits he'd just bought. It wouldn't have hurt to say goodbye."

"Did he look worried the last few times you saw him?"

"Not that I noticed. Johnny was always clowning about everything, always telling jokes, you know? You could never tell what he had on his mind, because there was always a grin on his face." Her mouth twisted in a pained smile, like she thought I was going to blame her for Johnny.

"Now tell me about the people who might want to talk things over with him."

"Well, on the top of the list there are cops in five flavours: local cops, provincial cops, the Mounties, insurance investigators and private cops. To say nothing of parole supervisors. They followed him to work and sat in front of the apartment all night waiting for him to make a move. Honest to God, you could trip over them just going to buy a pack of cigarettes."

"What about the three who went to the slammer with Johnny?"

"Those three!"

7

"Where are they all now? How can I contact them?"
Muriel Falkirk thought for a moment, and when she had the
information assembled, let me have it. Ian Todd, once a
lawyer, was working as a security guard for a furniture company, amid much publicity on the part of the owner who was
determined to milk the situation for all it was worth. Bill
Ashland, who had been a stock promoter before the kidnapping, was still working on the fringe of the market as a tipster.
The third man, Rolf Knudsen, had blown his contacts in
advertising and public relations, and was now selling insurance. That gave me something to start with.

"Then you'll see what you can do?" she asked, her smile
showing a nice set of white teeth.

"I'll play around with it for a few days. If I'm getting
anywhere, you can decide whether to keep me going. If I crap
out, you can always say you tried. I'll do what I can. For the
full treatment, and that means shoving everything else out of
the way so that this gets top priority, I get a hundred a day plus
expenses with an extra hundred at the start to keep me honest
and interested." I felt like a cop reading her her rights. "This
kind of thing, as I told you, is a little out of my line. That
Yates case was an exception. I fell into that. Have you got
anything else you can give me, Miss Falkirk? I can't see that
I'm going to get very far with Johnny Rosa's friends with my
private investigator's licence."

"I see what you mean. Information doesn't flake off
those guys easy. You could use my name. If they know that
you're working for me, they might open up a little more than if
you were the law. It's not much."

"You're right, it isn't. Okay, who else is after Johnny?
Have we covered the field?"

"I hate to say it, but I guess every hood in the country is
interested more or less. I mean, we couldn't go out like normal
people. It was like he was a movie star, only not so nice. It
always started friendly—somebody'd send over free drinks to
our table, then there'd be an argument and we'd have to grab
our coats. Sometimes there would be cars following us. Once
we were nearly pushed off the road. It was scary. So we didn't
go out much. Besides, he had shift work at the foundry."

"Tell me about that."

"It was something I was able to arrange. Something to satisfy the parole board. It's the Grantham-Niagara Foundry. You know, that red-brick building you can see from the High Level Bridge?"

"You said it was shift work?"

"Yeah," she said a little bitterly. "I thought I'd seen the last of a shift-working man ten years ago. Johnny used to duke in and out of that noise-works in my car. I couldn't see him on public transportation with a lunch pail, could I?"

"Has the car turned up?" She was looking at the big green stone in her ring again, like she was trying to remember where the secret catch was that opened it up. I wondered what she imagined was inside.

"It wasn't much of a car, but it was handy."

"Can you give me the details on it: the year, make, model, licence number, colour, that sort of thing?"

"Sure. It was a yellow Volkswagen, about ten years old and looking like it had been on the road closer to twenty. It was in and out of the garage once a month for repairs."

"Did you report it missing?"

"I didn't report Johnny missing. How could I report the damned car?" She had a point.

"Do you have the licence number?" She gave it to me and at last I had a fact to write on the yellow legal foolscap pad in front of me.

She now looked like she wanted to be going. She glanced to each side of her and then took her first impatient breath.

"Well," I said, "I'll certainly give the case my full attention."

She reached into her handbag and brought out a matched set of twenty-dollar bills. She laid them out on her end of my desk like she was setting up the bank for an evening of *Monopoly*. She also fished up a pencil stub from her bottomless purse, and, at my request, gave me her address and phone number. She wrote both in an unpracticed schoolgirl's hand. She folded the paper and handed it to me with a movement that was almost a flounce. Her eyes grabbed mine with a look of complicity. I kept mine fixed on the bridge of her nose.

I was already drunk on angora, and something of an expert after the last half hour in how the knitting stands up to regular deep breathing. As a respectable private investigator, I had to make sure that she didn't get the wrong idea about me. I guessed that in her time she'd met a few who'd got the wrong idea about her.

As soon as she'd gone, I looked at the money lying there so reassuringly and started wondering what I might do to earn it. For a minute, I played with the notion of picking up Johnny Rosa's trail, far from the February chill of Grantham, in the hotels along the ocean front at Miami Beach. I let this thought thaw me for a few minutes, and then came back to the reality of my mother's pet rubber plant and the dieffenbachias that had to be attended to regularly right here at home. My mother wouldn't be able to rub suntan lotion on her freckled shoulders down there if she doubted for a moment that I was on the job up here.

I was beginning to feel I'd earned lunch at least, and thought of closing up the shop. Before I did, I put in a call to the Regional Police and gave a voice, which sounded like it wanted its lunch too, the details Muriel had given me about her car. I left my name and the voice promised on its mother's grave that it would get back to me if anything developed. On the whole, cops shouldn't try to be comedians.

TWO

The wind whipped under my overcoat feeling for my liver. As I cut across St. Andrew Street in search of a bite of lunch at the United Cigar Store, all of February concentrated its power on the small of my back. I could feel needles playing with my eyeballs and my knees felt numb where they touched the cloth of my trousers. I was feeling pretty sorry for myself when I saw a girl come out of the United in a little jacket and a wispy skirt. She headed into the wind and out of sight. They must be built differently I thought. Inside the door of the United, I shed my hat and coat and stood for a while rubbing my red wrists like a car salesman closing a deal until something like circulation returned. A chill wind blew through the door whenever anyone went near it, and sent invisible fingers riffling through the magazine rack. In this weather, even the magazines that nobody picked up looked shopworn.

I perched in my usual spot at the green marble counter and ordered a chopped egg sandwich on white, toasted, with milk and vanilla ice cream to follow. The girl wrote it down like I was dictating the Ten Commandments in the original. There was a picture of a smiling waitress in a cap printed in blue at the top of the check she left beside the salt and pepper shakers. I compared the grim girl behind the counter with the portrait on the check, and wondered what the world was coming to.

I was at a complete loss as to how to go about trying to find Johnny Rosa. When a cheap hoodlum doesn't want to indulge in social intercourse, there are few ways to compel him to come out of his hole. I figured he was in a hole. He was alive in it or he was dead in it, but he was in there all right. This was a lot harder than standing under a dripping eavestrough waiting for a clear view of illicit love in bloom. I could start looking in Papertown, I thought. I didn't think I'd find out anything, but the word would be out that I was looking. If he could still hear and got curious, he could always find me.

11

Two teenage girls in nylon parkas blew into the store. The wind that followed them tried to grab the magazines from the dirty fingers of the regular boys in the chorus line who stood facing the magazine rack. The girls blew on their hands, tears glistening on their cheeks, as they cut through the line to find what they wanted. The boys were less direct. They didn't just buy the girlie magazines of their choice, as is every man's right in a free country. No, they preferred to look and to handle but not, in the end, to buy. Buying a girlie magazine represented life without a ginger ale mix; it was too strong a shot for most of them. One day, maybe one of them would change his luck, make a real commitment to life, and buy one. But I only half believed it. The two girls by this time had their magazines paid for and sat warming their hands on mugs of coffee.

I paid my bill, the waitress saluted me by tipping the toothpick in her mouth so that it pointed to her short nose, and I made it back through the February wind to my office. A bowel-clawing wind pushed me to my door. Safe upstairs and overheated again, I put in a call to a poolroom I knew in Papertown, asking the owner, whose falsetto surprised me, to get Binny Logan to call. Binny walked and talked like an extra from *Guys and Dolls,* but there wasn't much he didn't know about life in the south end. Naturally, I didn't expect him to be there. No self-respecting poolhall operator would deliver a message while it was fresh. Like fine wines, a phone message gets better the longer you hold on to it.

Then I called Ella Beames at the public library and told her I was coming down to read some old papers on the iron lung. She laughed and asked what dates I wanted. She knew me pretty well. I told her I wanted everything she had on the Warren girl's kidnapping. She didn't insist on my having the exact date. Ella was like that; she liked doing her job well.

The new library in town couldn't be more different from the old one if it tried. The old place had been full of books on racks in rows with people scattered all over the place, some reading under green porcelain lamps, some chatting to the girl at the check-out desk, sometimes exchanging views about the books around them. This new place started out trying to fool people into thinking that it wasn't a library at all but a picnic ground. There were pools and a fountain, and even a cobblestone bridge crossing a babbling brook. Wherever you went, you were followed by the sound of running water, which is not the easiest sound to live with when you've settled down to a good read. The carpets on the three floors were colour-coded, each being a slightly different shade of burnt orange. At the time the place opened, the *Beacon* carried a story about how the architect had been inspired by an empty egg-cup. I was glad that they'd brought people like Ella Beames over from the old place. You needed the human touch under those bright triangular lights.

I found Ella at her desk in the Special Collections department. She handed me three boxes of microfilm and a key to the microfilm room. It took me less than twenty minutes to find it, and half that again to fit the film on the machine. My machine was the only vacant viewer in a line of five. To an observer we might have been a bunch of paraplegic exiles from the magazine rack at the United.

The *Beacon* had had a field day with the Warren case. Only a war could have filled more space. There was a profile of George Warren, the wealthy chairman of Archon Incorporated, one of the largest and most diversified conglomerates on the exchange. I found that the cornerstone of the Warren fortune was shoepolish. First *Warren Blacking* in Britain, where the first of the Warrens employed the youthful Charles Dickens as a bottle labeller near Hungerford Stairs on the Thames. Then *Warren Shoepolish* in North America at the time of the first World War. It was after the second that the big push came: a branching out into wider and wider fields. In the records of Archon, the holding company that linked all these fields to a common Bay Street address, George Warren's name was prominent at the time, but in the most recent history his name was hard to find. For the ten years or so preceding the kidnapping, Warren appeared to have contrived to stay out of the papers.

There was a picture of the large house he had built up on the Escarpment so that it looked down on the few thousand acres of prime real estate he owned through one of his minor holdings. Passing mention was made of his private yacht club, built out of pique after a disagreement with the local millionaires-only club on the Niagara River, his fleet of Lear jets, his private island in the Caribbean, and his beautiful daughter, Gloria, who had become the focus of a kidnapping drama. There'd been an older brother, killed in a car accident shortly before the kidnapping. There was rather less said about him than the others, and I made a mental note to find out why. Warren's wife had divorced him for a handsome settlement a decade before and had quickly spent that and the remainder of her active life at the gambling tables in the south of France. Now she lived quietly in genteel poverty near Ste-Maxime.

I got the feeling that the family had been out of bounds to reporters on the paper before Gloria Warren's abduction. I wasn't surprised to see that Archon Incorporated owned the *Beacon*. Most of the pictures looked about thirty years old and came from out-of-town sources. Several showed the summer cottage at Dittrick Lake, a fashionable piece of vacationland not far from Grantham. The paper's artist had had a good time marking an X where the door to the frame cottage had been forced, arrows where the kidnappers' car had been parked and more arrows and dotted lines criss-crossing maps of the whole territory involved in the case.

Gloria had been staying for the long Labour Day weekend at the lakeside cottage. Her friend, Robert H. Jarman, had driven up for the day to go waterskiing with her. When they returned from the wharf to the cottage, about twenty yards distant, Gloria, entering the house first, was grabbed from behind. At the same moment, Jarman was sapped on the head. Neither saw a face. Jarman woke up tied hand and foot in the kitchen of the cottage with the ransom demand pinned to his beach robe. Immediately he got loose, he telephoned George Warren. He and Warren knew one another, but Jarman wasn't one of the family circle, I gathered. They contacted the Regional Police here in Grantham, and they brought in the Provincial Police because the lake was in their part of the forest. A joint war-room was established, the ransom note was studied and the police advised Warren to pretend to go along with the ransom demand. The kidnappers promised to return the girl unharmed on the payment of one million dollars. Warren was told to be at a certain public telephone booth in a crowded Grantham shopping mall at a certain time. He was warned not to go to the police, and told that his movements were being watched at all times. Very, very neat.

Warren and Jarman took the money in two suitcases to the phone booth. They only brought five hundred thousand, which was haggling a little, I thought. The kidnappers could take it or leave it and kill the girl. Warren figured they'd jump for five hundred and take their licking like the honest hoods they were. Warren had raised the money through a bank he directed on the side. Jarman got to carry it. The police stood by in unmarked cars, but might as well have been disguised in T-shirts bearing the inscription *Police Athletic Club*. A bugging device had been placed in one of the suitcases so that the bad guys could be traced and followed by the modern miracle of electronic tracking. Only somebody forgot to put in fresh batteries or something, and the modern miracle gave way to road blocks and tracking dogs on loan from the Provincial Police. At least they used real money. The temptation to use cut-up strips of paper instead must have been all but irresistible.

"We could have used phoney money," a senior policeman explained, "but anything could have happened. How much money is a woman's life worth?" I hope he asked George Warren that one. Not a cent over half a million.

Soon the money was exchanged. Again, nobody saw anybody. Warren and Jarman were told to move to another country phone booth and there they were given instructions about where to drop the money and where to go to discover the missing girl. They found her wrapped up in a sleeping bag, trussed up like Sunday dinner, in an abandoned shed, an hour's drive from where the pick-up was made. She was unharmed if you overlook a little shock and dehydration. She didn't see a face or hear a word. There was a photograph of her with her head lowered and Jarman protecting her with one arm and making an ugly gesture at the camera with the other. His was a face you wouldn't want to meet coming the opposite way along a cinder path.

With the failure of the electronic bugging device, the police sealed off all highways and secondary roads within the Niagara Peninsula. They searched thousands of cars, upsetting countless tourists homeward-bound after the long holiday weekend. When the cops began getting their breaks they came from tips. There were lots of those, but in the end one of them paid off. Someone drew their attention to some swinging bachelors who met regularly in Suite 616 of the Norton Apartments. After a few discreet calls, a few questions and answers, one group of men was isolated. In less than two weeks the four kidnappers were in custody. In three months, they had begun serving long sentences in Kingston Penitentiary.

Crime doesn't pay. Except that somewhere on the Niagara Peninsula, probably not twenty or thirty miles from where I was sitting, half a million dollars lay bundled up in two suitcases, just waiting to be picked up. I wondered whether I'd missed the item about the recovery of the money, but I hadn't. The money was still there all right, and only Johnny Rosa knew where to pick it up. I could get interested in Johnny myself with big bucks like that riding just over the top of the next hill.

That's the sap of what I found in the main newspaper clippings. Then there were notices of parole hearings, a journalistic flurry of agitation about the fact that the Grantham kidnappers were serving a bigger part of their sentences than some kidnappers from Toronto in another case, and finally reports of who got released when.

On my way out, I dug into a pile of recent *Beacons* for the account of Warren's death. I found it six weeks down in the stack. It told how the millionaire financier had drowned in his heated pool at home. He was 72 and in the habit of taking a morning swim. He'd been discovered at the bottom of the pool by a servant who'd brought him his morning coffee and paper. And it continued for a dozen more paragraphs telling about his estimated wealth—in excess of thirteen million a year—and the funeral arrangements. It gave another recapitulation of the kidnapping, and some speculation about the effect of his death on Archon Corporation. It ended with a bit of news I'd missed:

> Warren is survived by his daughter, Gloria, Mrs. Robert H. Jarman.

That fellow Jarman knew a good thing when he saw it, no mistake about that. I thought that maybe I'd pay a call on the couple. Since I was trying to locate Johnny Rosa, I felt practically one of the family.

THREE

I was surfing a few hundred yards from shore, just coming up beautifully on the crest of a wave that peeled away under me, when I heard a sharp warning from a big cabin cruiser trying for the same stretch of ocean. It hooted at me about fifty times, without changing course. It came toward me like a shark only a hundred times bigger. I shouted at the top of my voice, but it overwhelmed me and everything went blue. And then I was sitting up in sweaty pajamas with the phone in my hand and the bedclothes tangled about my knees.

"Hello?" I asked, wondering whether it was a complaint from the cockpit of the cruiser.

"You Cooperman?" a voice asked.

"Yeah. Who is this?"

"It's me, Binny. The word is out you want to talk to me."

"Binny, hold on a second." I reached into my jacket pocket for my cigarettes. When I was lit, and my hands had stopped shaking, I reached for the phone again. "Hello, Binny, what do you know, what do you say?"

"Little of this, little of that. You want to chat, ask me about my old man, and I should ask you are you getting much, Benny, or what do you want from my young life, eh?"

"Binny, have you seen Johnny Rosa since he got out?" I could hear the line hum between my hotel room and Paper-town, like somebody was hanging up his shorts on the wire.

"Cooperman, not you too? Everybody's looking for Johnny. You thing he's going to walk into the poolroom? He'd never walk out alive. I mean, if you can't buy a piece of half a million, you could grab a piece of Johnny."

"You know Muriel Falkirk?"

"What's to know? She used to be Eddie Milano's girl. I hear that she and Johnny had been keeping house in a quiet way since he got out. She's a good looking broad, what do you want me to say?"

"Is she straight?"

"What am I, a philosopher? What's straight, for crying out loud? She's been around, she's seen a lot. A lot of people know her. She thinks she knows everybody."

"What are the odds on Johnny being around next Christmas?"

Binny thought a moment, then: "Same odds as the Second Coming. Cooperman, what are you mixed up in?"

I could see the end of my cigarette in the mirror across the room. I couldn't see much more, although the neon light from the hotel sign was turning the pillow blue then pink. "Don't ask me, pal. I get roped into these things. If you hear anything about Johnny, I'd appreciate, you know."

"Sure, Benny. See you." And he was gone. I looked at the illuminated dial of my watch. It was nearly three in the morning. I knew that I wasn't going to get any more sleep, so I

18

pulled a paperback off the chair from under my shorts and read until the neon blinked out and the trucks began coming from out in the country to the farmers' market.

By the time I'd hauled myself out of the hotel and into the chair behind my desk, I could think of at least fifty things I should have asked Binny when he called.

I resolved to write myself a stiff note about it. One of the troubles of working for yourself is that there is no boss to tear a strip off you. What I needed was the kind of push my older brother had. He sprinted through medical school and didn't stop to catch his breath until he'd been appointed head of surgery at Toronto General. His left-over push is now devoted to collecting antique cars and fighting minor traffic violations. He could spare me a little. Not too much. I could overdo it. I could become such a success I wouldn't want to know me.

I looked up the address of the local office of the National Parole Board, and found it under Correctional Services of Canada. It was in the post office building, the one that was built just before a big general election, like all the post offices in this country. I spent nearly an hour trying to sort through the papers on my desk, putting answered correspondence in one file folder and unanswered correspondence in the same folder, until I got fed up. Even the prospect of trying to find Johnny Rosa or any other needle in any other haystack looked better.

A dark blue Mustang pulled away from the curb just after I turned the Olds up the lane and out into the one-way traffic. There were two men in the car, and I wouldn't have noticed them at all except that they were still behind me as I grabbed a parking spot with forty free minutes on the meter. The car went by me like a black cat on a Friday.

The door of the Correctional Services office was painted the sort of green you paint a door when you want it to say, "Come on in, this isn't as serious a place as you thought; we're real friendly here." They should have stuck with the bilious brown of the old days; the brown was honest, the new green looked like a lie. The general office pool was furnished with typewriters that looked as though they might have been acquired from a big metropolitan daily after having been used to write up the War of 1812. The girls behind them looked considerably newer. It was odd thinking that the machines were already busy at work when they were still in the nursery. It wasn't a big operation. One office looked like that of the boss, and I crossed to it without causing a stir. The name on the plastic plaque on the door read "Nelson Christie". I knocked. When I went in, Christie was seated behind his desk nibbling at his lunch which he'd spread in front of him on a paper towel. I counted seven green grapes, a sprig of green onion and a small piece of a sandwich. If he wasn't diabetic, he should have got a divorce.

"You're not McDade," he challenged.

"I never said I was."

"Well, what do you want? This is my lunch. I've got to be in Hamilton at noon. Talk to Simpson. *Miss Wright!* What do you want anyway?"

"I want to talk to you about Johnny Rosa."

"You're not a Horseman? Who are you?"

"Yes, Mr. Christie?" said a head in the door.

"Never mind, never mind. I asked you a question."

"I heard you. My name is Cooperman and I hold a private investigator's licence. My client is trying . . ."

"Come on, let's have a look at your paper. Can't be too careful. Everybody plays tricks these days." I handed him my wallet with the right plastic window open, and he looked at it and, with no apparent embarrassment, looked through my driver's licence, ownership papers, insurance and a few credit cards. I guess that parolees don't lean over the desk and grab their property back again. Neither did this private investigator.

"All right, Mr. Cooperman, how much do you know?" He rested his pointed chin on his folded hands, supported by elbows about a foot apart on the green desk blotter. He was grinning with large dentures which he kept immaculately, living proof that it was the second chance that counted.

"I know that he got out of prison three months ago, and that he came here and that he has disappeared."

" 'Disappeared'? That's a little melodramatic, isn't it?

He's been eliminated, that's what's happened, and, speaking off the record, why not? He has acquired a pack of enemies, you know, and a greedy lot they are. Today we are getting out a Canada-wide warrant for his arrest. We've done all we can do. I put my best man on it, and he hasn't found a thing in two weeks. I've suggested to the Mounties that they might save a lot of trouble by dragging the canal for him. That bandit Johnny Rosa is as dead as this desktop, if you ask me. He left his girl friend without a word, didn't even take the flash suits he'd bought. No, when he left town, it was to meet with his murderer, no mistake. What do you make of it?"

"Could be the way you plot it. Could be it was made to look that way. Did you know Rosa?"

"Of course I knew him. I get to know them all. We deal with the big criminals here, none of your penny ante provincial cases. All these people have done time measured in years, not months. All these files are fat, Mr. Cooperman." He got up from his chair and made the three steps to the filing cabinet without a wasted gesture. He straightened only enough to clear the opening drawer, pulled out a large file, pivoted, and was back in his seat removing a broad elastic band from the manilla folder. It was crammed with documents. "I should put some of these loose papers together with Bostitch pins," he said, thinking out loud.

"Bostitch pins?" I asked. He looked up, as though I had looked blank when he mentioned the name of the sovereign.

"Bostitch pins," he repeated, and reached for a stapler. With this he busily began to staple the pages together after shuffling them between his lean hands on the desk. He punctuated each push he delivered to the instrument by repeating the words for my benefit: "Bostitch pins." I wondered how could I possibly discuss anything with a man who called staples Bostitch pins. I was glad I wasn't here to see him about a minor breach of my parole.

"Well, now, Mr. Cooperman, that's better isn't it?" I nodded. He sat there in his green jacket and green tie looking mighty pleased with himself. It must be government work. It does that to you after a while. "Now, Mr. Cooperman, let's get down to cases. I have a train to catch in twenty minutes. If you think I can help you find Johnny Rosa alive, I think you're mistaken. Look at it this way: his confederates in crime were cheated of the money they all jointly earned. Illegally, of course, but you have to look at it the way they do themselves. Put yourself in their . . . what's the word? . . . space. Put yourself in their space. Johnny's robbed them, you see, and one or other of them has simply demonstrated to the rest of the world, to the criminal element at least, that they will not tolerate being pushed around, you see." I nodded, and thanked him for all these tips. He waved a generous hand and gathered the rest of his lunch in the paper it had been sitting on. He didn't leave much.

"What can you tell me about the other three? They all come in here?"

"Oh, yes. They come in every month now. They used to have to report every week, but they've been on months for some time. We've had no trouble with any of them. We rarely do with middle-class people." He got up and carried the folded paper to the wastepaper basket near the door. His trousers were green too. Three greens, all different, and a yellow shirt. His shoes were sensible black. Warren Blacking. "All of the men have jobs. That's the first step in not going back to serve the rest of their sentences. Working men are less likely to be involved in crime than idle ones. Parole, Mr. Cooperman, is a bargain negotiated between the man serving time and the people like me. 'I see here that you can't handle your drinking; very well; that's out. We want to know if you plan to leave town, buy a car, or get married. We don't want you incurring debts, or carrying weapons, is that clear?' And if the convict doesn't like the idea, he can go back and think about it for a few months, and then try to negotiate a better deal. It's not that we like to be officious, although there is plenty of that in government work, it's just that some of these people can't manage the responsibility of, say, the unlimited credit a plastic card seems to promise. It's too much for them. We try to help them first of all from the penitentiary back to the street with as few bumps as possible, and then offer advice and counselling when rough spots develop. Most of them slip into the old ways, of course . . ."

"Excuse me, Mr. Christie. Remember you've got a train to catch. I just want to know about Ian Todd, Rolf Knudsen and Bill Ashland. I'd like to have a clearer idea of the sort of man Johnny Rosa is, was, whichever, too. What sort of men are they?"

"Rosa's a thief. That's his nature. If he lives, he will always be a thief, in and out of penitentiaries until he dies. He's intelligent, he's amusing, even loyal in a primitive way, but quite impossible. He's a twister. When he got out on parole, he was supposed to report to Toronto. Most of them do. When he informed the board that he had changed his mind and decided to come here instead, we should have raised the roof, but—it's the old story of case-loads—we found that it was easier to pretend to be accommodating and understanding. Besides, he had some sort of job lined up pretty quick. He knew we'd put him back inside soon enough if he remained unemployed. He went to that foundry on the canal. You know the one?" I nodded and looked up at the clock. He went on more quickly. "Knudsen, now: he likes his beer. Phlegmatic, malleable, but tough. Cannon-fodder of this gang. Ashland isn't as likeable as the other two; he's quite bitter about all this. Thinks that he took a wrong turning somewhere and won handcuffs instead of pots of money. He'd like to replay the whole thing with himself coming out looking better. It's not a moral question with him. He's just a bad loser. We have a lot of amateurs like him."

As he talked, he began stuffing papers into files, and the files into a beaten-up attaché case. I thought that he might have fastened some of the papers together with Bostitch pins, they were sticking out in a disorganized fashion, but I kept my mouth shut. I was having enough trouble remembering all he was telling me.

He kept talking, now running a four-minute mile with the train. "Todd's a pathetic case: he really believes that initially he tried to stop it all from happening. Did you read what he said at his trial? Hog-wash, the jury thought, but I think he believed it. The jury was hard on him because he was supposed to have known better. A practicing lawyer letting the side down. One bad apple and all that. Some thought that they were hard on him because he was black. I guess if they gave him a lighter sentence than the others, the same people would have said that he got off easier because he was black."

"There are liberals wherever you look."

"He is nerveless, tough and dependable. But there's not one of them, save Rosa, who could have made corporal. And he's hardly officer material." He paused a moment and shut the attaché case with a loud clap. Then he was off and running again.

"You want to talk to them all, I suppose. Well, I shouldn't let you mess in this thing, but I can see you take an interest. That's worth more than rules and regulations, although I'll deny I said that if I have to. I'll have Miss Wright give you the addresses, employers and that sort of thing. Is that all right? And if you want to see me again, come some morning when I'm not in a rush. Get out of here now. I must collect myself. I hate trains." He waved a green arm at me and I shook something limp at the end of it and left. Miss Wright was as good as Christie's word. She pulled out a few hinged trays with plastic inserts, made the necessary notes, and handed me a list without looking at me. She had seen faces in her day and she had seen too many of them. When I came out of the post office building into the puffing traffic of Church Street, I had a list that made me feel pretty good. I was thinking that now I could bank a little of Muriel Falkirk's money with an easy conscience when I noticed a dark blue Mustang with two men in it waiting for spring to come to this happy valley.

24

FOUR

The name at the top of the list was that of Ian Todd. I was sitting in a hole-in-the-wall coffee joint in the middle of the market square where I could watch those two fellows overheating their car, waiting for me to move. I could also see three bearded Mennonites warming themselves over a brazier heating chestnuts. There weren't any horse-and-buggy Mennonites in the market this morning. It was too cold. But a few black-truck Mennonites and black-wheel Mennonites and even the odd chrome-wheel Mennonites were busily selling pieces of sausage and smoked pork to the few half-frozen customers. Funny how, in February, you could tell who was doing most of the talking, even at this distance, by the steady puffs of vapour over the chestnuts.

For a minute I wondered whether I could trust myself to go through the back door of the coffee shop, cut through the mall and come out on the sidewalk on the blind side of the Mustang. I sipped my coffee, looking at the list and trying to work out a schedule. Knudsen looked like the easiest target, Todd the ugliest. Professional men get bitter when you remind them of their scuttled potential. Ashland swam in the middle. I decided to get the worst over first. I found the pay-phone in the back of the lunchroom, behind a pile of cardboard cartons and plastic crates of milk.

"Sinclair and Ambridge," a rather weedy voice said.

"I would like to talk to Mr. Todd, your security man. Is he in?"

"Who is speaking please?"

"It's confidential. Security, you know."

"Just a minute." I felt the line grow cold, as I was switched to that realm of helpless loitering called "hold". When the voice returned me to the land of fish and chips, it was with the information that Mr. Todd was at lunch and wasn't expected back until one-thirty. A small exaggeration and a white lie got me the news that Mr. Todd ate his lunch at Nickie's Tavern, in the old papermill district. Not very choice maybe, but it was handy to the two-acre parking lot of the furniture warehouse. I looked out the window again. A man in a felt hat was breathing clouds of invective into the steaming insides of a blue Mustang. The uplifted hood looked like it was grinning at me.

I figured it would take me about fifteen minutes to drive to Nickie's. I didn't like the idea, but I had to earn my keep. If I had gone to law school, like Todd, I wouldn't be freezing my butt off in another Ontario February. I had that message tatooed on my heart in my mother's handwriting.

Nickie's was the oldest pub in town. The building was over a hundred years old, and the walls looked like they were two feet thick. In the old days the canal workers must have come to drink their lunch at the long mahogany bar. Then it was papermill workers, until the mills closed down in the Depression. Nowadays, it was hard to put labels on the clientele.

The only black man in the place, Todd was sitting alone at a table in the far corner of the noisy room. A waitress banged past me with a tray full of beer. She put seven glasses in front of two skinny men in faded parkas. They didn't object, so she put down two more. The room was fuzzy with smoke, and the sound of the juke-box sat on top of all the conversation. The table next to Todd's was free so I went to it and sat down. I was making up my part as I went along, and I didn't much like being so far from the door. Todd, having cleaned his plate, something with brown gravy, was drinking draft beer. He was staring into it, watching the effect created when he added salt from one of the shakers provided at every table for that purpose.

The waitress removed the remains of somebody's fried chicken: gnawed bones in a yellow plastic basket, and set down two draft. I was wondering whether I should start a casual conversation and work around to Johnny Rosa. In the end, I dumped the idea, deciding that a frontal assault would leave a better aftertaste. I leaned over.

"Todd? I'm Ben Cooperman. Private licence. My client is looking for Johnny Rosa. I thought that you might be looking for him too. Maybe we could pool our information. What do you say?" Todd's eyes turned cold, covering up an initial shock. He was going to try to blow me away without making a fuss. I thought there might be a clause in his parole agreement about busting private investigators in the nose. "Have you seen him, Todd?"

"I see Johnny? That's funny. If I knew where to find him, I wouldn't be drinking draft beer, Mister. You working for Ashland? I heard he's brought in professionals. He must really taste it."

Ian Todd looked like a thousand other guys. I couldn't spot anything special about him, unless it was the chill in those brown eyes. His hands showed long, bony fingers. There was a touch of the military in the way he was dressed, just a brass button or two. He looked like he could be a hard man to deal with, but I figured he didn't get excited too easily. I nodded back at him, neither confirming or denying that I worked for Ashland.

"Tell me about Johnny," I asked.

"Go take a flying leap at the moon," he said. I'd read somewhere that ex-cons are a passive sort. That as a group they tend to cave in to authority. I tried again.

"Did Johnny drop you from the car before he hid the ransom money?"

"Piss up a rope, Mister. I don't have to talk to you. Let me have my lunch. Scram." He was right, of course, he didn't have to talk to me. Anybody else in the business would now start talking about what a nice job he has and how it would be a shame if he lost it. I couldn't swallow that kind of stuff any more than I could the draft beer in front of me. So I just sat for a while.

"You don't think much of Ashland, I gather." I said it as a statement, hoping he'd treat it as a question. He looked across at me.

"Amateurs are whale shit, Mister, and there's nothing lower than that. Ashland howled from the moment we were pinched until he was moved to that minimum security place. Even there he yelled loud enough to get his nose broken. He was even an amateur inside.''

"You knew what he was like. Why'd you go along with it?''

"Ashland was the only weak link. He must have hinted or boasted to one of his friends. Not the whole story, but just enough to hint what a hard man he was. Jesus. The rest of it went like silk.''

"I thought you were trying to stop it. That's what you said in court.''

"And I did. I told Johnny to call it off as soon as he told me about it. I showed him all the holes in the plan. He had all the stuff about the snatch itself, he knew every detail of the cottage set-up. But the ransom business he didn't have so well. We would have walked into their open arms if it hadn't been for a few ideas of my own.''

"Was it your idea or his about the final dump for the money?''

"Johnny kept that to himself. It was a place he knew about.''

"Weren't you with him?''

"He let me out at Culpepper, a one-horse town off the freeway, and I caught the milk-run bus that stops at every other tree along the old highway. It took me two hours to ride forty miles.''

"Sounds like you trusted Johnny pretty well. Where'd you meet him in the first place?''

"Ever hear of the Kit-Kat Klub?'' I shook my head. "It's a joint, a sort of after-hours place. Night people used to drop by there: reporters, taxi drivers, people from the TV station, you know.''

"Do you think that Johnny meant to take the money and run as soon as he got out?'' Todd sipped his beer, ignoring my question.

"Damn it, Mister, you're turning my beer flat. I told you I don't want to talk to you. Get off my back.''

28

"I've talked to people who think we'll find him at the bottom of the Welland Canal."

"Some people read too many books." He got up from his seat, nearly upsetting the unsteady red table, and grabbed his meal check with a flip of his hand. He looked at it and dropped it on my table. "Thanks for lunch, Mister. Glad to see people give a break to a hard-luck con. Now, stay clear of me." And he threaded his body between the scattered tables and chairs until he got to the door. After a word to the waitress, he was gone.

Paying Todd's check made me feel as though I'd eaten something myself. I didn't like the smell of the food, so I felt ahead of the game; better him than me. Once out of the noise and smoke and into the sunlight, I could almost feel some heat through the shoulders of my overcoat. I'd parked my car behind Nickie's. It was looking salt-stained along the skirt at the bottom like all the other cars in the lot. You could almost hear them all rusting together. Everything back there looked dirty and neglected. A skinny cat was ferreting around the green garbage bags next to the back door of the pub and a signal on the railway track winked a cold eye at me as I climbed into the Olds.

FIVE

I had a hard time dragging myself up the stairs to my office. As usual they were dirty, drafty and smelled of bad plumbing. The metal edges were giving up their grip on the linoleum on each step.

I shared this second storey with Dr. Bushmill, a chiropodist who often ended his day by passing out in his own reception room. A couple of times I'd helped him into a taxi, or driven him home, when he'd had a "drap of the creature" in him. Frank was a sad man, sad to be in Grantham instead of Ireland, sad to be a chiropodist, and sad, I think, to be unwillingly gay. It went against his finer feelings. He and I used to talk, when a two-way conversation was possible, about books. He vowed that he was going to improve my reading habits which he deplored. His kindness was well-intended and it gave us something to wrap our time around when we met in the hall. He had given me three books by Flann O'Brien, a favourite writer of his, and an acquaintance of sorts, I gathered, but I hadn't had time to crack them.

Today there was no sign of Frank Bushmill when I reached the top of the stairs, breathing hard. I entered my overheated office and got rid of my coat on the great-uncle of all coat racks. As a matter of fact, it was a left-over from my father's store. For a few months, I shared the office with four nude mannequins, but I put my foot down and my father made a deal with Mr. Goldfarb across the street and down a block. Since then, whenever I pass Goldfarb's window, I'm reminded of my inhospitality.

The mail was strewn on the floor, fanning out below the slit in the door. From where I stood, it didn't look very interesting: envelopes with windows in them mostly, and others with pasted-on labels that suggested either the promotion of a new kind of microphone for electronic surveillance or a chance to buy an encyclopedia of crime unavailable to the general public at any price. Everybody was always doing me favours that cost me money.

I called the number of a stock promoter I knew, and asked if he had seen Bill Ashland. He gave me the name of another firm to try. Here I wandered again in the land of "hold" until a voice told me that Ashland only sometimes drops around, try phoning Friesen, Sunter and MacLeod, a new outfit in town. I did that, and a girl with a deep sexy voice said she'd give him a message to phone me. Then I went through the same routine trying to find Knudsen. I made seven calls this time and ended up leaving word to have him call me. When I finally hung up, rubbed my ear, and stretched my legs, I was beginning to feel like a real detective.

The next number I looked up was that of the Grantham-Niagara Foundry. There were a lot of Granthams in the book and my astigmatism was no help as my finger drifted down the page. I tried the number.

"Lithwick here," a voice shouted over a considerable din.

"I'm calling about an employee named John Rosa, who worked at the foundry for a couple of months."

"Who is this?"

"Taxation Branch," I said. I was going to ride the good feeling all day.

"Hold the line." Lithwick vanished and was replaced by Miss Mann, who had not only all of the facts and figures at her fingertips, she had a quieter extension.

"You want to know about John Rosa, yes?" Her accent was clipped, even military. She sounded like she'd never forget your social insurance number.

"Can you tell me exactly when he began working for you and when he quit?"

"Yes, I have that information, but it will take me a few minutes. You will call back, please?"

"Sure. While you're at it, I'd like to know the name of his foreman. Could you tell me whether the foundry owes him any back pay? I'd also like to know about any absenteeism, sickness, any irregularity in his work record. Got that?"

"This is unusual, Mr. . . .?"

31

"Ah, Watson. John Watson."

"Mr. Watson, we've never been asked to. . ."

"I know. This is a spot check. You probably won't be asked again until 2001."

"I see," Miss Mann said slowly. "You will call back, please, yes?"

"In an hour?"

"Oh, Mr. Watson, I hope I'm better organized than that. Half an hour will be sufficient." I said that would fit nicely with the plans of the Branch and hung up. I began wondering what Miss Mann's first name might be. I speculated on this for as long as it takes to retie both of my shoes—the heat in the office made my feet swell—and then I decided that lunchtime had finally arrived even for private detectives. I was thinking about that when the phone began ringing on top of the city directory. I put my hat back on the rack and grabbed it.

"Hello?"

"Is this Ben Cooperman?" For a moment, I thought that Miss Mann had a brother. It was another slightly accented voice. I acknowledged that I was Ben Cooperman. "This is Rolf Knudsen. I heard you wanted to talk to me. I'm at your service. What kind of insurance are you interested in, Mr. Cooperman?"

"It's not insurance I want to talk to you about, Mr. Knudsen. It's about Johnny Rosa and half a million dollars."

"I don't want to talk to you about that. Now, if it's any kind of insurance. Fire, property. . ."

"Theft?" That one was a mistake, I guess, by the book it was a mistake. But I figured that he'd heard enough soft words. "Mr. Knudsen," I continued, "I'm a private investigator. I'm working for somebody who knows Johnny, and who is worried about him turning up missing. I'm not interested in raking up dead leaves for the fun of it. I only want to go into it far enough to get a lead on where he might be, and whether he is still alive or not. As one of the people who will probably be questioned by the police about his disappearance I think it mightn't look too bad on your report if you can say that you were helpful to me in trying to find Johnny before the general search was started. What do you say?" For a minute I thought I was back on "hold", but I could hear him breathing at the other end.

"It will have to be tonight," he said, all trace of sugar vanishing from his voice. "You come to my place. It's a farm on the Louth Road. It's the first farm on the right after a right turn off Pelham. The name on the box is "Sanderson". Come after eight-thirty and don't bring any friends. I've got to hang up now." He did, without even saying goodbye. I'd just replaced the phone, this time on top of a pile of law books, when it started shouting at me again. I thought that maybe he'd remembered his manners suddenly. But it wasn't him at all, it was my client, Muriel Falkirk. I fidgeted, trying to unsnare the tangles in the coiled telephone wire. Whenever a client phoned, I thought I was about to get the axe between a couple of neck bones.

"Mr. Cooperman, I mean Benny, it's me, Muriel. I'm calling to see how you're getting on." She stopped talking, leaving a nervous silence on both ends of the line. The telephone wasn't Muriel's medium.

"Well," I said, "I haven't worked any miracles. But I'm making steady progress. I've talked to the parole board and Ian Todd, and am seeing Rolf Knudsen later tonight." I started the silence this time. I had all but one of the tangles out of the wire. Why didn't I think of untwisting it when I wasn't on the phone?

"Good." I had difficulty remembering what was "good". She sounded as excited by my news as if I'd invited her to a chess tournament. And then there was that silence again. I decided to try something.

"Miss Falkirk . . ."

"Muriel, please."

"Do you happen to know anyone who drives a dark blue Mustang? I've caught one in my rear-view mirror more than once today." Another long silence.

"Did you see who was driving?"

"Not really. Your pals don't drive Mustangs, then?"

"Sorry, you'll have to rule that out. Blue, you say?"

"Yeah, blue as tempered steel. Well, never mind. . ."

"Benny, you be careful, you hear?"

"Sure. Well, I'll hope to have more news tomorrow. Right now, all I've got is a full appointment book. Check in tomorrow."

"I will, Benny. Take care."

When she'd hung up, I wondered why she'd called. Was she just checking to see how her money was being spent? Could be, but she didn't ask for an account of what Todd or Nelson Christie had said. I couldn't figure her, but it was fun trying. I guess if she'd wanted fancy results, she would have gone to Pinkerton's. I looked at my watch. It didn't tell me the right time to call an heiress who had thirteen million a year sitting in probate. Still thinking of lunch, I pictured her sitting alone at the end of a fifty-foot table picking at a badly cut grapefruit. I tried the local directory. Naturally, there was no listing for George Warren. But I had better luck with Jarman, Robert H. The phone rang about three times before it was picked up. It was a woman's voice, but it had an unfeminine chill in it.

"The Warren Residence." No movie butler could improve on it.

"Could I speak with Mrs. Jarman, please?"

"Whom may I say is calling?" The *whom* was a reproach, and I'd scarcely said anything yet.

"This is Benjamin Cooperman. I would like to speak to Mrs. Jarman on a private matter."

"I am Helen Blackwood, Mrs. Jarman's private secretary, Mr. Cooperman. Could you please be a little more specific about the nature of your business?"

"Yes, Miss Blackwood, I intend to be more specific, but with Mrs. Jarman. Is she there?"

"Mr. Cooperman, I handle all of Mrs. Jarman's affairs. . ."

"I'll bet you do. Now, would you ask her to take the call. I have affairs of my own and I have to look after them myself." There was a moment of silence at her end of the line, followed by a sigh and then the "clunk" of the phone being placed on wood. It was the sound of solid, old, expensive wood. I played a tattoo with my fingers on the oak veneer of my desk and waited for about a minute. Then I heard the sound of another phone being lifted.

"Is this Mr. Cooperman?" It was another voice. This one spoke of private schools and not knowing how to make interesting casseroles out of left-overs.

"I'm afraid it is, Mrs. Jarman."

"Why were you rude to poor Blackwood? You should see her face. What do you want, please? I hope you aren't rude to everybody."

"My mother says I'm gentility itself. Are you alone? Can you talk?"

"That depends. State your business, Mr. Cooperman. I'm right in the middle of painting something, and I don't want it to dry out on me. What is it?"

"I'm a private investigator, Mrs. Jarman. . ."

"Oh, dear!"

". . . and I've been trying to track down Johnny Rosa, who, as you may know, has skipped parole and may intend to bother you. That's just a hunch on my part. But if he does, I would like to know about it. It may help to locate the missing ransom money and clear up a number of loose ends from six years ago. I'm just riding a hunch, but if I'm right, and you call me, we may be able to clear up the whole business without bringing in the police. They tend to be hard on the lawn and burn holes in your chintz among other things."

"I think it's highly unlikely that I should get a call from that man. So unlikely, Mr. Cooperman, that I promise to contact you. Is that good enough, or would you like me to sign an affidavit?" She was having a good time playing with me and I let her get away with it. If she were with me, I might even pull the old forelock. When she'd done I reminded her of the drying painting and gave her my number. She hung up, and then I said goodbye to Blackwood on the extension. I heard her suck in some air just before the click.

SIX

I went across the street to the United for a sandwich. The sun was getting lower, but it had to get full marks for trying this afternoon. The sidewalks were dry and the shoppers moving along them with bones a little less chilled than during the previous few days. The United was almost deserted, except for the boys at the magazine rack. I took my place at the green marble counter and waited to be noticed. Notice was a glass of water banged down in your vicinity by the waitress. It was a minimal kind of reassurance that I was visible and existed. Some days, that was a big boost; others, it was just a glass of water.

I ordered a chopped-egg sandwich, a glass of milk and some vanilla ice cream. It was an ordinary day; I ordered my ordinary lunch. The girl brought it and we exchanged nods. She wasn't being talkative this afternoon. I read through the menu for something to do, noting the price increases on all items since the printer had returned the three-colour job a few months ago. It was very depressing; a lot of things are depressing.

Back upstairs to the groaning of the heating-pipes in my office. They sounded like a midget with a mallet was working them over behind the filing cabinet. All the frost had disappeared from the windows now and I still hadn't had to turn on the overhead light. I wished that I could find a compromise between the intolerable weather outside and the overheated weather inside. I think the name of the compromise is Miami. I decided not to think any further in that direction and distracted myself by dialing the number of the foundry. Lithwick answered and passed me to his Miss Mann again. I wondered about Lithwick. He wasn't really taking hold these days. Miss Mann, the redoubtable Miss Mann, was doing all the brainy work. I told her I was the Taxation Branch, and was surprised when still thought of me kindly as John Watson.

"Were you able to find the information, Miss Mann?"

"Of course. Just a moment. There: John Rosa came to work here on the seventeenth of November last year. He worked regular eight-hour shifts with no overtime until the nineteenth of January. No absenteeism, only the usual time off at Christmas and New Year's Day. His foreman was Joe Strobel. I'll spell that for you." She did that. "If you want to talk to him this week, let me see, yes, you will have to catch him when he comes off at four in the afternoon, or at eight in the morning, when he goes in. Next week, yes, he works from four in the afternoon until midnight. Am I speaking too rapidly, Mr. Watson?"

"Not at all. Thanks. I'll look you up to say thanks in person when I come down there."

"I don't work shifts, Mr. Watson. I'm here from nine to five and not on weekends. If I can help the Branch in any other way, please call me. You have only to ask. Goodbye." Now was that a come on or was that a come on?

I knew that I couldn't think about Miss Mann or the foundry now. I had to put Johnny Rosa, Muriel Falkirk and all those people out of my mind for a half hour. I'd been postponing my next move for a couple of days, and I couldn't put it off any longer.

Before she left for Florida, my mother made me promise that I would take care of her house plants while she was gone. It was a chore she would not delegate to a neighbour, and when she heard me suggest that, she looked at me as though I'd wondered if anyone in our family ever ate their young. I'd still managed to ignore her injunction about daily visits to water the plants and throw them a little friendly talk as I plied between them with my watering can. Even in a condominium, I found it difficult talking to plants. On their own, I didn't mind plants: they helped fill a house with greenery; but the moment I thought of them as standing there in their pots on their stems waiting to hear me say something bright, they were transformed utterly into pushy, fleshy, grasping things that should find a horror movie to haunt. I buttoned up my overcoat again, pulled my hat about my ears and headed down the dirty stairs, gritting my teeth until my fillings went sour.

The automobile factory was changing shifts as I drove

37

along Ontario Street. The narrow road led straight as ten, jack, queen, king, ace between the steaming plant on one side and its parking lot on the other. Cars were trying to force their way from the lot into the solid line of stalled traffic, and I felt like I was trapped inside one of those plastic puzzles, a numbered square moved from space to space by a frustrated player. In the end, I forced my way through the snarl and beat past the greasy chin of the fast-food traps on either side of the road beyond the factory. In another minute I'd cleared the overpass leading to the Toronto-Niagara highway and was pulling into my father's parking space in front of Unit 57. I tried to imagine living in a unit after having an honest roof of a real house overhead for twenty years. Nobody'd ever say that a man's unit was his castle.

Inside, the sun was spreading muted gloom through the sheer tangerine curtains on to the tangerine couch and the tangerine broadloom. The Dresden china was standing at attention in the rear of the china cabinet, waiting to do its stuff again as it did in 1938, 1945, 1957, and 1967. I could hear the familiar tinkle of the crystal wine goblets as I took each step. I took a Coke from the double refrigerator and strangled my index finger pulling off the tab. The kitchen looked neat but dusty, and on the windowsills the ivy was looking thirsty. In the living-room the rubber plant stretched out its shiny leaves to me. The dieffenbachias looked terrible. I went to the kitchen sink and filled a pail with warm water. It was one of those taps that glide around and pivot according to its own rules. The ivy seemed to respond at once to my first aid. I mumbled something at it, and swore when I dripped on the ledge. I filled the large pot of the dieffenbachias and had to go back for more water.

"I'll be right back," I called behind me as I went. I finished up by telling the big guys a few of the snappy poolroom stories I'd picked up. Real knee-slappers. We were getting on famously, if a little one-sidedly, when the double chime of the doorbell sounded its tin-eared summons. Probably the paperboy inquiring about when my parents would be back from down south. "This will only take a minute, fellas." As I walked through the kitchen, I should have looked more closely at the blue mass outside my mother's cute Swiss-chalet curtains. It's easy to say that now. When I opened the front door, I found myself looking into the muzzles of two nasty-looking automatics. The boys in the blue Mustang had got it moving again. There it was parked at the sidewalk not ten yards away.

SEVEN

One of the gunmen was the tall weedy guy with the felt hat I'd seen weeping into the stalled Mustang. He wore a muffler that looked like his mother had knitted it for him and a heavy dark blue trenchcoat with a zip-in lining for winter. His galoshes were unhooked and they played jinglebells when he walked. His face looked sad more than anything else. The other guy was a stout, hairy man in a pale blue imitation-leather jacket. His trousers shouted "checks" and "plastic". His hair, worn long on his head but neatly barbered, was black and abundant. I could tell without looking that his knuckles were luxuriant and wouldn't have been surprised to find that after five o'clock his tongue produced a fine stubble. They both held their guns level with my trembling middle. I wanted to yell, but, under the circumstances, I invited them in.

The tall one made a fast circuit through the main floor then came back to me quick. "Where's the other guy?" He wasn't joking and he looked surprised and scared.

"What other guy? There isn't anybody here but me."
They looked at one another then back at me again.

"Come off it. Is he upstairs or down?"

"It's just the three of us," I told him, and nodded to the
hairy one like I was a neutral observer at my own interroga-
tion.

"Cut out the crap, we heard you talking," said the tall
one, waving his gun around in a manner that achieved exactly
what he intended.

"Oh, that. That wasn't talk. I was just muttering to
myself."

"Yeah? And I'm the man in the moon. I heard talk. I
know talk. I hear it all the time. Is he hiding upstairs or down?
Talk fast!"

"Search the place if you want. You'll see I was telling the
truth." I tried out a careless shrug. I got it to go up, but for a
second I thought I wasn't going to get it down again. The hairy
one pointed his gun in the direction of the door to the recrea-
tion room.

"You go first," he said. I did, and he nosed around in the
finished basement, inspecting my father's glass-brick bar with
the coloured lights behind, the cool-smelling laundry room,
and even the bookshelves with all my mother's whodunits leaning against my brother's discarded medical books. I could see
he liked my father's television set. I got good marks for that.
But he didn't waste any more time than necessary down there.
He wagged the gun and I headed back up the shag broadloom
stairs to the living-room. A second later the other guy came
down from the second floor. They shook their heads at one
another.

"Is there some other way out of here?" I motioned
towards the French doors, through which you could see a few
rabbit and cat tracks, the yellow stain of a dog in the snow, but
no footprints with shoes on. "Okay, friend, stop funning us.
We want to know where your friend went. Sit down." I sat on
the tangerine loveseat. The hairy one sighed and put his gun
away inside his jacket. I was right about his knuckles. He put
them into another pocket and brought out a roll of Lifesavers.

He took one and handed the roll to his pal, who made a mess of freeing a candy for himself. Me, he didn't offer.

"Okay," he said, trying to make the simple fact sit up straight in his head, "you were talking to yourself. Nobody was with you. Nobody heard us outside. Check?"

"Check." The tall one was inspecting the living-room, pointing his gun at the things that moved him particularly.

"Hey, that stuff in there's Dresden, you know that?" I tried a grin. He nodded, moving his jaw slowly as if in slow thought.

"I like this Chinese commode. This all your stuff?"

"No. This is my parents' place. They're away. I'm just watering a few plants."

"They got nice taste, your parents. Very nice." The hairy one, still standing in front of me, crunched his Lifesaver. After nodding approvingly at a couple of pictures, the tall one came back to his friend. The drooping automatic was smartly brought up to attention. I tried to grin seriously, to show that I was a decent living creature with thoughts and feelings of my own. I sat there for a minute watching the sad face of the tall one contort as a preamble to further talk, probably on a new subject. But it was the other who got started first.

"Listen, Mr. Cooperman. We got business with you," the stout one said. "Vito and me, we gotta make sure there aren't any third parties hanging around, you know what I mean?" Vito nodded. He now put away his gun, but kept his hand on it inside the pocket of his coat. The knitted muffler remained tied tightly around his throat, like it had been put there before he was sent out to play with the big boys.

"You been asking a lot of questions around town, Mr. Cooperman, and we want to know what it's all about. Asking questions isn't a hobby, huh?" the stout one continued. "Why are you messing in this thing? Who you working for?"

"Listen to Frank, and you'll be okay," Vito put in. "You're some kind of private detective, eh?" The "huh" made Frank an American, and the "eh" sounded very Canadian to me. "Level with us and we'll walk out of here like we walked in, quieter in fact." I tried to think of something that would make them go away. I could almost hear myself saying, but not quite, "You're nothing but a pack of cards!" But I held on to myself.

"Right," I said, looking from one to the other. "I work as a private investigator. I'm working for a client, but I can't tell you that client's name. I've been asking questions about Johnny Rosa. Obviously, I'm trying to learn what happened to him. You know everybody in the country is looking for Johnny. And you know why. I don't see why you've been tailing me. Did you think I didn't see you? That car of yours is as inconspicuous as the Batmobile at a three-legged race." I stopped. I could tell that that was a mistake.

"Keep talking, Mr. Cooperman, we hear you loud and clear," said Vito. I tried to think of what to give him next. I'd passed on all of the free stuff; the rest was going to cost me. Frank and Vito looked at me, not like I was a person, but like I was a talking machine. I didn't like the feeling.

"I only started on the case yesterday, so you probably know more about it than I do. And what I've discovered you can find out at the public library and the parole board."

"Gimme a break, Mr. Cooperman. I hate to go near that place."

"Sure, and the parole board's poison too."

"What can I tell you boys?" I heard myself saying in a voice like my father's. "You look like nice boys that wouldn't want to make any trouble. Do I look like I'm looking for the money for myself? I'm only doing my job: trying to find Johnny Rosa for a friend of his. Is that so bad? Is that worth coming into my father's house waving guns? Is that the way you behave in your parents' house? Why are you doing this to me?"

"How good a friend is Johnny to this client?" asked Frank. His voice was low, like burnt gravy.

"I told you I can't talk about that. You can understand that."

Vito and Frank exchanged glances. Vito's face was working again. I didn't like it.

"We're going to sit here until you tell us who's putting up

42

the money for this. We got all day,'' Frank said. Vito was off wandering again. He found Coke in the refrigerator and brought one for himself and one for Frank, putting them down on the coffee table.

"That's the real stuff," Vito said, tapping the table-top. They opened their cans and drank quietly. Vito was admiring the crystal chandelier. "Nice," he said. "Nice."

"Look, Mr. Cooperman, we ain't finished talking yet. We are still listening and you aren't saying anything we want to hear. I don't want to have to get tough with you, not here in your parents' house. I got feelings too, you know what I mean? But we gotta get some answers, gotta get them soon." He'd just said that they had all day, but I wasn't about to point out little inconsistencies at a time like this. Vito was wandering over by the French doors now, looking at the plants.

"What is this thing?" he asked.

"Vito, shut up!" Frank warned.

"It's a rubber plant." That didn't help.

"It could be plastic yucca as far as I'm concerned. I don't know my plants anymore." He took hold of one of the leaves of the plant and pulled. The fleshy leaf came away easily in his hand. I found myself half-way across the room, shouting at him. Crazy.

"Take it easy. Take it easy. It's only a plant. Not worth getting your head blown off for." Frank led me back to the loveseat.

"Well, tell your pal to stop ruining other people's property."

"Vito, you listening?"

"I'm listening. Only I don't hear any answers to the questions you're asking, Frank. You hold on to him, and see if I do any better." He took another leaf in his hand and looked over at me, his face sad as usual, but now mean on top of it. I knew that my mother had raised that rubber plant from a pup.

"I told you all I can tell you." Vito pulled slightly. The whole plant shivered. "Look, use your heads. You know I don't work for the Warren family. They'd get one of the bigger agencies. So who else is there? His former partners? I'm not working for Todd, Ashland or Knudsen. Who does that leave? Who else is a friend of Johnny? I'm not working for the Horsemen; they do their own prowling. I'm not with the parole board; they've already given up looking. Does that narrow the field down enough for you?" Vito loosened his grip on the plant. He grinned at Frank. I didn't much care for Vito's grin. It looked like a smiling death's head.

"You working for Muriel Falkirk, Mr. Cooperman?" Frank said.

"I'm not saying yes." Vito tugged at the leaf of the rubber plant again, so I added, reluctantly, "And I'm not saying no." That was enough for Vito; he dropped the leaf altogether and came back across the room.

"That's the right answer, Mr. Cooperman. I think we understand one another. Vito and me will be going now. Come on Vito. Let the man finish what he started in peace." Vito placed the leaf he had torn off on the coffee table.

"Sorry," he said with an awkward shrug. They backed to the front door, and in another moment I was alone with my mother's plants again. The hind end of a blue Mustang was disappearing around the curve and pulling on to the highway.

EIGHT

On my shaky way back to town, I could see that it was beginning to get dark. And with the dying of the sun, the winter took another night-time grip on the city. The manhole covers were steaming in the middle of St. Andrew Street. The stores had their display signs lit. In another half hour the streetlights would blink on.

After parking the car, I crossed the busy one-way stream of traffic and went into the United. If I'd been a drinking man, this would have been the time for a straight belt of whisky. As it was, I settled for a vanilla shake. After what I'd just been through, I needed to break the routine. The girl made it thick and set the aluminum container down with my glass. The straw stood up unaided in the centre of the froth.

I could hear my phone ringing while I was still climbing the stairs. I didn't hurry because those are the calls that stop as you rush across the room. I got the door open and it was still crying out when I plucked it off the cradle. It was Muriel. She sounded agitated, not the girl I'd talked to a few hours ago.

"Benny, what are you doing?"

"My best." What else could I say? "What's on your mind?"

"Nothing special," she said in a way that made me think she meant the opposite. "I'd like to see you."

"Any time. That's what you're paying me for, remember?"

"I'd like to see you soon, but not at your office and not at my place. Both places may be watched. Help me think, Benny." She sounded like she was trying to fit me into a tight schedule.

"How about the back row of the Capitol Theatre?"

"Benny, you're sweet. Think harder."

"What about the library? That's quiet. I want to tell you about a run-in I had with a pair of tough customers who drive that blue Mustang I was asking you about."

"The Public Library, you say?" She sounded a little abstracted from the here and now, like she was trying to talk with a manicurist working on both arms and a new hairdresser doing strange things to her hair.

"Sure, I think that's the best bet. I can think of at least two hoodlums who won't follow you in there. It's about a quarter to six now. . ." I was translating from my Japanese watch which read 5:42 in ruby digits. "Can you make it by six, or a little after? I'll wait for you in the Special Collections section. It's in a room of its own on the second floor. You got that, Muriel? Now can you tell me anything about what's happened?"

"I'll tell you everything in a few minutes. Until then, Benny, Lord love you." It was a fine and unexpected thing to hear her say. It passed on her fear to me.

Muriel was a hard woman to figure. She was as good-looking as a subscription to *Playboy,* and obviously, judging from the fur coat and a few other things, well appreciated by more guys that just Johnny Rosa. She had two grand to lend Rosa, and didn't appear to be terribly concerned over finding out where it went. She seemed genuinely stuck on Rosa and worried about his disappearance. She wasn't always straight about her answers, but I appreciated her efforts. I thought about the story she'd told in my office. An Academy Award performance. The inconsistencies glared at me. But a man in my position gets used to dealing with liars. I've had husbands trying to pretend they were paupers in order to get off with a gentler bite at the end of a divorce settlement, and wives swearing to cruelty that isn't in the porno books yet in order to get rid of an unwanted spouse. After a while, like Hammett says, you believe the money not the story. I've always found that it is perfectly possible to enjoy a normal working relationship with pathological liars.

For the fiftieth time, I put on my coat and hat, and shuffled out the door, clicking the spring lock behind me, then making it down the stairs and out into the butt end of the working day for this Tuesday. The streetlights were now on, washing the late shoppers in a mercury-inspired unhealthy tint.

46

It was just as cold as in the early morning and it felt as if this February would never end. I guess for some people, that was true.

I was glad to get behind the big glass doors of the library. A blast of heat hit me; it was spring again. The fountains were playing, the brook was running, the books were mostly circulating. I climbed up to the second floor and entered the Special Collections Room. Ella Beames had gone for the day. I didn't recognize the girl who sat at her desk. I found a chair at an empty table and pulled an old black atlas of the area off a shelf. It had been printed in 1878. I killed half an hour flipping through its pages, looking at the solemn bearded faces of the founders of these closely-linked communities. I wondered what they had to be so serious about. They looked like Roman senators, wondering whether they could afford to miss one of Caligula's poisoned feasts.

I looked at my watch: 6:11. I kept on with the atlas. Each of the old townships was illustrated with a map, showing all important roads, railways, churches, schools and mills. Each property had the name of the owner printed on it. You could see the same names clustered in a small group, the sons of the pioneer settler, probably. Occasionally a widow was going it alone. Some of the names were the same as kids I'd gone through school with.

When I checked again it was 6:44. I wondered whether I should call. I decided to wait another half hour, then drop around to her place. Back to the atlas. There were a few pages devoted to showing off the prosperous farms and residences of the county's best people. Some of them stood with their legs well apart, to sustain a comfortable paunch, with their hands held behind the tails of their coats. The houses looked new-built, the barns well-stocked, the steers Grade A beef, the cows oozing high butter-fat content. The toiler in the field rested a moment with one hand on spade, the other brushing the brim of a straw hat, eyes fixed on the distant horizon.

I heard my name. I turned and it was Muriel sailing between the tables like a playboy's yacht into an unfamiliar port.

"Sorry I'm late." She looked breathless from the stairs

and settled into the chair beside me without attempting to remove her coat. She looked around the room as though she had suddenly found herself backstage at the thought-works, where the books without pictures come from.

"I've never been here," she explained, and I nodded. It must have appeared to be a self-satisfied nod, one which boasted that I did all my reading here, because her face got serious and her fingers were trying to make up their minds about whether to take off her coat or not. They decided to un-button and I helped her put the fur on the back of her chair.

"You said you wanted to see me. Has something hap-pened?"

"Tell me about what you said on the phone. The men in the Mustang. Are *you* all right?"

"They wanted to know what I was doing and who I was working for. Have you any idea who they might be working for? It would make my job that much simpler." Muriel looked at me and opened up her blue eyes in a way that she had tried on me before. They were Little Red Riding-Hood eyes and I was learning not to trust them.

"I told you before, Benny. I don't know who they could have been."

"What about Eddy Milano? Could they be working for him?"

"What do you know about Eddie? What has he got to do with this?"

"You admit you know him, then. Why did you leave that part out yesterday?"

"Because, Benny, it doesn't have anything to do with Johnny. Eddie's only one of the people looking for Johnny. Sure, he can find muscle when he needs it. Maybe it was him. Go ask him if you want to know for sure." She'd placed her reddish leather purse on the table next to my atlas. It smelled like a luggage store. Inside I could see that she'd been shopping at two of the better stores along St. Andrew Street.

"Why did you ask me to meet you Muriel? It wasn't just to break up your shopping."

She was looking at her watch when I looked at her again.

Then she ferretted around in her bag and came up with an envelope with my name on it. "This is for you," she said. "Only don't open it unless you don't hear from me for forty-eight hours."

"Is it an insurance policy? Come on, Muriel, you've got to trust somebody." She stopped worrying the corners of her mouth and looked at the green stone of her ring for the first time since she'd come into the library. It seemed to be her calm centre, a rallying point for her concentration.

"Let me play it this way. I've thought about it."

"Okay, you're the boss." She put the envelope into my hand and watched me put it away in my inside breast pocket. Only then did she allow herself a healthy sigh of relief, which, as usual with Muriel's sighs, had a lot of incidental appeal.

She was in another sweater. This time it wasn't angora but it was blue and a size too small for getting away without causing a stir. Her navy skirt was slit up one side revealing a froth of white lace and long slim calves.

"Will you call me tonight?" she asked, tilting her head so that I forgot I was on the pay-roll. I nodded and grinned, and she started packing up. I helped her back into the Persian lamb and she gathered gloves and bag. We left together.

There was no Mustang parked in front of the library, but I walked her down the steps past the monumental pediment of the old library which had been re-erected on the approach to the new one. When we parted, she pressed my hand and gave me a peck on the cheek I didn't feel I'd earned.

"Call me tonight," she said again, but in a confidential, almost conspiratorial voice. "Try me around nine. I may have good news. God bless," she said, and moved off in the direction of Lake Street without looking back once.

49

NINE

Steve's Garage was a rusting, tin-fronted, overgrown shack that had been built back in the late thirties with the hope that it might last for ten years. It wasn't always Steve's Garage. Steve Tokarski had come on the scene fairly recently. He had installed pumps calibrated metrically and once in a while put up streamers when the oil company sent them. But he didn't know what to do about that rusting front. The stain slid down a new coat of paint the first time it rained. To the right of his small office were two large bays, with cars drawn over the pits. In back, he had an acre of wrecks. They looked like the remains of a metal-eater's lunch.

I drove on to the edge of the lot and put on the emergency brake. I was far enough from the pumps so I wouldn't be confused with business. I got out and walked toward the office.

Half an hour earlier, I'd got a call from the Regional Police telling me that a yellow Volkswagen had been towed to Steve's Garage on the Lakeshore Road near Niagara Street. I found Steve Tokarski in the back of the garage looking through a parts catalogue in an aluminum binder bolted to a workbench. He was a stocky, grease-covered man in his thirties, in a peakless peaked cap and a pair of overalls the colour of the last muffler I passed on the shoulder of a highway. He had a chubby face, and a one-sided smile that hoisted the left corner of his mouth into the cheek. His metal-framed glasses were streaked with oil as was the stub of a cigarette in the middle of his face. He didn't remove the cigarette to remove the ash, just blew hard without dislodging the butt. He had an oily rag to wipe his hands on when he saw company. When he saw me, he didn't touch it, but went on looking for the part he needed in the catalogue. A man with a safety light on the end of an extension cord glared at me. I waited and watched a crankcase drain its last oozings into a hubcap.

"Are you Steve Tokarski?"

"Yeah, I'm Steve. But I'm pretty busy right now, can it wait? I got both trucks out."

"It's about the car towed in earlier, the Volkswagen."

"Yeah," he grinned his lopsided grin. "What about it?"

"Well, I'd like to see it and hear where you found it."

"Who are you?" He had got suspicious suddenly. It sat well on his normal conservatism.

"Cooperman's my name. The car belongs to a client of mine."

"You a lawyer, eh? I spotted you for a lawyer. As soon as I saw that car, I knew there was going to be lawyers. You want to take it away with you? There's towing and storage on it. To hell with the storage. Let me have twenty bucks and you can drive it out of here."

"I didn't walk from town. I've got my own car. You hang on to it for a couple of days, and the lady who owns it will come for it. Where is it?"

"I'm not going to leave that heap of bones out front. Are you kidding? It's in back with the rest of the junk. I spotted it a week ago, off the road beyond the first lock of the canal. You know where the picnic grounds are? Well it was in the bushes there. It hadn't driven off the road or anything, it was standing there with the keys on the floor. I took a look, but didn't think too much of it. Then after a couple of days I started to get curious, wondering why it had been left there, you know? So I called the cops and I had Walter bring it in on Monday night. I haven't seen the cops yet. In the summer, that's a regular lovers' lane down there. If the car wasn't a wreck, I'd have figured it was hot, you know? But you couldn't hardly give away this heap of bones." He indicated that I was welcome to take the air and let him get on with his work, so I nodded my appreciation and walked around back.

It was a mustard-coloured VW with tattoos of rust everywhere. The winter had taken its toll a couple of times over on its poor blemished carcass. From the front, it looked solid enough. It hadn't bumped into anything, and there were no recent dints that I could see. Through the windows, everything looked in order. A religious medal dangled from

51

the rear-view mirror. The back seat looked crowded but ordinary. I opened the door on the driver's side. The seat had been pushed back so that some long legs could be freed from confinement. I looked at the ratchet along the floor. I could see the mark where Muriel had had the seat, nearer the wheel, and then, a little further back, the mark of Johnny's favourite position.

I was just about to close the door when my eye caught a dark stain on the back of the driver's seat. In my work, I haven't come across much dried blood, but when I saw this, I got out my penknife and chipped a few crumbs of it into an envelope. I shone a pocket flashlight around the floor of the car, front and back, looking for other clues such as used theatre stubs, hotel bills, or a bank draft for five hundred thousand dollars, but all I saw was the cellophane wrapper from a pack of cigarettes. I thought I'd better leave the cops something to look at, so I left it where it was.

Back in my car, I lit up a smoke of my own, and headed over the canal bridge to see if I could find the place where the car had been left. It wasn't difficult. A black patch in the snow stood out too well. I stopped the motor but left the parking lights on, and crawled out. These narrow two-lane roads are hazardous in the dark. If I'd been hoping to find footprints, I was disappointed. There were a couple of good ones from Walter's boots, but all other prints had been swept away by the stiff breeze blowing in off the lake.

I wandered into the main office of the Regional Police when I got back to town, and asked for both of my old pals, Sergeants Savas or Staziak. Both were off. But I left Savas the envelope and told him to check it for blood type. I didn't need to mention Johnny Rosa. Savas was a good cop.

When I left the Regional Police I bought an evening paper, and found myself feeling hungry again. I solved that problem at the Diana Sweets with the *Beacon* propped up in front of me. The front page carried the news that a Canada-wide warrant for Johnny Rosa's arrest had been issued. The kidnapping was chewed again like an old cud, but there wasn't anything I didn't already know. I ordered a bowl of vegetable soup and a well-done omelette. I hate runny eggs, and as usual, I had to send them back to the kitchen to be fried for another five minutes.

TEN

My headlights easily picked out the name "Sanderson" stencilled on the rusting mailbox, which leaned intemperately toward the road. The lane leading into the property was dark with naked poplars on either side. The black mass of a barn stood at the end of it, with the moon going down behind. To the left was the house, a typical Ontario farmhouse, its three-storeys squeezed into a narrow silhouette, as though it had been forced to move upward because expansion in other directions was impossible. In fact it sat quite alone on a fat ten-acre lot with nothing threatening it but a chicken coop, and that was fifty yards away. It was going to ruin slowly. The wooden shutters bracketed the windows precariously where they hadn't fallen off. White paint was peeling from the clapboard. The wooden porch subsided under my weight as I looked for the door. I rang the old-fashioned hand bell and waited. Light from inside lit up the porch from tall narrow windows on either side of the door. It was quiet on the porch, and I could hear the poplars. Even without leaves they made a poplar-like noise.

Something stirred inside the house and I could hear footsteps coming closer to the door. It was opened by a girl of about nineteen, wearing old blue jeans and a purple T-shirt. Her straight brown hair hung to her shoulders. "Are you Mr. Cooperman?" she asked, opening her dark eyes wider and arching her right eyebrow. I nodded and she led me through a messy hallway and kitchen to a messy back room. It had been a summer kitchen when the house was built, but now it had a woodstove and plastic over the inside of the windows. It didn't pass any *House and Garden* standards, but it looked comfortable. Rolf Knudsen was sitting in a wooden rocking chair with a guitar leaning against it. About a dozen empty beer bottles either stood at attention beside the rocker or had rolled to the low end of the slightly raked floor. The carpet was worn through in places. He looked up.

"Cooperman?" I nodded again, and took a seat on a brown couch against the inside wall. He inclined his head toward the girl. "This is Jennifer. Would you like a beer?"

Knudsen was wearing a heavy black wool sweater with a tartan-patterned shirt collar showing at the neck. He wore faded blue jeans too, with ragged cuffs covering his worksocks. A pair of yellow boots were melting into a pool of water beside the back door. Jennifer brought me an opened bottle of beer and left the room.

"Jennifer is the best," he said, when the sound of her footsteps had vanished. He looked me right in the eye and spoke with intensity. I figured that he had put away a quantity of beer, but that it took an ocean of it to shake his steady blue eyes. He kept rocking back and forth, easy and relaxed. He was a long, skinny man, in whom you could see the teenager he'd been. I couldn't picture him in a business suit trying to sell insurance, unless it was to university students. His hair was blond and he wore it long, but neatly. I tried to imagine him at the Warren cottage. Did he grab the girl from behind and gag her, or did he knock out her boyfriend? Maybe he just drove the car and kept his eyes on the road. Yes, I guessed he'd be able to do any of it without flinching. Christie from the parole board was right: he wasn't officer material, but he was the sort of soldier that officers depend on.

"You want to talk about Johnny? Okay, we'll talk about Johnny. I didn't see him after he got out. I expected that he would try to get in touch, but he didn't. I know that he has to be careful. They're watching him."

"Who do you mean?"

"The Horsemen. They want to find the money, and they hope he'll lead them to it."

"And you?"

"I'll wait," he said shrugging. "I've waited two years since I got out. I can go on waiting."

"You trust Johnny then? You think he will finally split that ransom money with you?"

"That's right. I could stub my toe on a gold brick too. I'm not holding my breath."

"Tell me about the snatch. Who did what to whom?"

"That's all in the transcript."

"I know. I want to hear it from you."

"Why me? I saw less than any of the others. I sat in the first car. When Johnny whistled, I drove it up to the cottage. They brought the girl out, all tied up, and put her in back. Bill Ashland got into the back too for a while, and we took her to the shed where we left her. We drove back to Grantham. That's all."

"How did you get involved in the first place."

"I knew Johnny. Don't remember when I met him. Maybe at the Kit Kat Klub. I don't go for the cards much, but you can always get a drink there. Johnny took me aside one night and asked me if I had the stomach to go after something big. I told him I had a very strong stomach. I was living on credit in those days, was in way over my head. I couldn't afford to know anyone who lived at the Norton Apartments, let alone live there myself. I was ripe for something as crazy as the Warren deal, and Johnny could see it. He was like that, Johnny. He laid out the plan for me and I couldn't see how it could miss. If Ashland hadn't . . ." He didn't finish. He took a long swallow of beer from the bottle in his hand and sat quietly for a moment.

"None of us had prepared alibis, you see." He looked up

and grinned sadly. "Once the cops started sniffing around our place, they were bound to stumble on to us. We were nearly home and dry. He didn't have the stomach for it, Ashland." He had now finished the beer he was holding. He placed the empty near the curved rocker by his right hand and found a full bottle on the window sill. He got up and removed the top on an opener fixed to the imitation wood panelling. The bottle was steaming from the top. He reminded me oddly of Nelson Christie, the parole officer; their economy of movement was the same.

"The word is that Johnny won't be coming back," I said, when he had settled his tall, lean body back into the rocker. He stared at the new beer bottle, looked at the label like it was a ten-thousand dollar bill. After a minute he shrugged.

"He was a good man. I'm sorry they're saying that. He always treated me right. I won't forget him, I'll tell you that." He nodded at his beer, like it was a holy icon.

"What do you think he did with the money?"

"The original plan was for the second car . . ."

"That was Johnny and Todd?"

"Yeah. They dealt with the money. We never saw it." He took another long swallow, his Adam's apple moved like a mole under the skin of his throat. Then he grinned: "I guess now I'll never see it. He said he had a good place for it, a place where it would be safe until it was time to divide it up."

"Any idea where that was?"

"You sound like Ashland." He got up and pulled another bottle from the window sill. He looked over at me, still struggling with my first, and came back to the rocker.

"Nobody likes Ashland," I said, thinking out loud.

"Look, I don't hate anyone. But Ashland is the one who could make me change. He was too soft for this business, you know, not hard enough. Then when they had us, he started to whine. That doesn't help anyone."

"What do you know about Johnny and Muriel Falkirk?" That one stopped him for a minute. He smiled.

"That's a good looking woman."

"What do you know about her?"

"She was Eddie Milano's girl. That's not a secret, except to Mrs. Milano. Milano's a respectable married family man. He goes to church. Supports the charity drives. All that stuff. But that's just the tip of the iceberg. He goes deep under. He's got investments in Las Vegas. He gets income from Miami, Los Angeles and San Francisco. Up here he's just a motel owner with an interest in horse racing and the tourist business at the Falls. Nobody has a sheet on him. He's too smart for that."

"Why did he split with Muriel?"

"Search me. Could be a dozen reasons. Why does anyone split up? It's chemistry. I don't know anything about chemistry. I stick to simple stuff like beer. I know that Milano has powerful friends. If he wanted to, he could crush Johnny like a gnat."

"Maybe he did."

"Yeah, maybe he did."

Something moved on the other end of the couch I was sitting on. I'd seen it before, but had taken it for a rolled-up ball of socks. The socks stretched and became a young puppy. It lolled, turned belly up, showing a light underside, whimpered and curled up into socks again.

"And you really haven't had any contact with him?"

"I told Jennifer I would have nothing further to do with that life. I gave her my word. She's the greatest." I smiled approval. "You'll never guess who she is. She's Jennifer Bryant, the daughter of the crown prosecutor. How do you like that? She was only little when I went to prison. I met her when I got out on parole. I had a job fixing boats. Didn't even know who she was for a long time. And when I found out, it didn't matter. She knew who I was right along. With her father and all, I guess a shrink would make something out of it. I'm just glad it happened." He tended to flatten his *d*s and turned them into *t*s, but apart from that his English was unaccented.

"Have you been in touch with Johnny?" I repeated.

"No. I'm through with all that."

"I know, but sometimes the past isn't through with us. Has anyone else been to see you? Have you noticed strangers hanging around, clicks on the telephone, that sort of thing?''

"Forgive my saying so, Mr. Cooperman, but you sound like a television show.''

"Tell that to the parole board. I think you know more about this than you're saying." I just tried that on him to see what the reaction would be. I could see nothing special, so I began making "I'm about to leave" noises. Then I thought of Muriel and asked to use the phone. It was in the kitchen: dark stained woodwork and cracked tile above a vinyl counter. I let it ring for about two minutes before giving up. Without thinking I was adding up the time since she'd slipped me the envelope.

When I came back, Jennifer was on the scene again. I said something about the farm and this sort of weather and Knudsen responded with something equally deathless. Jennifer was holding the brother to the puppy on the couch. I said goodbye to Knudsen, who didn't budge from his chair and followed Jennifer to the door. Her hair smelled of apples. She had her face pressed against the glass of the door as I went down the frozen path to my car. I had the feeling as I backed out of the lane that I had learned more than I knew I'd learned. I also realized that the itch at the back of my knee wouldn't leave me alone until I'd paid an unscheduled call on Muriel Falkirk.

ELEVEN

The illuminated dial of my watch showed 9:37. It doesn't deal in things like a quarter to or half past. With the moon down, the night looked blacker than when I'd started out. At Power Gorge, I could just make out the darker shape of the hydro-electric development, where a Niagara of water fell through a series of ten pipes to the benefit of all of us good citizens. It wasn't much to see at night, and, come to think of it, it wasn't much to look at in daylight either.

Lake Street was one of the streets that followed the lines first laid down by the earliest surveyors in Grantham. It formed one side of a parallelogram made by criss-crossing concession roads and side roads. Things worked this way on the edges of the township, but in the centre, where the city was, the old Indian trails, the Eleven Mile Creek and some discarded canals got in the way. Only once in a while, like here on Lake Street, did the streets run ruler-straight.

I found the address Muriel Falkirk had given me. It was a brick-fronted three-storey apartment building. You couldn't honestly say it was ugly, it was most of all forgettable. I parked the car in front, locked it, and went through the heavy glass door leading to the lobby. On one of the black and white speckled walls a group of bells and mail-boxes were arranged. I tried her bell, clearing my throat so that I would sound like me when she called through on the intercom. No answer. I tried again. I looked at my watch: 10:08. My mother was always reminding me that I should pay more attention to time. Of course, she meant not that it was ten o'clock not nine, but rather that "Benny, you're not getting any younger. Why not settle down with a nice girl. It's time." Sure. Who's arguing? I got ambitions, the same as anybody else.

I pushed Muriel's bell again. Still no answer. But now I could hear someone coming down the stairs. An old lady in leaf-green slacks and a paisley blouse under a fluffy, white imitation fur jacket opened the inside door from her side. She had a Siamese cat on a red leash. The cat smelled my trouser cuffs, but the woman left me alone. She took her cat and her blue hair and upswept rhinestone glasses out the front door. I caught the inside door before it clicked and went up the stairs to the second floor, where the corridor looked too clean and too bare. Muriel's apartment was at the back. I knocked on her door and waited. Nothing. I knocked again with no response. I was beginning to get that feeling I used to get when Nick and Nora Charles or Mr. and Mrs. North used to knock at the suspect's door and get no answer. I tried the knob. The door was open. Part of me decided that it was time to take back my overdue library books and declined to have anything further to do with this business. The apartment was quiet. I went in. I began to breathe more easily when I saw that the lights had been left on. She must have gone down to the laundry room or out for a quart of milk, I thought. Something mundane and sensible like getting new heels put on or having your hair cut. I called out, "Muriel?" No answer.

I was now in the living-room, which had wall-to-wall broadloom in a colour like old mushrooms. The furniture all matched, and reminded me of the ads that offer a room full of furniture for less than a thousand dollars. The drapes, which were drawn over the windows, were of the same material as the chairs. A game of cards was laid out on a coffee table, a half-filled glass of amber-coloured liquid stood beside it. Smelled like Canadian rye, but you could fool me. An ashtray full of butts completed the decor, except for the pictures. About them, the less said the better. I went on exploring. The bedroom was messy, the bed unmade. A small suitcase lay open and sprawled on the floor beside the pleated ruffle that enclosed the lower part of the bed. I recognized Muriel's scent in a bunch of perfume bottles on a vanity table under a mirror. I didn't much like the strange face that looked out at me from it. I should have taken my hat off when I came in. I did now, but it didn't help. In the closet, I found her fur coat, and a couple of cloth coats, and the whole registry of skirts, dresses, robes, negligees, nightgowns and about thirty pairs of shoes. If the coat was here, she must be down in the laundry room; certainly, she hadn't gone far.

The only other room, besides the kitchen, which in an apartment like this you could search in a fraction of a second, was the bathroom, and I almost left without peeking in there. I guess I must have thought that when Muriel walked in the front door with a hamper full of neatly folded linen on her hip, I could shout in my defence that at least I hadn't violated the sanctity of the bathroom. Whatever else I might be guilty of, I was free of that. But I could hear a tap dripping with loud drops. I couldn't resist. I opened the bathroom door, and there was Muriel with her head face down under a foot of water in the bath.

I found myself sitting on the white and black tiled floor of the bathroom with a yellow towel clutched in my hand. It was damp and clammy. From where I sat, I could see only the end of one of Muriel's legs poking up over the edge of the pastel blue tub. It didn't move. After I had caught up with my breathing, I came over to the tub on my hands and knees. Slowly, I lifted my head. It was all so quiet. The only sound came from regular fat gouts of water dropping from the shower head. They hit the water where Muriel's hair had fanned out on the surface. She was fully dressed, except for her shoes. One had slipped into the tub, where the polish was beginning to discolour the water. The other was near my knee on the bath mat. The water was cold but not icy. The back of her neck felt slightly warm. The pattern of her underwear showed through where her flowered dress was sodden. Only the back of the skirt remained dry near the hem. Elsewhere, even above the waterline, it had become wet. On the hand of the arm bent behind her, was the big green ring. Somehow I got up, found the door and the telephone. I was still holding the towel. I used it to hold the phone as I dialed the number of the Regional Police.

TWELVE

It was about eleven o'clock. I was sitting in Staff-Sergeant Chris Savas's office waiting for him to get back from Muriel's apartment. I had been surprised how fast the cops got me out of there. They let me let them in and show them to the bathroom, then I was driven back downtown to the Regional Police Centre on Church Street to wait for Chris. Chris and I went back a few years together, and Pete Staziak and I play a little gin rummy from time to time.

From the window, I could look down on the police parking lot, with overhead mercury lights reflecting on the decaying snowpiles. Beyond that I could see the blue and pink neon sign of the City House where my room was. If I hadn't played the good citizen and phoned the cops about Muriel I'd be watching the late news after a long hot bath, with the prospect of the next chapter of a thriller before lights-out. Instead, here I was waiting for Savas to turn up and ask me the same questions he could ask me in the morning, when at least I could wash them down with a cup of coffee.

For the last hour, I'd had the feeling that I'd forgotten an appointment or that there was something I was neglecting. Then I thought of the letter with my name on it. It was still where I'd put it in my inside breast pocket. I tore it open a little more savagely than I intended. I knew I couldn't change anything. Speed would not help Muriel now.

Besides the money, there was a single piece of notepaper from the desk of an infrequent letter-writer. It said:

Dear Benny,

Sorry I had to run out on you this way. Here is another hundred dollars, which should square us as far as work goes. You're also welcome to anything in the apartment. No need to get in touch. Don't worry.

62

You've done all you were supposed to do. I might get in touch one of these days, but don't hold your breath. God love you,

Muriel

So, she was running off and was interrupted before she got to slam the door. Poor Muriel. I slipped the five twenties into my wallet, thinking of that green ring of hers.

I looked at Chris Savas's desk. He was the best cop in town, but he was also the messiest. I could tell what he had eaten for lunch by the crumbs on his blotter; I could see that his desk calendar had got behind, and that he was giving himself notice of a meeting that had taken place three weeks ago. The big calendar on the wall announced that this was still January. Files were stacked all over the place: on top of the filing cabinet, behind the filing cabinet and on both sides of the filing cabinet. I was tempted to look, but I could guess that he hadn't thought of putting any files inside the filing cabinet. I was thinking this and other uncharitable thoughts when he walked in on me.

Savas is a big man even for a cop. He has a face like a boiled ham and shoulders that could buttress a cathedral. His eyes are steely sharp but there are lines that show he laughs a lot. He hung up his coat and hat without looking at me. Only when he had settled in behind his desk and lit a cigarette, did our eyes meet.

"Okay, Benny, let's have it. I'm tired and I want to go home. Never mind the stuff about finding her. You already told that to Kyle and Bedrosian at the apartment. I want to know why you were there and what she was to you."

"I told Kyle that too."

"Yeah, I know. But humour me."

"Okay, she hired me to find Johnny Rosa. He had been living with her since he got out of Kingston. He disappeared about a month ago, as if you didn't know."

"Only vaguely, Benny, and from far off. I got other fish to fry too. Johnny Rosa was big news once, but today he's just another parole violation. Let the Mounties find him, if they can. Why were you visiting the lady at such an unbusinesslike hour, Benny?"

"I'm in an unbusinesslike business." He got up from his chair and walked to the window. The mercury light came through the Venetian blinds and put stripes across his big face while he stood pulling his ear.

"And, before I forget it, how does all this mesh with the envelope you dropped off here earlier? I try to stay on top of things around here, but with you on the job I'm sliding all over the place."

"There's a tie-in, all right. The stuff in the envelope is suspected bloodstains, which I chipped from the driver's seat of an old Volkswagen, towed into Steve's Garage out near Lock One on the canal. It's on the Lakeshore Road near Niagara."

"I know where it is, Benny. So?"

"So, the car is registered to Muriel Falkirk, deceased of this city, and the last-known driver of it was Johnny Rosa. I thought it would be interesting to see whether the stuff I found happened to be blood to begin with and also if it happened to match Johnny Rosa's blood. . ."

"Which I've been trying to check with the authorities up in Kingston."

"But all I've got wouldn't convince a court-room janitor."

"So, who's doing all this killing, Benny?"

"Could be lots of people. Not even necessarily the same people. You know as well as I do who has been after the Warren ransom money. This case has got more angles than a crapgame has side-bets." Savas let his eyes roll up to the ceiling. "Did the coroner give you any dope on how long Muriel had been dead? Was it drowning, or did it just look that way?"

"You never give anything away, do you? Benny, you're off the case. Your client is going to have a post mortem in the morning, not breakfast." He didn't bother to throw a hand over a rather theatrical yawn and stretch. "You might as well go home and get some sleep. I'm knocking off myself. You want a lift back to your car?"

"Sure. It's not out of your way?"

"Naw, come on."

About ten minutes later, we were both sitting in Savas's car across from my car parked in front of Muriel's apartment. Neither of us said anything. We both got out and walked up the cement path to the front door. Savas opened it and the other door and we quietly went up the stairs to the apartment. He had a key to that door too. The fingerprint boys had powdered a few of the obvious places. The drink on the table was missing, although the cards were still there. Somebody without more interesting things to do had added a red five to the black six showing. Deft, I thought, and then, What a crazy business. We went into the bedroom. Chris held out the Persian lamb coat from the closet, looking in my direction, as if to ask, "Who paid for that?" We both noted three new suits of men's clothes hanging in the closet on the same rod as the coat.

"Johnny's?"

"I guess." Savas gave me one of his humorless smiles, which was just a muscular reflex.

The bathroom had been returned to normal. Somebody had even replaced the towels. Without Muriel, the room looked big and empty. She wasn't gone completely, just out of sight.

The contents of the suitcase had been turned out on the bed. The new leather purse was there as well, together with a buff plastic bag containing three large bottles of headache preparation with codeine and a phial of Gravol. There was also a new calf-skin wallet with a passport compartment. I clicked open the brass snaps and there lay the passport. It was made out to Ada Williams, but the picture was Muriel Falkirk.

"Oh, you found that?" Chris said, in an off-handed way. "There was some American money with it, which went downtown." It figured. I went back into the bathroom.

"Tell me about the bathtub plug," I asked Savas, as he was turning from the scene. "Was it in place firmly, was it half in, half out?" Chris shook his head, smiling.

"You trying to make this into an accident Benny? No way. This is homicide, trust poppa. You think she maybe hit her head on a cupboard door in the kitchen, came in here to soak her head and fainted into the bath? Come on. Who turned off the water?" I shrugged and followed Chris out of the room. Back in the living-room, I thought I'd ask a smart question.

"I see you've taken the drink downtown."

"Yeah, thought we'd see what prints were on it. Why?"

"I thought it might be nice to see what she was drinking, since there is no bottle around as far as I can see." Savas doesn't blush. Policemen as a rule don't. But he rolled his eyes up to the ceiling to take the pressure off his cheeks.

"Damn it, I've been over this place six times and I knew there was something. We got a cheapskate murderer on our hands: he comes with a bottle then takes it away when he's finished. A real sweetheart."

"Or worse: he could have removed the bottle that Muriel had when he got here. Either way, I wonder why."

"Maybe it's rare stuff."

"Or it could have been drugged. Maybe drugged her from it, then hit her with it."

"I don't care diddly for theories right now, I'm bushed. Call me tomorrow." He turned out the lights in Muriel's apartment and softly closed the door behind us. We didn't say anything as we walked down the stairs and out into the night. He crossed to his car, I to mine. I sat still in it after turning the engine over to let the heat circulate. Savas had been gone a couple of minutes before I put the car in gear and headed back to my hotel.

A gentle drone came from the beverage room of the City House. The last call had come and gone, and waiters were scooping up the remaining empty glasses from the beer-ringed tables. Through a blue haze, Dick the bartender caught my eye as I was about to hit the stairs to my room. He came over to me, wiping his hands on his dirty apron and jingling the change in his cash belt as he walked.

"Two guys been in looking for you earlier, Benny."

"Anybody I know?"

"Didn't look like it. I was happy you were out. I try to mind my own business, so I didn't ask any questions. You got another husband mad at you?"

"What time?"

" 'bout half hour ago. I seen them heading for the stairs, but I sent Gus over and he worried them out the side door." He looked at me hard, like he was trying to see whether I was more interesting than he'd ever suspected. I shrugged, thanked him and as I walked up the squeaking stairs began wondering what kind of protection the lock on my door provided when a visitor wanted to get familiar before being invited.

There was no one in my room, not even under the bed or in the closet. The bed had the look of the usual chambermaid; everything in order, but nothing done too well.

I set the beat-up alarm clock and pulled off my clothes. It had been a long day, and I already had the feeling that the night was going to be longer. I counted out enough pills into the palm of my hand to rub out the picture of Muriel Falkirk's legs hanging over the edge of the tub, and drank them down with a glass of cloudy tap-water. For a minute I thought I'd see if the local news would have anything on the murder, but I knew it was too late. A murder has to happen before noon to make the late local news.

I turned on my set anyway, and found myself in the middle of a late night talk show, with the earlier guests I'd missed strung out on both sides of the host and the lady writer he was interviewing. He was pretending that he'd read her book and didn't sound very convincing. But he had to try. A couple of nights earlier he'd used the frank approach and confessed that he hadn't had time to "finish" the book he was talking about. His researchers must go crazy. The lady writer was telling him that she had recently discovered what it was like to be a human being. He said that was nice, and soon they were talking about the recent theft of her jewelry, which seemed to suit her as well as talking about being a human being. I started to nod, so I reached over and turned it off. I fell into a deep sleep wondering what she might have been before she was human.

THIRTEEN

I don't know what time it was when the phone woke me. All I remember is that the insistent ringing pulled me off stage where I was pretending, in blackface, that I was the real Larry Parks pretending that he was the real Al Jolson.

"Hello?"

"Mr. Cooperman?" The voice was little and far away. It sounded as though it had been crying.

"Yes. Who is this?"

"Jennifer Bryant."

"Who? I don't . . ."

"Jennifer. Rolf's friend? You came to the farm earlier."

"Oh, yeah. That Jennifer. What can I do for you that can't wait for daylight?"

"Mr. Cooperman, Rolf's gone. They came for him about an hour ago. What am I going to do?"

"Just a minute, Jennifer. Take it slowly from the start. What time is it to begin with?" I eased my body out of bed and tried to focus on the face of the alarm clock. It said 2:30 in the morning. I fished a smoke from my pocket and twisted around on the bed feeling for my matches like a blind man in a movie, bumping into things that weren't even close. I finally found them and surprised my eyes lighting up in the dark.

"It was after one when they came, Mr. Cooperman. There were two of them, big men, and they made Rolf go with them. Will I ever see Rolf again? Will . . . I . . . oh, Mr. Cooperman, I can't . . ."

"Listen, Jennifer. Jennifer? Listen to me." I was beginning to see that it was difficult to control things from my end of the phone. She had drifted off her end, and I wasn't sure she could hear me any more. "Jennifer, can you hear me?"

"Mr. Cooperman? Are you still there?"

"Yes, I'm here. Listen, Jennifer, I'm getting in my car and coming over to your place. Do you understand? I'll be

68

there in about twenty minutes. Will you be all right until then? Can you hold on?''

"I think so. I'll try. But please, hurry." I promised and hung up. I pulled my pants and an old sweater on over my pajamas and looked my last at the bed. The footsteps echoing down the linoleum corridor and then down the stairs were my own. They met the deadly hush of the silent beverage room. The empty chairs were all looking at me as I went out the front door.

It didn't take as long to get over to the Louth Road at that time of night. It wasn't fifteen minutes after I heard the frightened voice on the phone that I slowed down for the second time in twelve hours looking for the lane with a mail box marked "Sanderson".

It was bloody cold when I got out of the car. The slamming door echoed off the wall of the barn and set a dog barking over in the next concession. The path froze my feet through the soles of my shoes as I made for the porch, where a flashlight was showing me the way. As I reached the door, Jennifer's white arm opened it and let me in.

Funny, I hadn't really noticed Jennifer on my earlier trip. Now with red eyes and nose, dressed in a faded flannel nightgown, she ran to me, and I held her. I rested my chin on her heaving shoulder, reminding myself that I was here as a family friend. I heard myself making comforting noises like "there, there", patted her back and smoothed her long brown hair, then led her to the couch. Neither of us said anything until her sobs stopped.

"Now, tell me," I started in a voice that frightened me, it was so loud. I tried again a little softer. "Jennifer, try to tell me every detail about the men who came for Rolf. Try not to leave anything out."

"Okay," she said, trying out a smile on her small, tear-stained face. "I didn't get a good look at the car. There'd been a moon, but it went down early. It was very dark out there; I could hardly see anything but their headlights from the house. There were two of them. Both big and slow. One of them asked if Rolf was in. They stepped into the hall and I went to get him." I nodded to show that all of this was helping, and she began speaking less hesitantly and without doing more damage to her nose with a battered Kleenex. "Rolf had had more beer after you left, and I had been smoking, sitting next to him, here."

"Smoking?" I asked raising my eyebrows slightly.

"Smoking. You know." She tried to grin, but it didn't work. "Rolf got up and came out to them."

"Did he appear to know them?"

"I'm not sure. He didn't get time to say anything, really. One of them called his name, and they both walked over to him. If they said anything else I didn't hear it. They turned around and he followed them. He threw me a short glance, but didn't say anything. The men looked at me, but they didn't talk either. Rolf got his coat and they helped him into it, both of them. We all watched him put on his boots, and when he'd done that, they left. I ran out and tried to get the number of the car, but I couldn't get it in the glare of the lights, and besides, I didn't have my contacts in."

"Contacts?"

"Contact lenses. I'm blind as a bat without them." She looked almost confident now. A brilliant recovery, I thought. But I couldn't think of a thing I could do to help her. So I kept on asking questions. She told me that the men were dressed alike in heavy twill trousers and khaki parkas with similar fur hats and boots. They hadn't shouted at her, just went about their business as though she wasn't there. One had smiled at her briefly.

Jennifer had quietened down now and was trying to help. She even asked if I wanted some coffee. I needed it all right. The pills I'd taken earlier were trying to shut off my lights. I could feel the little beggars inside me crossing the wires and shorting the main connections. When she returned with the coffee, she had thrown on a blue terrycloth bathrobe. That would help me concentrate on the coffee and the matter at hand. The coffee was strong and went right to work.

"Rolf told me your father's a lawyer."

"That's right."

"Can we count on his help, if we need it?" She frowned into her coffee.

"I haven't seen Daddy in over a year. You see, Mr. Cooperman, Daddy didn't approve of my living with Rolf. He tried everything he could to break us up."

"Would he have gone this far?" My eyes caught hers for a second, but she broke the connection.

"Oh no, he'd never sink that low. I don't think. No. He might agonize over my being here, you know, but he wouldn't do anything so overt. That's not his psychology at all. He wouldn't even try to bring me back by force. He wants me to see the error of my ways and come home like a prodigal daughter. He wouldn't try anything that might possibly cause a scandal. Not Daddy." She ended up smiling at some picture in her mind, but didn't share it with me.

"Where did you meet Rolf? I gather not in prison." She smiled again, and tugged at the blue belt of her robe.

"When Rolf got out on parole, the board helped find him a job at the yacht club. Rolf is wonderful around boats. I met him the summer before last. He seemed to be so much more grown-up than the boys in my gang. He made their smartest schemes sound dumb. I don't mean that he was always putting them down. Just the opposite. He rarely opened his mouth. It's just that he was busier, quieter, more mature, I guess."

"And Daddy didn't take to him?"

"At first he didn't say anything, and then, I guess when he found out who Rolf was, he did everything he could to see that it remained only a summer romance. Bribes: Europe, an American college, the whole bit. Anyway, in the fall, Rolf left the club and started selling insurance. He made contacts among the younger gang at the club and he knew the campus up at Secord University pretty well too. He has two years towards his degree, you know."

"Sorry, I didn't. Has he every spoken to you about the Warren business?"

"Naturally, but what's that got to do with all this? He's paid for that mistake. When are they going to leave him alone?" She was losing control again, and I didn't blame her.

71

"Look," I said, "I think you should try to get some sleep. Do you have anything that will help make you sleep?"

"Sleep? Without knowing where Rolf might be? I couldn't, I just couldn't. What do you think they'll do to him?"

"Depends on whether he has any guilty knowledge. Has he? Does he know anything about the missing Warren money? Has he heard from Johnny Rosa?"

"No. He told you the truth. He wouldn't lie, especially about Johnny. Johnny was a crazy sort of god to Rolf, even after what happened."

"So he would help Johnny if he was in trouble?"

"Yes . . . but I'm not sure how far he'd go. I know that he doesn't want to risk going back to prison, or have his parole revoked . . ."

"Never mind. I didn't really expect you could answer that."

"More coffee?"

"No, I think I'll try to get some sleep. Do you mind if I curl up here on the couch?"

"No sweat. If the pups don't get in your way. I'll bring you a blanket." She disappeared, and I pulled off my shoes. My socks were damp. When she returned, she was carrying a maroon blanket smelling of mothballs. She told me where I could find the bathroom and where to turn out the light. In spite of the mugs of coffee inside me, I found myself drifting into a deep sleep within seconds.

In my dream I was being chased over a winter landscape by two howling hounds while the tree I knew I could climb to escape them kept disappearing as I reached it, reappearing at the top of the next hill. Somehow, although I could never grasp the tree, the dogs could never quite reach me. It was one of my good nightmares.

I awoke to the sound of sizzling in the kitchen and the peculiar smell of frying fat coming from the same direction. I felt weak and dirty. I found the bathroom, splashed some water around, injured myself on the inside plumbing and cursed the luck that had brought me out in the middle of the night. To clean my teeth, the best I could do was to wet the end of a towel and give them a lick and a promise. In the medicine chest, a piece of home carpentry with a toothpaste-spotted mirror, I found a shelf devoted to Jennifer's contact lenses, wetting solutions, concentrated cleaners, storage solutions and a little plastic container with two tabs, like miniature toilet seats, marked right and left.

Jennifer was in the kitchen, wearing jeans and yesterday's purple T-shirt. She smiled at me and asked how I'd slept. She talked in a formal voice, like she was talking to the neighbour. She was feeling shy about me, and I figured I should take it as a compliment. There were two mugs of tea on the big round table. I sat down behind one and Jennifer sat across from me, sliding a white ironstone plate in front of each of us.

"There'll be toast in a minute," she said. I looked into my plate and saw the bacon. It was bacon, all right. I'd know it anywhere.

"What's the matter?" she asked.

"Matter?"

"You've gone white. Your face. Are you okay?"

"Sure." She brought me a piece of buttered toast, and I absent-mindedly began chewing at it while she devoured her three strips of curly bacon. I could see no way out. I closed my eyes and took a bite, seeing in my mind's eye the earth opening up to swallow me. It didn't. Well, it didn't right then.

FOURTEEN

My phone was ringing while I fumbled with my keys trying to unlock the office door. I leaped over a pile of mail and reached the phone just as it stopped. If it was important, they'd call again. The mail was also a disappointment: bills and junk mail. Do I want to own a replica of a rare Dutch clock? What about a hundred and fifty piece set of socket wrenches? A magazine company offered to send me their magazine at a price that undercut the price paid by subscribers. A poor deal for subscribers. And a note from my bank began, "In order to serve you better. . ." I reminded myself to wince whenever I ran into that phrase. Like a lot of things, it meant the opposite.

When the phone rang again, I was able to reach it before it finished the first ring. After all, I was in business, and my only client was in the morgue.

"Hello?"

"Mr. Cooperman?" The voice was cultured, male and sugary.

"That's right. Who's speaking?"

"This is Bill Ashland. I got the message you left with Friesen, Sunter and McLeod. I hope I can help you. What exactly did you have in mind? Something in the stocks line? The market is very active this week."

"Yeah, I heard that. I wonder if I could talk to you?"

"Thinking of taking the plunge? I have a few hot numbers."

"Anything as hot as the number where I can reach Johnny Rosa?" There was a sudden hush at his end of the line. I'd expected it. The hot air went out of him like he had the football and the opposing team knew it. My own knuckles were looking white on the phone, so I don't know why I was feeling so smug. If I hated eggs, what was I doing in the poultry business, as my father used to say.

"Who are you and what do you want?" He said this in a flat voice that had lost its carnival manner.

"You've got my name in front of you," I said, "and I want to talk to you about half a million dollars. My bet is that you'd like to know where it is, and that you think you'd know how to spend it. Problem is, you don't know where to look. That's why I want to see you."

"Look, I don't want anything to do with you or that damned money. I've paid plenty for it already. I'm not going to lay down any more time."

"I'm full of sympathy, Ashland. My stony old heart is bleeding for you. The way I see it, there's no harm done in trading a little information. After all, the case is over and done with. I don't want to talk to you about anything you haven't already paid for. And, you never can tell, I might know something you don't know."

"Talk's cheap, Mr., uh, Cooperman. Where did you trip over such valuable information? Who are you anyway? What's your angle?"

"I'm a private investigator. You can look me up in the book. I've already collected a pocketful of information."

"I don't have a Toronto book handy, but I'll check you out, Cooperman."

"I'm local, Mr. Ashland. We've got P.I.s here in Grantham too, you know: sidewalks, electric light, and now private investigators. And I've been paid to find Johnny Rosa. I think you know he's away without leave?"

"Who doesn't? But I still don't see why I should talk to you."

"I'm not bending your arm. I'm only making a suggestion. You could be right. Maybe I shouldn't be talking to you at all. It's not as though you're the only one interested, is it? I've been wrong before. There are other trees I could bark up. I've got a list of them."

"Okay, okay, I'll talk to you. But I'm a busy man, and I don't want to take too much time. I've got to go down to the CN Station just before five on business. I'll see you there at five. In the waiting room, and no tricks." He hung up abruptly. I didn't even get to ask what kind of tricks he expected. Maybe he thought I'd have all my assistant operatives disguised as baggagemen and departing passengers. If I had assistant operatives, naturally, that's what I would do with them.

I was beginning to feel like I'd spent the night curled up with a blanket smelling of mothballs on a couch that was shared with a pair of pups of an expanding territorial disposition. My stomach was not the stalwart companion of my youth either. After my first breakfast of bacon, I felt the dark angel both in the pit of my stomach and riding the hot air currents above my head. I went next door to see if I could bother Frank Bushmill for a handful of aspirin, or any other cure that a practising chiropodist is privy to.

There were three old ladies with three shades of gray hair sitting in the bright waiting room. The one that had had a blue rinse was reading *Time* magazine, catching up on the New Deal. The one with the pinkish rinse was deep in a book-sized magazine on ornamental gardens. The third had brought a lending-library book of her own, and was now well along the way to discovering who murdered Roger Ackroyd. Her hair had a yellowish tint under a fine hair-net to protect the manufactured wave. I grinned at the ladies, who took in my old sweater, but I hoped didn't guess at the pajamas I was still wearing underneath. After a minute, Frank, demonstrating again that he has the ears of a bat, came out of his surgery and gave me the top of the morning with his smile. The three ladies studied him over their bifocals. He acknowledged them with a curt professional nod apiece.

"Good morning, Benny. I thought I heard you. Isn't it a grand day for the polar bears now? I was hoping you'd drop by, I've got a good book for you. You're killing yourself with that television."

"Could you spare some aspirin, Frank?"

"Sweet Heart of Jesus, are you dying on my doorstep, Benny? I've got the stuff to fix you up, and no mistake. I'll be right back." He retreated into his sanctuary for a moment, and was back in front of me in short order holding a frothing noisy drink in a paper cup. "Drink this down, Ben, and it'll

76

have you fit in no time. These good ladies don't mind my taking on an emergency when it comes along. Am I right, Mrs. Dalrymple?'' Mrs. Dalrymple, the one with the blue rinse, nodded agreement, and the others bobbed approving heads too. I drank down the mixture, an old fashioned Seidlitz powder, the effervescent bubbles tickling my nose, wishing everybody long life and happiness. Frank brought out the Irish in me. His company put my normal speech in a fine disorder. My stomach ache even began to go away. I guess, when I was feeling Irish, I didn't mind the bacon so much. I could feel violent things beginning to happen in my insides, so I excused myself and retreated to the toilet. I began thinking about poor Frank. He probably had bacon for breakfast three or four times a week and never gave it a second thought. And here I was, four thousand years of dietary laws going up in the fat of the frying pan.

I pulled myself together and returned to the office. Once again the phone was ringing. I had a feeling in my solar plexus to let it go on ringing, but made the mistake of answering it.

"Hello?" I tried not to sound too encouraging. Like I didn't need the favour of anybody's business. I was going crazy.

"Mr. Cooperman?" I'd heard that voice somewhere.

"Yes."

"Mrs. Jarman would like to see you this afternoon. Could you make it at two?" It was the private secretary.

"Sure, Blackwood, I wouldn't miss it. The little place on the hill, isn't it?"

"Mr. Cooperman, you might save your comic side for those that appreciate such things. May I take it then that you will come?"

"Wouldn't miss it. See you at two. Bye."

"Goodbye, Mr. Cooperman." Blackwood must have grown up with her own print of *Rebecca*. She was playing Mrs. Danvers well, but at an absurdly young age.

Before the phone could ring again, I decided to use it myself. The earpiece was still warm against my right ear. I dialed the number of Savas at the Regional Police. I waited

77

while the switchboard shunted me around the wire maze for a minute and then Savas gave me his usual greeting.

"Cooperman? What the hell you want? I though we had your only paying client in the refrigerator?"

"You know what I want."

"Okay, okay. Here it is. Muriel Falkirk: apparent age, twenty-eight. Subject well nourished, evidence of good care and attention. Height, five-foot five; weight, one hundred and thirty-eight pounds. Are you still with me, Benny?"

"Sure, I wouldn't want to miss anything." Savas was in a good mood, for Savas. I was getting more curious. "Keep it coming."

"Here it comes: ecchymoses under hair at back of head, none in face or anywhere else. No marks of restraint or struggle. Dead between 7:30 and 9:30 pm, Tuesday, February 12th. Cause of death: drowning while unconscious. Do you want the internal details, Benny? We've got a fracture at the base of the skull, water in the lungs and rye in the stomach. There wasn't much food residue, so she hadn't been taken out to dinner first. Oh, yeah, in case you think you're some kind of smart ass, we checked the water in her lungs: it was the same as in the tub. Just in case you want to say the murderer had fancy dime-novel ideas. Satisfied?"

"What kind of rye was she drinking?"

"Tell you tomorrow. That stuff goes to the Liquor Control Board lab in Toronto. They tell us good, but they take their time about it. Except of course when private investigators ask for favours. Then they bust their ass."

"You got a report on the blood?" Now I knew why he was beaming on his side of the phone.

"Yup. It just came in. I found out that Rosa's blood type, as noted at Kingston, was Group O Rh positive. The stuff in the envelope, which was blood all right, proved to be Group B. When I was just about to call you up with that piece of damning news, I got a call from the head serologist in Toronto, who said that they'd done more tests and now the blood in your envelope was known to be Group O Rh positive. How much are you paying serologists these days, Benny?" I think he could sense the grin that I was transmitting down the wire. I was suddenly feeling like not such a bad detective after all. "Is there any other work," Savas was enjoying this, "that an honest cop can do for the private sector this morning? If not, I'll get back to the public. G'bye."

If Blackwood thought I was a comedian, she would love Chris Savas. I could picture the two of them romping on the big front yard with the Warren mansion in the background. I tried to think how the latest news from the coroner changed my life. Frankly, I was feeling so terrible, that I couldn't think of anything. I backed out of the office, turned off the overhead light, and slammed the spring lock behind me. It wasn't noon, but I'd had the office up to my eardrums. Home is where the heart is, and that's where I was headed.

FIFTEEN

After a shower and a nap, I got up refreshed, then dressed to present my better self to the gang at the Warren place. I slicked down my hair with both of my military brushes, cleaned my nails and darkened my ankle under the hole in my best black socks with a dab of Warren Shoepolish. My shirt was clean, even if it had never reconciled itself with the shape of my neck. A conservative tie with a fat knot in it hid most of the problem. The face in the mirror was recognizably my own, except for the blotches where I'd scrubbed it a little too enthusiastically. My shoes dulled the shine on my trousers when I rubbed the uppers against my trouser legs, but picked up a little of the afterglow.

Everybody knew the Warren mansion. It hung over the edge of the Escarpment from its highest point. You could see its lights coming over the highway late at night from the Falls. I'd heard that old George Warren used to entertain celebrities up there over the years. The names never got into the papers. Warren wouldn't stand for that, although he would sometimes allow a discreet society note: Mr. and Mrs. George Warren entertained Lord and Lady Whozzis at their Mountain home last weekend . . .

Knowing the location of the mansion was one thing, getting there was something else again. I cut off the four-lane highway, twirled around a cloverleaf or two and found myself on a straight macadamized road heading for the Mountain, as some of the locals called the Escarpment. When it reached the slope, the road curved to the right and began a series of switch-backs, each mounting higher, until the well-sanded hairpins gave way to a straight razor cut through a forest of young beech and poplars. There was a gatehouse with large stone pillars to the left, and piles of dusty snow on either side of a clean black lane that arced up to the house. The view was inter-rupted by the box hedges and tall ornamental trees, some of the smaller ones with winter bags over them. The drive was designed to make the mansion look impressive and it did. It would have taken more than a discarded back seat from a '58 Chevy or a rubber tire swing hanging from that silver birch to spoil the effect of that much ivy covering that much wall. Each of the windows, the same number on each side of the big front door, was divided into a dozen panes, and each was winking at me differently; telling me that this was the wink of old glass. A *porte cochère* jutted out from the front door. I left the Olds with the keys in it. If they wanted it moved, the help could do it.

It was a serious-faced, attractive young woman with beautiful eyebrows who let me in. I told her my business, and without speaking, she indicated that I follow her. She led the way past a few museum pieces in the front hall. She didn't bother taking my coat, but moved up the curving staircase, which was made of dark wood with slender, turned balusters. Climbing ahead of me, the girl was also slender, with easy movements. The prints on the wall were engravings of classical ruins, massive arches seen through other arches. After the fourth or fifth of these, I became distracted by the gentle rustle of the skirts just in front of me. Then, suddenly it hit me. This was Blackwood, the Mrs. Danvers voice I'd scuffled with on the phone. From the landing at the head of the stairs, she led the way through a long passage to the back of the house and motioned me to stop before a closed door. She knocked and went in, leaving me to stand in my own meltwaters. In a second, she was out again and called me by name. It was Blackwood, all right.

"Mr. Cooperman, come in please."

"Thank you, Blackwood," I said, trying not to sound too smug. Her eyebrows came together in a very attractive way, and I walked past her into the next room.

It was a huge studio, with north light, an easel as big as the Ritz, lots of work-in-progress hanging on the tall walls, which went up through where the ceiling ought to have been to a roof about thirty feet above the floor. A table near the easel had been mustered to serve as a palette: a piece of plate glass was nearly covered with blobs of pigment. At one end of the room, a balcony jutted a dozen feet into the room. To reach it, a black wrought-iron spiral staircase beckoned to the sure of foot. A door from the third floor of the house also led to this balcony, which held a large piece of sculpture and a shiny leather couch that I bet didn't open up into anything. In the middle of the studio, Gloria Jarman, the Warren heiress, was sitting on a tall stool in old jeans and a paint-smeared man's shirt. She got up and started walking to me with a paintbrush in her teeth, like a pirate with a dagger. She was tall and slender, a brunette with the white skin that should always go with it. Her eyes were green and friendly.

"Mr. Cooperman, I'm so glad you could come. Sorry to welcome you in such a mess, but I'm preparing for an exhibition in the spring and I've got at least forty more pictures to do. I hate working in the winter, don't you? You have to steal the light. I've ended up putting in artificial. Otherwise I'd be here till July with nothing to show for it. Come over here, I'll show you what I've been doing." Without taking a new breath or looking back, she raised her voice, calling: "Blackwood, we'll have some tea in here, I think. You'd enjoy a cup of tea, wouldn't you, Mr. Cooperman? I know I would." She picked up a rag and began rubbing her hands, as though she wanted to shake hands with me, but the timing was wrong. She gave it up after a nervous minute.

The canvas on the big easel was a painting of a broken doll. The head had been split open. The painting was precise to the point of pedantry: every blotch on the face, every tear of the clothing was rendered faithfully, perhaps too faithfully. The pattern of the doll clothes, the texture of the composition head, the glassy stare of the eyes all announced that Gloria Jarman, or Warren (I didn't know then that she exhibited under another name entirely), was a very accomplished artist.

"I've been working in acrylic for the past year," she said, looking at one of the pictures with her head tilted to one side and pulling at a loose strand of hair.

Wherever you turned in the studio, pictures of dolls looked out at you with a gaze that was strange and frightening. Blown up on the canvases to twice the normal size or bigger, they made me want to avoid eye-contact. They weren't all battered like the one on the easel; some sat with dignity, some stood. All were Victorian with cream complexions and long dresses. It was as if each of the figures were expressing some half-stifled emotion that had been under control for a hundred years. Each was so slyly drawn that it was impossible for me at least to tell how the painter had shown the greed or anger, fear or pettiness on their unmarked faces. Otherwise, all looked exactly like the dolls in the basket of old dolls lying in a heap near the outside wall.

She led the way to another leather couch at one end of the room. Here the light came from behind me, and the view of the studio could be seen without blinking. She didn't quiz me about her pictures, but she'd watched my face carefully as I'd examined them. There was a large slab of marble in front of the couch with heavy art books on it. Gloria Jarman took a seat opposite me and looked at me intently, like she was trying to decide if I could hold a pose in the nude for twenty minutes at room temperature.

"You're not very big, are you?" she asked smiling and giving a toss to her head to suggest that she was talking in italics.

"No, but I'm wiry," I told her. Funny, I didn't mind her staring at me. It gave me a democratic chance to stare back at her with equal frankness. Her dark hair was a mess, pulled back from a high, calming forehead with a polka-dot red bandana. Her cheekbones were covered with the glow of the work she'd interrupted, her mouth was generous with full lips, and her chin came to a point which tended to make her face a little top-heavy. Her hands were large, hanging at the end of nicely turned arms under the paint smears. Her shirt hung free at the waist and covered the designer label on the well-cut jeans. Her shoes were brown and English. The top three buttons of her shirt were undone, and that ended up, as usual, the main focus of my attention. As I looked at her, I felt suddenly sorry for George Warren. It would be easy to recognize fortune hunters buzzing around a plain daughter, but when the heiress was a great beauty, how could he sort out the drones?

"I'm sorry," she said, "I was staring. Very rude."

"So was I. We're both rude, but even." Now she tried out her let's-get-down-to-business smile. It was my cue. "You asked me to come up here, Mrs. Jarman, so I braved the hairpin turns, and here I am. Do you have a problem? I could use the business."

"You put it so appealingly, Mr. Cooperman. How could I resist?" She tried another smile and shifted in her leather chair, glad the meeting was under way. "Let's get down to cases. I had a phone call this morning. I think it was Johnny Rosa." She looked at me trying to see the effect of her words.

I tried to show as little surprise as I could get away with. After all, she'd told me that she'd call only if he tried to reach her.

"I see," I said. I let her have that much and a serious frown. "Tell me about it."

"It was about eight o'clock, or a little before. I honestly didn't check the time. I thought about it later. I thought that it might be important. It was around then, around eight."

"Keep talking," I said.

"He asked for me. Blackwood wasn't here. I was still in bed. I thought it might be Bob, phoning on the kitchen extension to tell me something before heading off to work, but it was this different voice. I don't know how to describe it. It was full of menace, I guess. It sent shivers, anyway."

"What did the voice say?"

"It asked if I was Mrs. Jarman. I said yes. Then there was a pause, as if he hadn't expected to get me so quickly, and then he said something like, 'You were the one. It had to be you. You've got to see me, I'll wait for you at the hole.' I think that's what he said. 'All I want is what I earned. Come alone at noon tomorrow.' "

"I said I didn't know what he was talking about but then he hung up. Some of his words may have been different, but that's the gist of it. Do you think it was Johnny Rosa? I can't think of anyone else it might have been."

"Do you know what 'the hole' might be?"

"No, it doesn't make any sense to me. Maybe I didn't hear him correctly. Why do you think he telephoned me, Mr. Cooperman? If it is Johnny Rosa, why is he still pursuing me? Why doesn't he stop or find someone new? I'm sick to death of Johnny Rosa and the lot of them. Do you understand?" She looked as though her hair was going to come loose; it had been thrown about as she added expression to her recounting of the conversation. I tried to think like a detective for a change and pulled my gaze away from Gloria.

"Well," I said, pulling a Player's from the nearly empty pack in my overcoat pocket. I found a light more easily than the next thing to say. I lit the cigarette elaborately, watching

Gloria's eyes follow the whole process. I felt like a magician who knew there was no rabbit up his sleeve. "Well," I repeated, "if that was Johnny Rosa, then my former client went to a lot of trouble trying to make it appear like he'd been killed. That's pretty funny."

"I don't understand." She lifted a chin that in this position didn't look so much pointed as aristocratic. I guess she led with her chin quite a lot. I liked it.

"She hired me to find Johnny. Now it sounds likely that she knew he wasn't really missing. Maybe she was trying to impress a friend, or a couple of friends."

"Why the mystery? Ask her."

"Can't. She was murdered last night."

"Oh dear. I mean, that's awful."

"For her, yeah. She paid me to find somebody that wasn't lost, and somebody drowned her for doing it. Anyway, she didn't get what she paid for, so, in a way, I still feel like I'm on the case. For another couple of days at least."

"And then?"

"Then I'll be working for you. Frankly, you need me. I'll try not to be so careless this time." She smiled, but her paint-smeared hand went involuntarily to her throat just the same. At this juncture, Blackwood came in wheeling a tray with a large silver teapot and a few very small pieces of bread and butter.

SIXTEEN

After the last of the crumbs had been cleared away on the tea trolley, with Blackwood following in its wake, I was settling into the prospect of further talk about business, but Gloria had caught me watching Blackwood's retreating backside from the room. As backsides go, it was one of the nicest I'd seen, and it was all the nicer because it didn't appear that she took much notice of it.

"She's a treasure," Gloria said.

"What?"

"Blackwood, she's wonderful. I don't know what I'd do without her."

"Where'd you learn to talk like that? Do you normally call people 'a treasure' and say you don't know what you'd do without them?"

"I see what you mean. It makes me sound older. Sounds like my mother talking through me. I'll try to watch it. I find myself imitating people I respect. I have to watch that in my painting. But I should really draw the line at Mother." She'd ignored a rasp of class envy in my voice. Breeding had to be worth that at least. She went on about her mother.

"She became one of those despicable rich women who haunt the casinos in the south of France. I think I keep seeing her in the movies. I haven't heard from her in years. She didn't even send a card when Daddy died, although, of course, we heard from her lawyer."

"Where did Blackwood come from?" The question surprised me too, since it led away from the territory I wanted to explore.

"Oh, the usual places. She was well recommended, and she really is very efficient. It's true, whether I say it in my mother's voice or my own. I've never met anyone so organized. I've only seen her rattled once, and that was when she mixed up the mail the morning Daddy died."

"Oh?"

"Detectives! Always on the lookout, aren't you? Well, the great letter mix-up happened *before* Daddy drowned. It was Blackwood who dived fully clothed into the pool after Daddy. She was too late, unfortunately. We were all too late. You should stop barking at her." She didn't look straight at me when she said this, and I made a mental note. She was playing with the hem of her shirt-tail, winding it around her fingers. It made her look about twelve.

"Did you have bad dreams after the kidnapping?" I asked, wondering what sort of effect the question would have on her shirt-twirling.

"I still have them. Not as often now, of course, but sometimes. Even in the middle of the day, I can feel someone standing behind me about to pull an evil-smelling hood over my face. If you get to know me better, you may see me suddenly go bug-eyed and turn around quickly. I was under a doctor's care for over a year you know. It seems silly, I guess. I mean, I was only a prisoner for a few hours."

"For most of a long weekend."

"Just the same. Apart from tying me up, they didn't actually hurt me. They didn't even threaten me, or talk to me at all. I remember being so thirsty. I'm sorry. I shouldn't be encouraged to talk like this."

"Tell me about your life before the kidnapping. Were you happy?'

"I should have been. I had every reason to be. I had everything I ever wanted from the cradle. I was never the poor little rich girl. Until two months ago, I had a father who loved me dearly. The George Warren that everybody knows from the business world wasn't Daddy. When he was with me, there was never a word about business. He was good and kind, and only wanted the best for me. Sometimes we disagreed about what 'best' was, but we agreed in theory anyway."

"You said you should have been happy."

"Did I? Well, I suppose I must have been."

"You had an older brother, didn't you?"

"Yes. Russell. He at least was spared the horror of the

kidnapping. He died a couple of months before it happened. We were very close, Russ and I. When we were little, we were more like a pair of twin brothers than brother and sister. Especially at the farm. We felt free there, truly free. Pop was alive then. My grandfather. He showed us his secret world where he could escape his wife and the others. The three of us were always staying clear of my grandmother's search parties. Like three kids. Russ and I never fought the way most brothers and sisters fight. Well, I guess we had our disagreements, but they were trivial compared to our everyday fondness for one another. He would have died for me, and I for him. I miss him, Mr. Cooperman.''

"Call me Benny. Everybody does.''

"I sometimes think of things that I want to tell him, and then, when I remember that he's gone, it hurts all over again.'' I was watching the shadows creep across the floor of the studio and crawl up the walls.

"He was killed in a car accident, wasn't he?''

"Yes. I don't like to talk about it. He always liked fast cars and he drove them fast. He was a wonderful driver. He used to drive his Lotus in car rallies. I remember feeling so proud one day when someone asked me if my brother was Russ Warren, the driver. Imagine that: 'Russ Warren, the driver.' '' She grinned at me and I gave her the best I could manage. I saw hers fade quickly as she faced again the irreparable loss. I thought I'd better try a new line for a while.

"How old were you when your mother went away?''

"How tactful you are, Mr., I mean Benny. I must have been twelve or thirteen. Russ was two years older. He sheltered me from that too. Nobody knows what a wonderful person he was, Benny: a really wonderful human being.'' I nodded and tried not to picture Russ Warren. I haven't met many really wonderful human beings in my time. Maybe I thought the compliment was a cheap label that tended to mark down the merchandise. She went on: "We were staying at the farm then. Of all the places we've lived, I think that those summers were the best. You can take the Riviera, the Costa Brava, Malaga, Sardinia. I'll take the old home farm any day.''

88

"Is it still the home farm, or is it now a housing development?"

"Oh, Daddy wouldn't have sold the farm. Never. And now I won't. It has too many memories for all of us. It was Daddy's home, where Pop raised his racehorses. When Pop died, it went to his oldest son. We didn't see much of it then, but when Uncle Henry died, four years ago, it came back to us. To Daddy, I mean. Sell the farm? It would be like selling part of your own body, an arm or a leg. You must see it sometime and try to imagine what it was like when it was being worked. I hate to go there now, because I always think that Russ will swing down from the hay mow, or jump out at me from a loft in the barn. He would go to great lengths to amuse me, Benny. We used to hide from the old folks, Russ, Pop and I. Pop had a store of old Scotch. Russ and I used to smoke cornsilk cigarettes and later we blew our first grass. I do so miss him. I don't know what I'd do if it weren't for Bob. Bob's helped me so much."

"What did your brother do, exactly, Mrs. Jarman?"

"Russ? Why, Russ could do anything. He could fix a motor or build a box-kite or find May morels or get me to stop crying. But, of course you mean what did he do as a job, don't you? Well, Russ never settled to anything. Sometimes he worked for Daddy. He couldn't stick wearing a tie, though. He hated jobs in the city. He had a lot of memberships that he attended to. You know, clubs."

"But he didn't work in the sense of 'I work', 'you work', 'he, she or it works'?" I could see she didn't like that, so I let it drop. "Can you think of any reason why Johnny Rosa, that is assuming it was Johnny Rosa, why he would want to see you after all this time?"

"Of course not. I only saw him at the trial, remember."

"Is there a chance he might think you know something that in fact you don't know?"

"I can't think what that might be. He can't believe that I know anything about the ransom money. Maybe he wants *more* money. Maybe he's trying to blackmail me."

"Why?"

" 'Why?' How should I know what a criminal like that thinks he can get away with? It's not funny. I didn't hear anything in what he said that sounded in the least familiar. It seemed intended for somebody else."

A door had opened on the balcony, and for a minute a tall male figure had looked over the balustrade, then begun to descend the spiral staircase. He didn't hurry.

"Do you think he will bother me again, Benny? Do you think I was right not to go directly to the police?" She looked over at the staircase. "Oh, Bob! You've missed tea. I'll have Blackwood get you something." She jumped up and stopped Jarman dead in his tracks with a massive hug.

"Hey! What will people think?" He was well over six feet tall, and bald on top but with a fashionable moustache over a whole keyboard of smiling teeth. His eyes were penetrating and blue, his handshake bone-crushing. "Glad to know you, Mr. Cooperman," he said when his wife had made the introductions. "Never mind about bothering Blackwood, dear. Maybe Mr. Cooperman will join me in a drink." He looked up at me conspiratorially, and made for a sideboard with a tray of bottles on it. Inside he found ice in a small refrigerator and a shaker full of left-over martinis. I said I'd have a light rye with water. He passed a drink to Gloria and sat down beside her. He didn't look so big once he'd been partly swallowed by the deep leather couch. His suit was immaculate, but he'd given his blue and white tie a pull and a shift that said 'I'm home'. I could picture him in an office easily. I could see him in a boardroom making the tough decisions, getting on airplanes bound for distant places, wearing a hard hat on a building site or by an oil well. He crackled with the kind of energy that governments don't tax.

"Mr. Cooperman's been giving me some advice about that call I told you about."

"Good. I'm glad to hear you're taking this seriously, Gloria. It's nothing to fool around with. I can't imagine why this man would be harassing my wife again, Mr. Cooperman. You'd think 'Once burned, twice shy', wouldn't you?" I shrugged. I was no expert on what is usual or unusual among half-successful kidnappers. Besides, I was still getting used to the idea of a living Johnny Rosa. Jarman was still talking when I tuned in again over the top of my glass. "Are you thinking of re-opening the kidnapping case, Mr. Cooperman?"

"Hardly that, Mr. Jarman. I . . ."

"Bob's the name. Please go on."

"I was just going to say that I have no intention of re-opening anything. I can't think that you'd want that either. Besides, I don't have a reason. You can't take an anonymous phone call to court. I had a hunch a couple of days ago that one of the hoodlums might try to contact your wife, and I was right. That's why she asked me here."

"I'd like you to take charge of this, Benny," Gloria said, with a sidelong glance at her husband, who nodded his approval. "If he phones again, I'll tell him to deal with you."

"Fine. You know, you should consider getting the police involved. I mean that seriously. They could put a man at your door if that would make you feel more comfortable."

"Right now, Benny, I think I'll get more sleep knowing that you're at the other end of the telephone."

"Darling, I hate to break this up, but we have tickets to the Moscow Circus tonight. We're picking up the Bryants and the Attorney-General for cocktails in twenty-five minutes. Have you seen the Russian circus, Mr. Cooperman? It's the damnedest thing. Sorry to break up the meeting," he said, getting up and offering me his hand again.

"I'll call Blackwood," Gloria said pushing a button on the telephone.

"Don't trouble. I can let myself out. You'll get in touch if anything happens?"

"I promise. I feel better already. Thank you for coming." She extended her hand and I took it, still smarting from Jarman's grip. She savaged my fingers too. It must run in the family. Her grip came out of a boiler works or a karate school. I let go and the hand went on stinging as I crossed the studio floor, found the door, and let myself out.

I didn't get far before Blackwood caught up with me.

"Mrs. Jarman wants you to have this," she said, holding

an envelope to me. She had a good face, but it was troubled. It was the face of a poised young woman, but as vulnerable as one of Gloria's dolls. She was about three inches shorter than Gloria Jarman, and insecure enough that every hair was in place. It was light brown hair and rolled under at the end of a cascade that circled her face. Her brows were arched, clear and wide with eyes set well apart. Her neck was slender and her shoulders narrow. The dress, which was ochre or some earth colour, was loose-fitting in front, but caught tightly at the waist. It flared over her hips and fell down to mid-calf. She was almost smiling.

"No thanks, Blackwood. I don't think Mrs. Jarman owes me anything yet. I'll keep track, though, and will get in touch when I've done some work on her business. You hang on to it for me, will you?"

"As you choose, Mr. Cooperman. I assume you've discussed this with Mrs. Jarman?"

"It didn't need discussing. I thought it up by myself."

"Why do you talk like that, Mr. Cooperman? What have we done to you? You sound so belligerent and prickly."

"Guess I'm not used to having tea wheeled in on a trolley. Where I come from, we dip the bag in the cup and pass it on. You ought to try it sometime. It's fun."

"Don't let the packaging fool you, Mr. Cooperman. Mrs. Jarman's a wonderful human being. She doesn't need all this. She waved her hand around the darkening hall we were sharing with a few display cabinets full of the spoils of Greece and Rome. "Gloria Jarman is a rare person, Mr. Cooperman. In time you'll come to appreciate her rare qualities."

"In which she abounds, I'm sure. Look, Blackwood . . ."

"Stop calling me that! You make me feel like there's a collar around my neck. My name is Helen Blackwood."

"All right, Miss Blackwood. I get along fine with your boss. You can save the build-up. I've got wonderful human beings behind every pillar in this place, and frankly my opinion of the human race is tapering off. Your boss treated me fine. I don't have any complaints." She took in her breath and turned heading for the stairs without saying any more. We went down the curving staircase with more of the same and she didn't turn to me again until we were both at the front door.

"So long, Miss Blackwood. Don't take me too much to heart. Remember that under this stony heart of mine lives a stony liver."

"Goodbye, Mr. Cooperman." She opened the door for me and I had one shoulder into the snow-flurry that had started while I was in the studio when I thought that it might be profitable to talk to her about all this.

"Is your job a sleep-in job, Miss Blackwood?" I took a second run at it. "What I mean is, do you ever get into town?" The explanation didn't help. I tried again. "There are some angles to all this that are still vague. Things I didn't want to trouble Mrs. Jarman about, what with the show she's preparing and all."

"Oh, I see, you'd like to talk to me." She considered the proposition for a moment, frowning. "Now let's see what I can do." Then she looked me right in the eye and fired. "Look, Mr. Cooperman, I think we've made a bad start with each other, and I'm sorry. I've developed a manner in this job. There's nothing personal, I assure you." I nodded my willingness to take her word for it.

"You're just a little protective of the boss."

"And she pays me very well. Look, I get off about eight. If this snow-flurry doesn't develop into a blizzard, I could drive into town and meet you around nine, say, in the lounge at the Beaumont Hotel?"

"Sounds fine."

"All right. Until nine, then? Goodbye."

I let myself be pulled out into the weather, which caught hold of my coat like a pool-room bouncer and yanked me into an eddy of blowing snow under the *porte cochère*. The Olds was where I had left it. It hadn't turned into a pumpkin, but it was wearing a white dinner-jacket.

It took me five minutes to clear the snow from the windshield, after a struggle to get the motor going. I decided to ignore the hairpin turns I'd driven over on my arrival. I wasn't that suicidal. I turned left at the bottom of the Warren drive and pieced my way along the straight but unplowed road for a couple of miles until the road was intersected by a highway. From there on the normal hazards of winter driving prevailed, and as the snow came blasting at me from a single point ahead, I could picture my mother and father sipping cocktails beside a Miami pool.

SEVENTEEN

On the way back into town, I stopped at a pay phone and tried to reach Savas. He was out, so I left my name. Savas is a good man, but he's never around when you need him. On the other hand, I always seem to be around whenever he decides to upgrade my eating habits, aided and abetted by Staziak, his partner. It's no use my telling them that I like all my bad habits. I've got professional countermen and short order cooks feeding me, and I eat three times a day, more if I want.

By the time I'd reached St. Andrew Street, the snow had stopped. Storekeepers on both sides of the street were cleaning it away from their stores, sweeping it across the sidewalk and into the gutter. The merchants of St. Andrew Street were all getting older. They looked like my father, and he was retired. Their stores had come to look like them. I parked illegally in front of the Regional Police Headquarters, scribbled a note to Savas and delivered it to the man in blue at the desk. He looked at the name and told me the sergeant had just returned. He pointed the direction.

Pete Staziak was leaning in the doorway to Chris Savas's office. He was tall, in a three-quarter length winter coat and a green tyrolean hat, a size too small, perched on the top of his large head. We were once in the same chemistry class, and I was in a school play with his sister.

"Ben," he said, "I keep missing you. Chris said this morning that you were a regular visitor. How come I don't rate with you any more?"

"It's your personality, Pete. You just don't have it the way Chris does."

"Yeah, you're right. I'll always be Watson to Chris's Holmes. Whatcha got, Ben?"

"Are you working the Muriel Falkirk case with Chris?"

"Sure, we even go to the john together. What's a partner for, Ben? You wanted to know about the booze that she'd been drinking? We have a report on it now, and it looks like she was drinking top-grade booze: Crown Royal."

"Still no sign of the bottle?"

"Nope."

"I wonder whether you still have the keys to her apartment?"

"We got keys. What's on your mind?" He had inched his way from the door-frame to the inside of Savas's office with its metal furniture and view of the parking lot. He kept his shoulder to the wall as though he knew something about the contractor that I didn't.

"Well, I'd like to borrow those suits we think belonged to Johnny Rosa for half an hour. I want to check out the labels."

"You think they were Muriel's? Benny, your mind gets cuter every day. You know I can't let you have evidence. Ben, what's the matter with you?"

"Does that mean you'll talk to Chris about it?"

"What do you think it means?"

"I think you learned about answering a question with a question from me. It's a cheap trick. *I* don't even do it any more." At this moment Savas strode back into his office, adjusting his belt. As soon as he'd frowned his greeting, a messenger in blushing acne and blue uniform handed Chris a folded newspaper, like a marathon runner passing on the baton. Chris opened it.

"We're getting ink," he said. I caught the headline: WOMAN'S BODY FOUND IN BATH. The story gave most of the details, adding for the prurient that the body was fully clad. I was glad to see that they'd left my name out of it. There was nothing new in the story but I read without skipping because it's strange to see your life turned into those simple declarative sentences. They get the details right, but somehow miss the bigger meaning.

Chris's face looked weary as he threw himself into his noisy swivel chair. He sighed at a dirty, coffee-stained mug on a pile of file folders.

"Afternoon tea's over, Benny. You missed it."

"I had mine up at the Warren place, thanks. They do a nice tea up there, I'll say that for them." I watched the eyes in both their faces widen.

"So that's the league you're playing in. Nice going. Your client's successor, Benny? Gotta hustle, eh?"

Pete gave me a look and said lamely, "You want some coffee? We always got coffee."

"Never mind. I got the car running outside. Mrs. Jarman's had a phone call from somebody who claims to be Johnny, and she thinks that it probably is."

Savas was looking sheepish now. I thought I'd get out before I started losing again, and left them standing there.

The car was still where I'd put it and I hadn't been given a ticket. I headed west, across the High Level bridge with its clear view of the Eleven Mile Creek at the point where it becomes the First Welland Canal. The shift was changing down below at the foundry, a huge red brick shed with a chimney that worried the provincial pollution critics. My only stop before the station was at Binder's Drug Store for some cigarettes.

I recognized Bill Ashland sitting on the end of one of the waiting-room pews. He was wearing a business suit, and didn't have a rolled-up mattress with him or two baskets of eggs like a couple of his neighbours across the room. Twenty years hadn't dulled my recollection of the smell of the place. They must be using the same oil on the floors now as when my father used to show me the newly-hatched chicks in crates, ready for the Toronto night train. The pictures of a train crossing the Rocky Mountains were no longer the only wall ornaments and the telegraph noises were gone, but the echo was the same.

Ashland's buff coat, furry hat and paisley muffler were folded neatly next to him. It must have been the first three-piece suit in the place since Mr. DePue, the station agent, retired. Ashland brought a pair of quarterback shoulders to this outfit and the rest of his frame didn't make them conspicuous. His face was flat and hard, with a pair of unlikely gold-framed glasses sitting on top of his broken nose. He'd taken his hair to the beauty parlour and had brought it away with a thousand clusters of blond curls. I guess he thought that his Zorba moustache and massive chin protected him from wisecracks. His eyes were piggy and gray, a little too close together to get him far in the banking business. He didn't look up at me when I came in through the puddle of salty water and melting snow that hung around the door like porridge on a spoon. As I settled into the space beside his coat, he lowered his *Toronto Life* and inspected me like I'd just flaked off the ceiling.

"You're Cooperman, are you?" His smile revealed some gaudy dentistry leaning heavily on the precious metals.

"Sure I am. Thanks for coming."

"I don't have all day, Mr. Cooperman, so, if you'll state your business . . . ."

"Sure. First, it would help if you filled me in on how you were first brought into the Warren scheme."

"You don't want much for nothing, do you?"

"With private investigators, Mr. Ashland, it's like doctors. It's routine with us. We don't care whose feet are in the stirrups. I personally get no thrill from asking a lot of questions. As a matter of fact, I'd just as soon be down south right now."

"What do I get out of it if you do all the asking and I do all the answering?"

"Don't ask me. But the technique gets results." He

looked dubious, so I added: "How can you tell for sure I'm not going to drop the missing piece right in your lap? You can't know for sure, that's why you can afford to take the chance. Besides, you've nothing to lose by telling me how you got involved in the first place."

Ashland pulled on the corner of his moustache with his right hand, thought for a while, then said, "I was living with Knudsen in the Norton Apartments, and Todd was always dropping by. I was spending lots of money, had a steady flow of chicks. It was a crazy time. We once got through ten cases of beer on a weekend. There was always some girl wrapped in a bedsheet on her way to the bathroom. You could smell the action when you got off the elevator. One day Rolf brought Johnny around. He fitted in. He liked to groove a bit, play a little cards. He went in for very young stuff, and I used to think he'd get the apartment raided. But in spite of the girls' school uniforms, they could out-curse a stevedore with a backache." He took out a fine slender cigar and lit it with a disposable French lighter.

"How did Johnny bring you into the scam?"

"One weekend around the middle of May, we'd had a marathon drunk and were all shagged out with no beer in the place and no food, and not one of us had a dime in his jeans. We finished the last beer by taking turns drinking a shot-glass-full each. If we hadn't been bombed out of our minds already, we could have got stoned all over again. I think that Todd had to go out around six, and Knudsen was taking one of the chicks home or for a walk, I can't remember. So that left Johnny and me. We were just talking. First it was about this young chick he'd seen, and then it was something else, and before I realized it, we were talking about snatching this girl I'd only read about in the papers. Johnny knew all the details, and it looked like it couldn't miss. I'd never been involved with the law in my life, I mean nothing was ever proved, but, I mean, how many times do you get a chance to grab half a million dollars over a weekend? We figured heavy traffic would reduce the chances of getting caught, so it was planned for the long weekend. Johnny said she'd be at the lake and there she was."

"Did Johnny ever say why he'd picked this girl?"

"What was there to tell? She was the daughter of the richest man in town, one of the richest men in North America. It was a natural."

"He didn't tell you where he got all his information, did he?"

"Johnny just swatted it up. He was a whiz at things like that. He used to be a good people-reader. He would watch a guy and then after a time say something that knocked him out of his chair. I remember one time . . ."

"Sure. You were in the first car, the one that took the girl, you and Knudsen, him driving? Right?"

"He tell you that?"

"What are you so jumpy about? I don't have a tape-recorder. What you need is a new head looking for the details that got lost somehow." He caught me in those piggy eyes, and then he began to split. It started slowly, then it was like he was in the confession box and I had my ear to the grille.

"Yeah, well Johnny, Todd and I were waiting in the cottage when they came up from the dock. I grabbed Miss Warren; Todd grabbed her boyfriend. Johnny stood by giving orders and help as it was needed. I knew that it didn't matter about the screaming, because we'd checked that out, but just the same I was glad when I got a gag fixed. The sleeping bag was a great idea. It kept her from kicking and scratching. First thing, I got her head covered so that she couldn't see any of our faces. She fought every inch of the way and it took both Johnny and I to do most of it. Meanwhile, Todd had hit Jarman, the boyfriend, and started tying him up. I put a long piece of nylon rope around the sleeping bag, and when I was ready, Johnny went out and whistled for Knudsen to bring the car around. Johnny and I carried her to the back seat of the car and we set out, Rolf and I."

"Could she have heard your voices during any of this?"

"Johnny was the only one who said anything. He didn't say much, just the few commands, and then the whistle."

"Would you recognize Johnny's voice if you heard it on the telephone?"

"Not necessarily. It wasn't that special. It was the way he

had of talking that made him special, not the voice."

"Okay. Todd says that you shot your mouth off about the snatch."

"Todd's full of it, the black bastard; I kept as quiet as the rest of them. Some people have to have somebody to hang things on. I think our friends in the building could sense that something funny had happened. We were quiet for days afterward. We didn't party it up. Nobody drank any beer, the girls wandered off home. It was a real drag. I know how my father must have felt. He was in the war. After that, nothing back home ever caught his whole attention again. I'm glad he didn't live to see me go on trial." Then his face grew angry. "Damn Todd, and damn the others! Any of us could have shot off our mouths. It didn't have to be me. If Johnny Rosa wanted professionals, he should have paid for them."

A train was due, and people were moving out to the platform with suitcases and magazines. I remembered the black front of an old locomotive emerging from a shroud of its own steam. I knew that I would lose another of life's cherished illusions when a diesel puffed in on Track One.

Ashland saw that I'd been distracted, and grabbed me by the coat. "You got me here to listen as well as talk. Seems like I'm the only talker so far."

"All right. You know that Johnny Rosa's gone. Maybe you don't know that the car he was driving has been found abandoned near the canal and that there were bloodstains inside on the seat. It's not just a parole violation inquiry any more. It looks like murder. And I would say that your name might be high on the list of suspects. He got you involved in the Warren affair. He took the money without sharing with you. You've got a record. I'd say they'll be talking to you before the week's out. They won't wait until his body floats out into Lake Ontario and comes up in the spring."

Ashland shook his head. Instead of imagining Johnny Rosa's body floating out into the lake, I think he pictured five hundred thousand dollars floating out of his reach forever.

"Then there's another thing that's happened: Muriel, Johnny's girl got herself bumped."

"I didn't hear about that," he said, shaking his head in an easy sentimental gesture. "Damn shame. She was a gorgeous chick, one gorgeous chick."

"Besides that, what do you know about her?"

"Nothing." He said that too fast, then added: "Eddie Milano used to buy her clothes for her before Johnny got released. He used to spend a lot on her. They didn't keep house, or anything like that—there's a Mrs. Milano out in Fort Erie, I think—but they were known as a twosome in the joints, and he used to hang around that apartment of hers, I guess having a closer look at what he'd been paying for. Then, when Johnny got out, she pushed Eddie over again and shacked up with him."

"*Again?*"

"What?"

"You said *again*. What did you mean by that?"

"Oh, well, Muriel had seen other men even when she saw Eddie. I've even bought a whisky sour for her on a couple of occasions. She was a nice chick."

"Yeah, a wonderful human being."

"You said it. That's her to the life."

"Tell me, in Eddie's crowd, how does it look when a guy out on parole, working in a foundry, beats the time of a big wheel like Eddie?"

"Well, she ain't going dancing with anybody tonight, is she?"

"Is that the way you figure it?"

"It computes; what more can I say? It's easy to figure, but hard to prove."

"Why?"

"Eddie never makes a step without being seen somewhere else. The night Muriel got it, Eddie was probably at the policemen's ball winning the raffle and getting his picture taken with the chief's wife. Eddie Milano isn't going to get caught with the elastic in his shorts busted."

"Your pal Knudsen has disappeared. He was snatched in the middle of the night. Same night Muriel got it. Better look under your bed when you get home tonight."

"Climb off, Cooperman. None of us knows anything that didn't come out at the trial. If I had a whiff of that money—if any of us did—do you think we'd be sitting around Grantham? By the way, what's in it for you? Who hauls your ashes?"

"You'd be surprised." I knew that wouldn't hold him, and I could see him looking at me sideways.

He sucked in his breath after a minute and asked: "Where do you think the money is, Cooperman?" I think he really meant it. He was a greedy little man, in spite of his size, and his pride wasn't hurt at all by asking me.

"Well, from all the people who are looking for it, I guess it must still be out there."

"That doesn't get us anywhere," he said testily, looking a shade prissy around the corners of his mouth. "I thought you had some information to trade, Cooperman, but all I hear is the same sort of chat I could get in any poolroom in town."

"You're not getting much joy from the professional you hired?"

"How do you know about Handler?"

"I keep my ears open and my mouth shut for a start. I was tipped. Somebody thought I was your man, and didn't like it."

"He's costing me enough." I guess I must have sneered a little. I'd meant it as a smile, but you don't get to check these things after you set them up. Ashland exploded: "I can see you don't think much of me. If you think I'm bitter and angry, well, you're right. I wanted that money bad. I wanted it more than the others, I needed it more and I knew how to spend it better. You think it's easy for somebody like me to take a plunge? You think I found doing that time as easy as Johnny Rosa? You're crazy. Rosa and I come from different planets. I think I'm getting mad, Cooperman, you better watch out." He got up, scooped up his magazine and coat and struggled into it on his way through the lake by the station door. I watched him leave, then followed him into a turquoise compact with a hatchback. He raced the wheels, trying to get moving, spraying slush ten yards behind him, but not moving

102

forward. He turned his wheel and tried to back up. He rocked the small car backward and forward with violence for a minute, and then by a fluke he got away, heading downtown at a noisy intemperate speed.

EIGHTEEN

The Kit Kat Klub had been closed up by the police a couple of years ago. A dance school had replaced it and when that failed to make a breakthrough, it gave way to a small-time commercial artist with a couple of cute helpers on the silk-screen. It looked like they were confining their art to the T-shirt medium. From the artist I learned the name of the landlord, and a few more calls brought me to a broken-down, pebble-dashed house on Facer Street out near the canal. The land was flat. It had been under cultivation before the war, but had been lost to farming during the post-war housing boom. Looking at Jack Gowan's house, with its weather-worn blue porch lurching toward the right, I could feel something of the hopelessness of living in a row of houses that were slowly rotting. Tarpaper was showing through Gowan's neighbour's house. His own roof looked dodgy, and I could almost smell the oil cloth on the table and the Quebec heater before I knocked on the front door.

Gowan didn't look the sort to run an illegal gambling den and blind pig. He looked more like somebody ran him, and, not satisfied with the mileage, had ditched him. He was a little guy with a big head, which he kept cropped like he might have in the army, if they took men that short. His plastic-framed glasses had been mended with adhesive tape in the middle and the temples were stained with neglect. He wore a surprised ferret-like expression, like I'd awakened him from a bad dream, and a T-shirt which hung big around his small chest and arms.

"You Jack Gowan?"

"Who wants to know?" I guessed that in some circles, friends had to be won.

"The name's Cooperman. I'm a private investigator trying to get a line on Johnny Rosa. I was hired by his girlfriend, who was worried that he may have been killed, just like she has now. I've got a few questions I hope you can help me with."

"I don't have anything to say to you. I don't know what you're talking about, and I don't have to talk to you."

"Look, Mr. Gowan . . ."

"Get your foot out of the door."

"I'll get it out in a minute. Look: one person has been killed and there may be more. You can help stop that. I'm not going to put anything in the paper. I don't have to answer to the cops. I'm in this on my own. If we come to something you don't want to answer, just let me know."

"Cooperman, you say?"

"Yeah. Ben Cooperman."

"Any relation to Manny Cooperman?"

"He's my father."

"Hell, why didn't you say that to begin with. Come on in." Here he opened the door, easing the pressure on my big toe.

The living-room of Jack's place looked like it had been fixed up nice in 1945 and that the wife who'd done the fixing left forever in 1945 and a half. All of the pieces of that period were still in sight, including some plaster dogs and flights of birds on the wall. Above the couch hung a faded tapestry in velvet, showing a stag at bay with six or seven snarling hounds nipping at his flanks. Even faded it was strong medicine, and

I'm glad I missed it when it was new. A floor-model radio stood in one corner, with a small black-and-white television set above it. Gowan turned off the sports news and showed me to an overstuffed chair with a gold thread running through the upholstery, except where the stuffing was coming out.

"So, you're Manny Cooperman's son!" he said, shaking his head. "I've lost more money to Manny than I ever did to the mob. Your father is the best gin rummy player in North America. He has a gift. That's the only word for it, a gift. I call him *The Hammer*. How is he? I was thinking about the old son of a gun just the other day."

"He's down in Miami. I'll tell him I was talking to you."

"You do that. Tell him I was asking about him."

"I'll do that."

"Manny Cooperman's son! Heh!" He was shaking his head with a wide grin on his large face, which had lost its ferrety look. "You want a beer? I was just going to have one myself."

"Sure. I'll join you." He got up and disappeared. I heard the refrigerator open and close, and the uncapping of two bottles. He returned with them and a glass for me.

"I never waste a glass anymore. Less washing up. Here's to Manny." We both drank in silence for a minute. I was feeling just a little smug about stumbling on one of my dad's haunts. I remember that an hour after dinner he used to make the excuse that he "was just going downtown to check the cash".

"Well, now, what were you saying with your foot in the door? Is this a survey or something?"

"No, it's about the club on St. Andrew Street."

"Manny's store was just down the street. He retired?" I nodded, and he joined my nod with a nod of his own. We nodded in deep thought for a moment. Then: "They closed up the Kit Kat a few years back. I've been on unemployment mostly ever since. Can't seem to find nothing. I help out at Mac and Tom's from time to time, but I'm too old to be emptying ashtrays and racking balls in a poolhall. Besides people remember, and it embarrasses hell out of them to see me doing dirty jobs when they know I had my own place once.

But I help out at Mac and Tom's. It gets me out on the street, you see."

"Do you remember Johnny Rosa?"

"Do I remember him? Sure I do. He was a very funny man. I never saw him have a bad word for anybody. He paid up when he lost. Manny beat him every time they sat down at the table. Your father. He was quite a fellow."

"A truly remarkable human being."

"That's right. That's right. You sure have the right words to describe him. Well, now, what do you want to know about Johnny?"

"Did he come to the club alone?"

"Sometimes. Sometimes not. It depended on whether there were other people with him."

"I see what you mean." At last, a careful witness. "Do you remember any of the people he brought to the club, people who came on their own maybe later on?"

"Let me think. There was the Swede. I don't remember his name. Might not have been a Swede, but that's what some of the fellows called him. Tall thin fellow. Used to drink beer like it was soda pop and never laugh much."

"Rolf Knudsen?"

"Could be. Never had any trouble with him. He could look after himself. Yes, I guess that's the Swede. Never had to cut him off. Not like that rich kid Johnny used to waste time with. He was always three drinks past his limit. Trouble, you know what I mean? And then there were the girls he brought. He liked them young."

"Rich kid? Which rich kid?"

"The Warren kid. Young moneybags himself. Only he didn't live to spend it, did he? I always say that . . ."

"Did he come to the club often?"

"He was a regular for a few years. He dropped a lot of money on the tables. Used to bring these girls up, and everybody'd look at me like the club was a Sunday school. I couldn't make rules in a blind pig, none I could enforce. I never kept no bouncer."

"So Johnny and Russ Warren knew one another."

"Like I know your old man."

"Do you remember any of the girls?"

"Nope. I never had a head for remembering women at all. Not that I don't like them—even though they make a mess in the toilet that you gotta see to believe—I like women fine, but I can't hang on to their faces much. Johnny's girls and Russ's were always good looking. I'll give them that. But I can't . . ." He stopped and tore his beer label for a moment. "You know who you should talk to? You remember Kate Rodman? Even I remember her. Kate was the daughter of a Baptist minister out west some place, and he was killed over in Europe in an accident, so Kate was brought up here by her uncle, another minister. I guess he wasn't as broad-minded as her father, because he had her jumping through hoops she never heard of until she came here. He had to take her out of the high school after a term and put her in a private girls school. St. Audrey's up on the hill. She was smart as new paint, but she couldn't stand the discipline. I used to see her smoking stogies on St. Andrew Street before she was fifteen. I remember one time hearing her trying to talk a bunch of girls from the business college on James Street to come with her to watch a murder trial at the court house. Now, she was a woman to remember! She went with Johnny for a while, during the time you're talking about, then she went off to Toronto like most people around here. Now Kate would be able to tell you names. Leastwise if there wasn't any trouble for anybody."

"Do you know where I'd reach her in Toronto?"

"Hell. Toronto packed her up and sent her back years ago. She's been teaching school here for years. Her name's O'Neil now. Married Willy O'Neil, you remember him? Your father would." I put down my half-empty glass of beer and thanked Jack Gowan for all his help. He stood at the door with his skinny arms protruding from his short sleeves, waving after me as I retreated down the walk. "Don't forget to remember me to Manny!"

"I promise."

It was after seven, nearly seven-thirty. I went into the Diana Sweets for a fast sandwich and a glass of milk with

107

some ice cream. With that disposed of I tried the phone book. After two wrong numbers, I had Kate O'Neil on the line.

"My name's Cooperman, you may remember my father from the Kit Kat Klub. He was a gin rummy player."

"I'm sorry, it's been years since . . . I don't remember any of the people . . . I mean, I was a different person in those days.'

"Do you remember Johnny Rosa?"

"Sure. Hey, what's this all about? Are you, what are you?" Her voice was like black coffee with brandy in it. Her words weren't up to much, but her voice made up for it.

"Look, this would be a lot simpler if I could see you for a few minutes. Could I come over right now? It would really help." I didn't get an answer right away. Maybe she had to go out. Maybe she had to get dressed. I admit it, I was asking a lot on short notice. Then I said that, and she said to come over right away. I wrote out the address, which was on lower Queen Street, past the YMCA and the law offices, just a short walk from Montecello Park.

For a minute, I thought I caught the glimpse of a Mustang running a few cars behind me. I couldn't get the colour. There must be thousands of Mustangs on the road tonight. I'd better try to get Frank and Vito off my mind. Of all the possible candidates for Muriel's murderer I could think of, nobody wore that tag better than Vito and Frank.

I parked a few houses past where I was going and walked back without seeing a blue Mustang show up in the streetlights. The park looked dark and cold. The verandahs along the street were dark, except for a couple with illuminated doctors' shingles. I found the number I was looking for attached to a round white pillar, one of a pair which supported a porch with a classical pediment. A black mailbox with the silhouette of a Scottie dog did some damage to this traditional package.

The woman who met me at the door was wearing a dark blue corduroy skirt and a white blouse. She was a little taller than me, but I was used to that. Her figure, as I judged it retreating along a corridor to a den or study, was tidy. I could believe that she could face a roomful of thirty teenagers and tell them about Julius Caesar or William Wordsworth without losing control. Her face was a calming combination of good straight features, good skin and a high forehead. She wore her brown hair brushed back from her brow and it tumbled straight down past her ears and ended abruptly at a sharp line. Her eyes were hazel and nicely spaced. I tried to picture her smoking a cigar on St. Andrew Street at fifteen.

"You're Mr. Cooperman? I'm Kate O'Neil. Willy's out right now, so maybe we should get right down to your reason for coming. I did a lot of crazy things when I was young, Mr. Cooperman, and my husband knows all about them. He wasn't a choirboy either, so we get along. We drink a lot of coffee and we go to our A.A. meetings regularly. I've been sober now for nearly five years. I've been working steadily for three years and have had two promotions. So, you see I'm putting some distance between the person I am today and the girl I was when I knew those people at the club. Would you like a cup of coffee, since I mentioned it? I make a very good cup." I nodded and followed her into the bright kitchen. The coffee was on a back burner, looking black and strong. A red clock told me that I'd better hustle if I wanted to get to the Beaumont Hotel by nine. Kate O'Neil poured the coffee with a steady hand into a blue-and-white mug. It took a lot of cream to lighten it. We nodded over the mugs and she did her best to help me ask my questions, beginning with a big smile which didn't darken at the corners the way some do.

"You asked about Johnny Rosa? Yes, I knew him for nearly a year . . . through a good friend of mine."

"Russ Warren?"

"Yes. Russ was, I guess, more than a good friend. I was precocious, anyway, for those days. Russ was the first man I ever loved and the first that really loved me. I nearly died when he was killed. Even though he wasn't with me any longer, it nearly killed me. I knew that he would go violently. That was his way, wasn't it: fast cars, all that drinking and living? He lived at too great a speed to last. Trouble and early death were written all over his face."

"What was troubling him?"

"I didn't know in those days, but since then I've been thinking about it. I've read a lot of psychology, Mr. Cooperman: Freud, Jung and even Reich. I don't know what you think of such things, but I'm certain that Russ harboured some unnatural affection for his sister. I think that he loved her more strongly than a brother normally should. I say *should*. I know that *ought* and *should* have no place in this kind of talk. What happens, happens. Poor Russ couldn't handle it, and in the end, it killed him."

"I see," I said. "What about Johnny Rosa?" Her face darkened.

"Johnny was all right. He was a lot of laughs. He was the right man for the mood of the time. But later Johnny seemed to force the pace when we were trying to settle down a little. I didn't like Johnny's girl either. No. That's not strictly true. I liked her at first. She looked like she could be a calming influence on Johnny. I mean, she wasn't knocked out every time Johnny drained a glass of straight scotch at one go. She could do that and so could I. But then, she started paying more attention to Russ than to Johnny, and I didn't like that. She ended up taking him away from me. We were both children, of course. I guess it's ridiculous to talk about it in such melodramatic terms, I mean it's rather novelettish in adults, isn't it? But children! Oh, I loathed that girl. I haven't thought about her for years now. See how you bring it all back? Sorry. I didn't mean that. I used to think that if Russ had stayed with me, it wouldn't have happened. His being killed I mean. But I know, I really do know that it would have had to happen sometime. That was Russ." She paused. "Is this the sort of thing you wanted to know? I'm sorry for running on and on. I've just not thought about those days for such a long time. I don't even think I asked you why you wanted to know all this."

There was only one other thing I wanted to know, and I had a feeling in my gut that I wouldn't like the answer. But I was getting paid by a dead woman to ask these questions, so I asked it.

"Do you remember the name of the girl?"

110

"The girl?" She looked surprised. I think we'd both dropped a stitch in the silence that followed Kate's long monologue. "The girl? You mean Johnny's girl. Of course I remember her name. She's Helen Blackwood and she works for Russ's sister as a private secretary."

NINETEEN

I parked the Olds in the crowded lot behind the Beaumont Hotel and wove my way from the parking attendant, who wanted to know how long I was planning to stay before I'd even arrived, to the dimly lit entrance to The Snug, the main lounge of the hotel, one of the few licensed places in town where it was un-chic to ask for draft beer. There had been a half-hearted attempt on the designer's part to make the room look like an Irish pub, but he had been waylaid on his path by helpful suggestions from several uninformed quarters about the true nature of the Irish pub.

Helen Blackwood was sitting at a table for two in a dark corner. She was wearing a soft print dress. Her hair, though pulled back, didn't look as though it impeded her eyes from blinking anymore. There was even a trace of make-up on her lips and cheeks. She smiled at me as I came across the floor, struggling out of my heavy coat.

"I've already ordered a drink," she said, pointing to a partly finished whisky sour. "I hope you don't mind." She was sporting earrings and a gold chain around her neck. I noted the effect, but I couldn't figure out why she was turning on the charm in my direction. In spite of all I've overheard when my mother gets talking to her cronies over the teacups, I have a fairly level-headed view of myself, and none of the persons I am are the sort you wear tiny pearl earrings for. Maybe this was just an extension of her job: "Blackwood, be a dear and see what that Cooperman fellow really thinks." I wouldn't put it past Gloria to use her in this way; at the same time, I could see Blackwood keeping the interests of the Jarmans and Warrens uppermost in her mind. I wondered when she'd last done something special for herself. I sat down opposite her in the management's idea of an Irish chair; she was seated on a padded banquette which followed the contours of the room from the mock-Irish bar to the mock-Irish turf fire. I liked the idea of getting to know the real Helen Blackwood if she still existed under "Blackwood" and all the other poses.

"You've become a rye drinker?"

"You really are a detective."

"Sometimes I just get lucky. Today my luck took me to Jack Gowan and Kate O'Neil, Kate Rodman to you."

"Yes, you have been busy. My compliments."

"You hadn't tried to hush any of this up. It was all there for the asking." She was rubbing her finger around the rim of her glass. Not being an expensive wine glass, it made no sound. I think she was blushing behind her make-up, but I am only guessing. Her slight shoulders seemed to hunch together.

"My chequered past would take a lot of hushing. I don't make that kind of money."

"Have you run into people who offered to try?"

"For a price, yes." She smiled a brief smile over her glass. "I guess I wasn't interesting enough to gain their full attention."

"I see," I said, trying to show my best bedside manner. "How did you meet Johnny in the first place?"

"I went to a house party with an older girl I knew. She asked me to tag along. Johnny was there. We sat on the stairs most of the night talking. He had a way with him, Johnny did. He wasn't good-looking, he was short and sort of ugly, really, but he had an electricity about him. You felt that you'd get a shock if you touched him, and you wanted to touch him. He asked me to tell him about myself. To me, that was wonderful. Nobody'd ever asked me about me before. He got in touch with me the next night. I don't think he knew how young I was. Maybe he did, but didn't care. I learned to drink that week. Johnny taught me to drink Scotch. I drank it until after Russ was killed, then I stopped drinking altogether for about a year. Now I drink a proper lady's drink. Will you have something?"

"I've not much of a head for drinking, frankly. I get dizzy. A friend in the Regional Police says I was born two drinks below par. I don't play golf either, so I'm not sure whether that's good or bad. Maybe I'll have what you're drinking. Or is it exclusively a lady's drink?"

"Oh, it's unisex, as far as that goes. You're a funny man."

"What makes me a funny man?"

"Well, you bluster so, and put up such a noisy show, when you're really rather shy and unworldly."

"I could say that about you too," I said. She thought a moment and then admitted the possibility. I think she took it as a compliment. At least, I think that was when we stopped jousting with one another.

"Did Johnny strike you as a criminal in those days?"

"All I knew was that he was lots of fun, and that he liked me and that he took me seriously. I think I wanted to be taken seriously more than anything else. He used to bring me things that I knew, vaguely, hadn't come from over the counter. He took me to the races, and we met some of his friends. When he was with them, he seemed exactly like them; when he was with me, he wasn't like that at all. He had a chameleon-like quality, I guess. When he was with Russ Warren, you'd have picked him out as the son of a millionaire, not Russ. He was one of those people that should have been born rich. He sensed that, and went to prison for trying to change it.'' Her glass was empty, and I was able to mime our order to the waiter without his actually having to cross the floor and speak to us.

"Do you think that the Warren money went to Johnny's head?"

"It might have been that, but I don't think that's why he got involved in the kidnapping.''

"Why then?"

"I don't know. But I'm sure it wasn't just for the money.''

"Had he and Russ had a falling out before Russ's death?''

"I don't think so. Johnny could sense that I was moving towards Russ. He didn't say anything. He wasn't the sort to let a miserable woman come between friends. He was *macho* in that way, as well as in a number of others. By then he may even have been relieved to get rid of me. I was jail-bait, remember.''

"Did you feel differently about Russ, after Johnny?'' She thought about that one for a moment. The waiter, in the meantime, had arrived with our drinks and a tray of assorted food: meatballs on toothpicks, pink shrimp and sausages wrapped in a crust. Helen Blackwood tried the shrimp. I helped myself to a handful of peanuts that were already at the table.

"Johnny Rosa occupies a special place in my life, Mr. Cooperman. Every girl had a Johnny Rosa at one time in her early life. But Russ was special too. He didn't seem to give a damn about conventions or about his family name or any of the things he was supposed to care about. I think he belonged to the golf club, not so much because it was hard to get into, as you might know, Mr.— may I call you Ben?—or because it was expected of him, but because it offered him more opportunities to cut up and have fun. He once mixed up the keys to all the golf carts; it took them hours to sort them out. That was a typical Russ Warren trick. He loved to see the fat, wealthy WASP customers getting red in the face about the delay, but too far gone in their degeneration to swing a bag of clubs over their shoulders and get on with the game. It sounds silly the way I describe it, but Russ got eloquent on the subject whenever he got smashed."

"Was that often?"

"Regularly. Russ was a drunk. I loved him with all my sixteen-year-old heart, but I can't escape that one. There was something bothering him that he couldn't talk about."

"He got along with Gloria?"

"But not with many others. He and his father hadn't spoken for about a year before the accident, the result of one of his pranks. Mr. Warren hated the inability of his son to value the family's achievement and imitate it. Not only couldn't poor Russ make it on Bay Street in Toronto, he couldn't leave the secretaries alone. It is rare that a son of a board member gets fired, but Russ did. Several times. Mr. Warren didn't have enough subsidiaries or cowed flunkies to accommodate his randy son. Russ couldn't even sit in an office and collect his pay."

"I guess some rich people can't take being the inheritors of the easy life. You got away from Gloria pretty quickly. Was that on purpose?"

"There's not much to say. Gloria and Russ stood apart from the rest of the clan."

"How did the clan take to you?"

"I heard that there were some monumental rows about me. I can see why now, though at the time I didn't see anything wrong with a grown man living in sin with an intelligent teenager. After the accident, however, Gloria looked me up and asked me to come to work for her."

"To keep things quiet?"

"Maybe initially. I can admit that now without it hurting. But we liked one another from the start and we both so loved Russ that there's never been any problem."

"Had you started work when the kidnapping occurred?"

"I'd started at the beginning of August, a month and a half after Russ was killed."

"It was a car accident wasn't it?"

"Yes. He loved speed and drink. They killed him."

"I'm sorry."

"So am I. I hate waste, and I think he was wasted."

"Sorry. I'm rambling in my questioning. I should be a regular machine-gun of short direct questions."

" 'Where was I on the night of December 16th?' "

"That's the sort of thing. How about the Labour Day weekend?"

"I was here that weekend. I never went to the lake when I could avoid it. It's an allergy I have; something in the sand or water. I come out in hives or at least a running nose and watery eyes. Also I burn easily in the sun. So I was at the house when Bob Jarman called from the lake. I answered and ran to get Mr. Warren. He was tinkering with something in his shop. That was his special kind of joy. He loved machinery of all kinds. I guess after the abstractions of his business interests all week, it was the perfect relaxation for him."

"Did Jarman tell you what had happened?"

"Yes, he told me to stay calm, that Gloria had been abducted, and that he had the ransom note."

"Did he and Warren talk long on the phone?"

"Just a few minutes. Mr. Warren said that he would contact the police at a high level and that Bob, I mean Mr. Jarman, should drive down from the lake as soon as he felt well enough. He left about half an hour after he phoned."

"How do you know that?"

"It's an hour's drive. He arrived here at three-thirty, an hour and a half after he called."

"Was he calm? Did he look badly beaten?"

"He had a goose-egg on the back of his head that looked very tender. I put a cold compress on it, but there wasn't much I could do about it. He and Mr. Warren met with the chief and an inspector for about another hour. I didn't hear any of that."

"But you don't miss much, do you?"

"Information is power. I want to survive." Both of us had done with our drinks by this time. I'd eaten the piece of orange that came with my drink, and Helen Blackwood was leaning across the table in a very friendly way. The impish, or gamine, quality I'd recognized in her face kept darting out at me from behind her gray eyes. I had a strong desire to reach

116

across the table and touch her, just to make sure that she was real.

"What sort of place did you come from? Where were you going when you bumped into Johnny Rosa?" She sighed, as if reluctant to go back into the past again. I couldn't blame her. It was her free night.

"I was born here in Grantham. My father was a writer, whom I didn't see much. My brother and I were brought up in my grandfather's house by my mother who looked after all of us. I was very close to my grandfather, didn't like my mother much, and idealized my absent father. I can see how unfair that was now, but as a teenager I could see no future in washing dishes and ironing dimity blouses. My dad was Edward Blackwood. Did you every read. . .? I'm sorry, I'm embarrassing you. I'm always doing it."

"No, no, really. I'm not much at reading novels, but what sort did he do?"

"Oh, he didn't do novels. His closest to a big success was with *Algonquin Rambles,* a history of lumbermills and canoe tripping in northern Ontario. As well as books, he did magazine articles, and once went to Hollywood for a year. He was staying in Guatamala when he died. The woman he was living with wrote a very kind letter. My mother still has it. As far as I was concerned, I took two years of university at Secord before I finally gave it up. The Warrens paid for it. I guess I'm almost one of the family now: Russ's young unofficial widow." She smiled, but there was no joy behind it.

"Did you ever meet a woman named Muriel Falkirk?"

"She was a friend of Johnny's, wasn't she? No, I didn't see Johnny after he came out of prison."

"He never spoke of her when you knew Johnny first?"

"He may have, but I didn't retain it. I'm sorry, is it important?" Her beautifully arched eyebrows were up, adding poignancy to an ordinary question.

"Right now, I don't know what's important and what's the bag the potato chips came in. Half of what I was asking was just trying to get to know you better. You're not at all like that grim voice on the telephone."

"I acquired that voice with the job. It saves time in the

long run. You have no idea the number of people who have been trying to push Gloria into one scheme or another since her father's death. 'Is she having weekend guests? May the paper know their names? Is she going to Europe this summer? Will she be staying with Princess Grace in Monaco? Will she be attending the Royal Winter Fair? Will she and her husband be going to the opera gala?' ''

"Anyway, I like your real voice. Though now that I think of it, even your Mrs. Danvers voice didn't stop me."

"My what?"

"Never saw *Rebecca*?"

"Or read it."

"Mrs. Jarman told me that you found her father in the pool. That can't have been much fun."

"No, not much. If I'd been there five minutes earlier, I might have been able to do something. As it was, I pulled him out and called for help, but even then I could tell it was too late. I tried mouth-to-mouth but there was no response. They told me that when the ambulance crew came they couldn't pull me away from him. I don't remember that part. I just remember how little he looked, sort of half-kneeling on the bottom, when I came in with his paper and coffee. I guess I've burned that image into my brain."

I shrugged and didn't say anything. She sent a sad smile past the empty glasses. I found it necessary to take a deep breath.

"I don't have any more questions, Miss Blackwood. You have been a great help. I don't know exactly how right now, but I'll let you know." I grabbed the waiter's eye, wrestled it to the ground and forced him to take my money. We came out of the hotel and into the parking lot together. She had put on a dark fur coat, one of Gloria's minks of a few seasons back, I guessed, and on her it looked good. I was walking close to her, close enough to still be aware of the perfume she was wearing.

We were standing close to my car, she was just about to say something, her head was turned toward me and a smile was working up behind her eyes again, when I heard the first slug tear into the door of my car. The hollow echo of metal was still just getting started when a second bullet creased my shoulder and went into the right back window of the Olds. I didn't think any more. I grabbed Helen by the arm and we tumbled into the slush and, where lucky, on the asphalt of the lot. I could hear her breathing in my ear, and remember seeing some mussed hair and frightened eyes. "Keep your head down!" was all I can remember saying as I tried to pull myself ahead of the next car. The loud thumping I heard was the sound of my own heart, the other was the sudden gunning of a motor. I looked up and saw the back end of a car pulling rapidly away from the curb. It could have been a blue Mustang, but in that light it could equally well have been a turquoise compact with a hatchback.

TWENTY

Helen Blackwood was still hugging the ground when I got back to her. She turned her head, looking up at me as though she thought I was the man with the gun. Her face seemed set for the finish. When she saw that it was me, she was comparatively glad. She got up and tried to brush herself off, but the pair of us were work for the cleaners. I was happy to see that she could get up. I honestly hadn't thought too much about her when the fireworks started; now, somewhat guilty, I was concern itself. I asked her the normal questions under the circumstances, and she asked me who was doing the shooting and why. I shrugged that one off, saying it could be an angry former husband from any number of dead and dying files. But I knew that the bullets had come from closer to current business than that.

"Can we take your car? I don't think that it would be very smart to take mine. I can come back for it later. Are you really okay? Would you like a shot of something?"

"No. I'm fine, honestly. Just a little wobbly that's all. I'll be all right. Were you hit?" Her eyes were wide with the excitement of a woman who has just been shot at. I tried not to take her interest too much to heart.

"One came close to my shoulder, but it's just a crease." She tried to laugh, as though I'd just been cracking wise or something, and then she leaned over toward me and practically fell into my arms. She didn't faint, she just wanted to feel that there was somebody who wasn't shooting at her for a second.

"Let's get out of here," I suggested. "I'll drive if you like."

She nodded like a waif being told for the third night running that there would be no supper. She slipped me the keys which were lying near the top of her handbag, and led me to the two-door Volvo. The instrument panel lit up like a Boeing jet when I found a place to bury the key. She rested her head back against the leather headrest with her chin thrust forward: another victim for the guillotine. By the time I'd cleared what remained of the cars in the lot, she was looking a little calmer. But when I put on the brakes near the place where the shots had come from, her big eyes were questioning me again. "I'll just be a moment," I said, and held her arm for a moment. Then I reached for my pocket flashlight and hoped that the batteries were still alive after a year of nearly constant neglect. They were, but barely. I found what I was looking for without very much difficulty. The brass shell casings were shining under the street lights where they had been ejected by a powerful rifle. I put them in my pocket and returned to the car.

"Why did you stop?" Helen asked, a little healthy annoyance displacing shock.

"Just looking for something on the road."

"Did you find it?"

"Yes. I'll have you home in ten minutes. Try to relax a little." She let her head fall backwards against the rest again.

A man of my word, I drove for the second time that day along the curved drive leading to the Warren mansion. Helen kept her eyes tight shut until I pulled up under the *porte cochère*. It took her a few seconds to realize where she was.

"Keep on driving and take the driveway that goes around to the right. I have my own way in. You will see where I usually leave the car." I did what I was told, wondering whether she came in the back way because she was, even in her position of private secretary, still the help, or because of its convenience. We left the car on the edge of a parking lot the size of a tennis court and Helen began rummaging in her bag like an obstetrician. She found keys, and opened the dark door under the drab wooden porch. A stairway which looked as though it had been painted in old coffee, led up to her private apartment. I muttered something about using the phone, while she nodded and slipped her coat off her shoulders so that it fell half on a couch and half on the oriental rug. I dialed the Regional Police and asked for either Savas or Staziak. They were both off. What I got was Sergeant Harrow, who hated the guts of all private investigators in general and mine in particular. I didn't have the heart to play games with him, so in a falsetto I said that I was sorry but that his party hadn't waited and hung up. I started dialing again, but when Helen heard that I was calling a taxi, she pushed one of the two little buttons and the phone went dead.

"Have another drink first. I need one, and I hate to drink by myself. I fear that once I get started, I'll have begun another long chapter. You don't have to go quite yet, do you?" She went to a tea trolley stocked with bottles and lifted a bottle of Canadian Club. "Will you stay with rye, or would you like to move on to something else? Would you like some cognac?" She replaced the rye and found a dusty textured bottle and a couple of wine glasses. While she poured, I pulled my coat off. The bullet had scorched the shoulder only slightly. Helen was sitting next to me. Her hand was shaking as she handed one of the amber-filled glasses to me. She sloughed her shoes without touching them and let them sit on the rug where they fell. She drank deeply of the cognac, letting her head fall back, until a shudder brought her head back and her slender shoulders together when the alcohol hit her stomach. That put some colour back in her face. "You're not drinking. Go on. It will help." I did what I was told.

The cognac burned the way it was supposed to, and I felt as though my feet were in a tub of hot water. I tried to smile, to say something, but nothing came out. I looked down and my wide tie was looking luridly up at me in all of its various colours. She took another long sip, and urged me in the same direction. I scorched my esophagus again to please the lady, who was looking very pretty sitting next to me. I blinked and she had my feet up on the couch. I blinked again, my head was in her lap and she was bending down to kiss me. I don't know where my hands were, but they did nothing to stop her. She kissed me long and urgently. Her perfume was all around me. I felt my hand on the back of her head. Her clothes made a whispering sound as she stretched out beside me. Wherever I touched her it felt good. We held one another and kissed, until the sound of the two high-powered bullets disappeared into other sounds, and the smell of the cordite of the shells was eased by that of perfume and freshly washed hair.

TWENTY-ONE

It was a very early morning taxi that took me back to the hotel. The blue lights of the snow-removal machines were swinging across the empty expanse of Market Square. A policeman with red hair was trying the locks along King Street. The hotel was deserted, and the stairs creaked loudly as I climbed up to the room. Inside ten minutes I was asleep and miraculously back at the top of the mountain.

I threw something at the clock when it went off and turned off the day for another couple of hours. When the phone started in, I gave up.

"Benny?"

"Yeah?"

"It's Pete. I've got some . . ."

"What the hell time is it?"

"Come on, Benny, it's eleven already. Remember that 'sunlit pallets never thrive.' Up, boy, up!"

"Pete, go bother somebody who'll appreciate your memory for poetry better than me. You weren't drinking cognac after getting shot at last night. Call me in an hour."

"Who was shot at? Benny, what are you saying?"

"In the parking lot of the Beaumont Hotel. Check over my Olds, I didn't move it. I've got the casings and I'll bring them over in an hour. But right now, I don't like the look of the day. G'bye Pete, see you at noon." I tried putting my head under the pillow, but it was no good. Once you know that there's light out there, it isn't the same any more. So I slowly rolled out, showered and dressed. I put on yesterday's tie because I'd left most of the good ones in the back seat of the car. At one time I used to think that I could utterly transform my appearance by a deft change of neckwear. But in those days the highlight of my life was losing two dollars to another detective who was watching the same couple for the other side. They took hours in the motel unit, and we devised a spitting game to break the monotony. He was the best spitter I ever

123

met. He should have been on television I thought, although I hear he went into real estate.

Outside, it was dry and cold. A little puff of vapour preceded me to Bagels, the place that never had any bagels. Naturally they were out of them, but the coffee helped. Thank God the owner hadn't called it The Coffee Shop. Breakfast was good and it helped me feel like something better than egg shells and coffee grounds in the garbage. My shoulder hurt, but so did the rest of me. Even my hair hurt, what was left of it.

It was about ten after twelve that I went through the glass doors of the Regional Police Headquarters. The fresh nectarine-cheeked faces of the cops walking up and down the corridor made me feel like one hundred and seven. Savas was in his office with a few file drawers pulled out like he had been working. A Hollywood director couldn't have made it look more convincing. I dropped the brass shell casings on his desk and he removed the transistor radio earplug and slammed a drawer closed.

"Why is it you make so many people mad at you, Cooperman? These guys weren't fooling. Those slugs came from a gun that is tough enough to mess you up even if you were inside the car. It usually comes with a sight that's good enough to read what you had for lunch on your tie. Why not go into retirement for a while? These guys could have laid you out."

"Sure. Give me a job emptying parking meters, and I'll give up my life of crime. What can you tell me about the gun besides that?"

"Probably next to untraceable. For my money it's a mail-order weapon picked up in New York State. But that's guessing. I'll send the bullets we took out of your car to the Forensic Centre. They may see something, but I doubt it." At this moment Pete Staziak walked in, smiled and sat on a chair the wrong way around. He repeated Chris's warnings and told me to go into the hand-laundry business and get my thrills pressing skirts. I enjoyed their concern, but when you have a client that gets knocked off, it's bad for business not to do something about it. Then Pete grinned at me: "Benny, I had a brainwave last night. I sent a man with those suits we found in Muriel's closet around to the tailor's where the labels said they came from."

"So?"

"So, the tailor's never seen Johnny Rosa, but recognizes the suits as the ones a good-looking blonde bought off the rack in ten minutes a couple of months ago. He said he thought she was laying out her seven dead brothers she bought them so fast."

"The other news," said Savas putting in his share, "is that the suits were all too big for Johnny Rosa if he still looked like he did when he left Kingston. Now, it is possible that he might have put on a few pounds, but he didn't add two inches to his legs, and one and a half to his arms."

I looked at both of them; they looked like the cats that licked up the cream. "Brainwave," Pete said. I could swear I planted the idea on him the last time I saw him. Maybe I'm getting too old for this game. Maybe I should retire, or at least lay low for a while.

"Come on, Benny, I'm buying lunch." Savas grinned one of his rare grins, which made his face look like a ham with a gash in it, and Pete got up fast, like he thought Chris had said that he was buying everybody a new Cadillac. We went down the corridor together, with me dropping in behind whenever we passed a large object like a showcase full of prizes and trophies won by the police athletic teams. Once out on the street, Chris clapped me on the shoulder. "Benny, if you can only crack the mystery of the missing bottle of rye, we'll have this case sewn up."

"Go on," Pete said. "We'll figure that out over lunch. Where, incidentally, are you taking us?"

"Little place I know off Academy Street. Nothing fancy. . ."

"Wouldn't you know," put in Pete.

". . . but nicely prepared. I hope you like Greek food?"

"Yeah," said Pete.

"Benny?"

"I'm game for anything." I tried to keep up with their

long legs as they walked up the south side of Church Street, past the library and the convent across the road, and on up to Academy, where the ruin of the first secondary school in the district stood. An architect had thought he could take a good example of a building of the middle of the last century and, by stripping off the eaves, the pediments and other classical features, deliver to the Board of Education a brand new school for the middle of this century. Nobody admitted that it hadn't worked. Nobody wrote in the paper that the school looked as silly as a tutu on a prizefighter. I get angry about the school because I went there for a year.

Once on Academy Street, Chris took the lead. He cut across below the bus terminal and followed a path between two old houses, one now a beauty parlour, the other an insurance office. He stopped when he came to a large lean-to café that had been thrown up in back of the beauty parlour. Chris was first through the door, where he was greeted in Greek by a giant with a handlebar moustache under a real chef's cap and dark suspicious eyes. The greeting was noisy and we were excluded for the first minute or so, during which time both Pete and I stood with grins on our faces. Chris did a little describing of each of us to the chef in Greek, and he looked at us evenly. A dark-haired woman came into the room to see what the noise was all about, and the introductions were made all over again, still in Greek. It was very rude: Chris didn't care whether we knew who they were. The woman wiped her hand on her apron and thrust it out at me. "How do you do?" she said. "Good, better, best. Bring, brought, brought." I shook her hand warmly and when I looked around we were all attached to one another in this fashion.

In another minute we were seated at a vinyl-topped table and Chris was ordering for all of us, and before long, the chef and his old lady laid a table before us fit for some sort of celebration. There were about twenty small dishes, each with its own specialty, and there was Canadian beer to help it all down. I tried a few things. Nothing huge, you understand. I liked the meatballs best, and there was some fried cheese which went down well. Once the beer had been uncapped, Savas started in on me.

"Okay, Benny. Who killed the Falkirk woman?"

"Get away from me, Chris, I'm eating my lunch! How am I supposed to know what has outwitted the combined forces of the Regional Police?"

"Hey!" Pete put in. "It hasn't outwitted anybody, it's just that you were in it a couple of days before we were, that's all. We want to know about why somebody tried to fake Johnny Rosa's disappearance with those suits and then bumped him off in a car that can be traced as easily as your shorts."

"Right," said Savas, eating something with a fin on it. "And what's going on between you and the people in the house on the hill?"

"Tell the truth, you didn't have to spring for lunch to find that out, Chris. I was invited by the lady of the house. I told you. She thinks she had a call from Johnny." I was nibbling on something chewy with nuts in it. The chef and the woman were grinning as we made each selection. I tried something that tasted like seaweed. When I asked Chris what it was, he confirmed my suspicions. I could see that I was going to have to sing for my supper, so I took a long gulp of beer and started spinning out what I could make of the whole deadly ransom game.

"Somewhere out there, hidden by Johnny Rosa, and unknown to anyone else, is half a million dollars. He put it in a hiding place and went to prison believing it would still be there when he got out. Unfortunately, when that happened, he was being watched. Ashland, Todd and Knudsen were watching because they wanted their pay for the kidnapping job. The Warren family wanted it back too. You never get so rich that five hundred thousand dollars can be written off with a grand gesture. I think that Muriel was interested too, and she let Johnny move in with her to keep a closer watch on him. She may have been in this alone, but the better bet is that her partner was Eddie Milano." Pete, who had been holding a burning match about half an inch away from doing any good to the cigarette he was trying to light, suddenly yelled and put his finger in his mouth.

"How do you get that?" he said, cooling it in his beer.

127

"It just makes sense, that's all. Up until Johnny got out, Muriel was Eddie's girl. There's only one smart answer to why she changed the shoes under her bed."

"Smooth work," said Chris, sucking on a fishbone.

"Polished marble beside those lunk-heads from the RCMP."

"How do they come into this?"

"Same way you do, only you haven't picked up one of the kidnappers and hoped that he could be scared enough to start talking. Knudsen may not be too quick in most ways, but he's not soft. The lake will boil over before he tells the Horsemen anything."

I let the image sit in the air above the table for a few seconds while I tried my first black olive. I'd just tasted something waxy that Pete identified as avocado. I was really mixing it up in the food department. I tried another morsel, something salty and vaguely fishy. Savas was eyeing me steadily without blinking. The old couple had given up on us, since we were not going to return to talking Greek. I wet my mouth with a sip of beer.

"Let's go back to Eddie. I know that Eddie was busy checking out Muriel's little drama. I discovered last Tuesday, the day after Muriel hired me, that I was being followed. When the two mugs finally caught up to me, all they wanted to know was who was I working for. When Eddie heard that, he could see that it fit in with all the other stuff he'd discovered, and some I'd brought to you."

"The bloodstains in the Volkswagen."

"Yeah, along with the abandoned toothbrush and wardrobe."

"But he found out it was all a trick, and took it out on Muriel." Pete looked happy after saying that.

"Could be. But then again, he may not have had a hand in her death at all. I still haven't figured out about the missing bottle yet." Savas grinned at Pete, but neither of them said anything.

"Another way to look at it is that something fell through from Johnny's end. Something must have stopped him picking up the ransom money. What else do we know? We know that he has broken cover, abandoned being dead at least as far as Gloria Jarman is concerned. That is, if we take that call Mrs. Jarman says she got as genuine. Supposing it was from Johnny. Why would Johnny contact the victim of the kidnapping about it after all this time? Why would he tell her, 'You were the one. It had to be you'? Supposing that refers to his discovery that the money was gone, isn't it odd that the first thing to pop into his head would be that the victim of the snatch moved the money? It suggests that Johnny had reason to believe that Gloria Warren arranged her own kidnapping. It's an incredible idea, but not, as you know, unheard of. If Gloria arranged the whole scam, why did she tell me about hearing from Johnny Rosa? Why was Johnny so sure that 'It had to be you'?" I took another sip. The beer was getting tepid, and I was running out of gas. The remains of the lunch lay spread out on twenty plates between us. Savas stretched in his chair. It was something to watch, like he had started to grow, to double his size before your very eyes.

"Well," he said, "it sounds good, but I haven't heard a word that sounds like proof or evidence. It's just a plausible explanation which happens to fit most of the facts. It doesn't solve the death of Muriel Falkirk, or tell us where the money is."

"It's more than we had before lunch, Chris. Admit it."

"Well, I don't know, Pete," he said playing with his leftovers the way he'd been taught not to. "Some of it sounded pretty arbitrary to me. Like that stuff about the Horsemen taking Knudsen in for questioning. Have you anything stronger than a feeling in your stomach that it was the RCMP? Come on, you're talking through your lid on that."

"Why don't you check?"

"What do you mean? You think I should just call them up?"

"If you won't," I said, brave on beer, "I will."

"Let it be you then. The only Mountie I ever got along with got fired for wading in the goldfish pond at the Banff Springs Hotel while in uniform and under the influence. He bought his first three-piece suit wearing sunglasses. No thanks. You can have those guys. I know they're supposed to co-operate with us. Yeah! Like racehorses coming into the stretch they co-operate.''

Pete shook his head silently.

"Chris," I asked, getting the feeling that the party was almost ready to break up. "You ever hear of a private operator named Handler?" Savas sneered and exchanged a short look with Pete.

"Luke Handler? How did he get his feet into this barrel of cement?"

"He's snooping for Ashland. What do you know about him?"

"He used to get paid by the Hamilton police force. A big guy, quick with the muscle. Didn't like that part of the police manual that said he was essentially a peace officer. Liked to cut up a lot. He quit and went private, working out of Hamilton. He put his neck in a sling when he broke into a lawyer's office to see what kind of case was being prepared against his client. A judge called 'foul' on that and the last I heard he was suspended. If he's snooping without a licence it better be as a friend of the family."

"He's a lefty, Benny. If he takes a poke at you, watch his left hand," said Pete. "A better tip is not to get involved." I nodded thanks to both of them grimly. That's all I needed in this case, a little sadism and brutality.

We all squeaked our chairs away from the table at precisely the same moment, like we'd rehearsed it that way. I muttered a syllable or three by way of thanks at Savas, who waved it away with his big hand. "The guy that runs this place is a cousin of a cousin of mine." We were sent off into the street with a Greek benediction, and the three of us parted on Academy Street. Pete shouted after me that I could pick up my car at the police garage. I'd have to pay for the window they fixed, but I could collect most of that on my insurance. Before they were out of hearing, I thought I heard Savas tell Pete Staziak, "The peeper's okay." It was nice to hear. Nice to know I hadn't wasted my days working the divorce grind, getting rained on and sworn at, and generally feeling like I was looking at the world through orange peels and egg shells. I shouted after them not to fix too many tickets before knocking off for the day. I wondered: would my mother prefer me to be a cop in uniform, or just one of those people they wouldn't give one to.

I paid an arm and a leg to get my car away from the mechanic at the police garage, and signed the papers that would put me back on the road again. As soon as I got back to the office, I checked my calls. There were three from Jennifer Bryant, all from different numbers. Before I got a chance to try any of them, the phone rang and it was Pete Staziak.

"Well, to what do I owe this?"

"Benny, Savas and I feel crummy about something, and we decided on the way back to tell you about it after all."

"You've got Johnny Rosa locked up in the drunk tank?"

"No, but we do have an apple off the same tree. We found out that Eddie Milano drinks nothing but a certain kind of booze. It's a calling card with him."

"Crown Royal, right?"

"You son of a bitch," Pete sputtered, "I'll bet you knew it all the time!"

TWENTY-TWO

I tried all of the numbers that Jennifer Bryant left in reverse order and got nowhere. I wondered what was so important. I hadn't exactly covered myself with glory on Knudsen's behalf. He'd been gone for about thirty-six hours and I hadn't done anything except tell the girl to keep her chin up and babble to Savas about the Mounties. Once again, I put both Knudsen and his girl out of my mind. I phoned the Warren place. I was getting used to the tender-flaky upper-crust.

"Hello? The Jarman residence."

"Helen?"

"Benny. I hoped you'd phone. Are you all right? Did you find out who shot at us last night?" I was glad to hear her, and she seemed to be having a good time too.

"I don't have anything now, but I might have later in the day. I'll call. Promise. Meanwhile, I need to talk to your boss. Is she taking calls?"

"No, but I'll put you through." There was a dead sound as I went on hold.

"Mr. Cooperman?" It was Gloria Jarman. I heard Helen on the extension as well.

"Yes, Mrs. Jarman. I wanted to know whether noon came and went without incident."

"I don't understand."

"You said the message from Johnny Rosa talked about noon tomorrow. Well, noon's long past. Nothing dire going on?"

"Nothing remotely dire, Mr. Cooperman. How nice of you to call."

"I was wondering whether you might have figured out the place that Rosa meant? A place known to you and to no one else?" There was a middle-sized pause at her end.

"I'm afraid not," she said at last. "I've been racking my brain but nothing's jelled. I'm sorry."

"Remember, Mrs. Jarman, when you were telling me about growing up. Something in what you said about how you, Russ and your grandfather were often at odds with the others in the family. You spoke of a place where you learned to smoke cornsilk cigarettes and your grandfather kept a store of old Scotch."

"Pop's hole! I never thought of that. He did say 'hole'. But no, it couldn't be there. It's impossible."

"Why?"

"Well, it's family; it's at the farm. It's part of a secret that nobody knows about but me. Both Pop and Russ are dead. I've never told anyone where it is. I haven't been there since well before Pop died."

"Think a minute. Could that be the place?" I held my breath, I even muttered a prayer.

"Mr. Cooperman, Pop's hole *could* be the place. But I can see no reason why it *should* be. How would Rosa know about it? The whole thing frightens me more than that phone call. What does it mean?"

"Let me untangle that. As soon as I can tell one end from the other, I'll let you in on it. What you can do is tell me more about Pop's hole. Where is it for a start?"

"It's on Gillingham Creek, Swayze Township, third line. I think the sign's still in Uncle Henry's name. We never got around to having it changed. It's about half-way between Effingham and St. John's."

"I'll find it. Now the details."

"I told you about Pop. He was an alcoholic. He tried all the cures. He endowed a treatment centre in town, but he grew to hate the place. He really liked his Scotch. And out at the farm he didn't hurt anybody with his drinking. But his wife, my grandmother, 'didn't hold with it'. She was always after him. When he was on a tear at the farm, he used to keep a cache of drink in an old root cellar under the ramp that goes up to the big barn doors. The entrance is on the lower floor, where the cows and work horses used to be. He covered the entrance with boards and put a tack-mending bench in front of it. The door opens when you pull the bench away from the wall. Russ and I used to play in there when we were little. Even after he died, we kept Pop's secret.''

"What's the farm being used for now?''

"Why nothing. It's just ours. Daddy loved it; we all loved it, and maybe I'll get it going again. It's part of the family, Mr. Cooperman. Why, the day before Daddy died, he went out there just to look around.''

"And at the time of the kidnapping what was going on?''

"I don't understand.''

"I mean, was it being worked? Who was living there?''

"Oh, nobody was there that summer. When Pop died, the farm went to my Uncle Henry. Then Uncle Henry had a stroke and was in the nursing home at Hatton. He didn't get on very well with my father. He didn't get on with anybody, really. So there was no-one living at the farm after he had that stroke.''

"Is there a watchman on the property?''

"Mr. Lyon has a shack on the land. He doesn't live there any more but he keeps half an eye on things. The place is boarded up. I don't think that anything of value's been left there.''

"I think I may drive out there this afternoon.''

"Good. What time do you expect to be back? I'm asking because I'd like you to drop in later. My husband and I would like to see you again. Perhaps the two of us together will be able to persuade you to accept a retainer. Is that the word? If it is, I must have learned it on televison.''

"Sure, I'll drop in. I want to ask your husband a few questions about the kidnapping from his point of view.''

"Certainly. Could you come around seven, then?''

"If I don't get stuck in the hay mow.''

"I'm sure you're far too clever for that, Mr. Cooperman. Goodbye.'' I heard one click on the wire and before a second one, I heard Blackwood say, "Be careful, Benny.''

I still wasn't finished on the telephone. I couldn't get the thought of Jennifer Bryant out of my head. I thought I could smell bacon cooking somewhere. I knew I'd have to do something about it, or the smell would follow me all day.

Although I'd shot my mouth off to Savas and Pete about

134

the Mounties, I didn't have anything more than an itch at the back of my knees to go on. But I have very intuitive knees. I smelled horseballs in this from the beginning. I dialled the number of the RCMP and asked for the Criminal Investigations Division. A corporal answered and identified himself.

"Hello, this is Barney Reynolds from the *Beacon*. We've just had an anonymous tip that you've got Rolf Knudsen in for questioning on the Johnny Rosa case. Our information is that he was picked up late last night at his farm, witnessed by his girlfriend—just a minute, ah, here it is: Jennifer Bryant—and that he has been in custody for about thirty-six hours. I wonder whether we can get a confirmation or denial there, Corporal?" I hoped that the real Barney Reynolds wouldn't mind my borrowing his name this once.

"Can you hold the line, please, Mr. Reynolds?"

"Sure." I waited a minute until a deeper voice came on the line. It was deep enough to be Renfrew himself but going under the name Richard Blackie. I repeated what I had said to the corporal.

"Well, Mr. Reynolds, we are not making any statement about that one way or another at this time."

"Okay, let me just check to see that I've got your name spelled right. I guess you've got your belly full of this Rosa disappearance, eh? We had to dig up all our old files on the Warren case. And me, allergic to dust. So, officially speaking, you're not saying anything. Off the record, which way do you think it's going to go?" I was trying to sound like George Harmon Coxe's *Flashgun Casey* as best I could.

"Well, strictly off the record, we don't have anything to say, either."

"Come on, Sergeant, give us a break. The old musical ride isn't doing for your image like it used to."

"Mr. Reynolds, I don't have authorization to say anything about the Rosa case."

"Have it your way. No sweat to me either way. I pick up my check Thursdays whatever happens. But the word around the paper is that Rosa got out on parole pretty early for a guy who hadn't told where he held the money in safe-keeping.

135

They figure that you Mounties have been shadowing him since he got out in hopes of being led right to the promised land. The guess is that Warren and all he stands for applied a little pressure on the Attorney-General, and the Attorney-General used his powers, unofficially, of course, to obtain the early release of Johnny Rosa from Kingston, with the assurance that you boys in red would be skulking in the shrubbery close at hand. Now that's all talk. I don't put much faith in it, but I don't hear any alternative theories either, so . . ."

"Look, Mr. Reynolds, your paper had better not print any of that."

"Who said anything about printing? We've got a watching brief on this, that's all. You know who owns the *Beacon* as well as I do. Well, it's been nice talking to you."

"Just a minute. You know, Mr. Reynolds, that we try, through our different agencies, to maintain a good relationship with the press. It's damned hard to do sometimes, what with Royal Commissions and inquiries of all kinds, manufacturing charges. So, have a heart, eh? We're only human."

"Well, a couple of humans picked up Rolf Knudsen at his farm the other night. There hasn't been an arraignment, no charges laid, no statements to the honest toilers of the fourth estate."

"Okay, off the record, understand, I will look into the unsubstantiated rumours that you've reported. I doubt if there's any substance to them, right, but I'll check them out. How's that?"

"Wonderful, Sergeant. Much obliged." For some reason, my suitcoat was sticking to me like it was the middle of a heat wave. I felt the little spiders of sweat walking down my sides from my armpits. If anybody ever asked, I could say I fought the good fight this fine day. At the same time, I hoped they hadn't tried to trace the call. Next time I feel that brave, I'll be brave on a pay phone.

I was just sitting there looking at Dr. Alekhine's *My Best Games of Chess,* which I hadn't opened in two months, when the phone rang. I jumped up faster than light, checked the frosted glass of the door for shadows and the window for a fast way out. When the Horsemen move, they don't fool around. I answered the phone in a voice I'd used in a high-school play twenty years ago. It was high and adenoidal. Jennifer Bryant was on the line.

"What's the matter?" I said in my own voice, as soon as I'd found it.

"Benny, a man came to the farm! He asked a lot of questions. I told him to leave me alone, so he left. But he's been following me. I can't shake him. What shall I do?"

"Where are you?"

"There's a fish and chip store across from the Lincoln Theatre . . ."

"I know the place. It's just up the street from me. Sit tight and don't move."

"He's outside. He keeps looking in the window at me."

"Order yourself a chocolate malted. I'll be right over."

"Yuk! Goodbye."

I pulled my coat off the rack and hurried down the twenty-eight stairs two at a time. A freezing wind was blowing down St. Andrew Street. It caught me in the pit of my stomach as I tried to move as fast as I could along the curve of the main drag. I cleared Dunn's Tailors, the Radio Lunch, Leon's Furniture, the Capitol Theatre, the old Fire Hall and the Palace Theatre. From about the Murray hotel, I could see the tall sign of the Lincoln clearly ahead. It was about eight blocks in all and the front of my shins were calling "uncle".

As I was crossing St. Andrew Street, Harvey Hinden called my name and looked like he wanted to chew my ear off. I waved and kept on going. Harvey could say more about less than anyone I ever met. I ducked into the alley between the Wool Shoppe and Lady in Waiting, a maternity store. It led to another that ran behind the north-side stores. The trouble was not all of them identified themselves in the rear. You had to go by the "No Parking" signs and the look of the garbage. I recognized the "Stop Me And Buy" van behind the fish and chip place. The back door was closed and marked "Privite" by an unskilled hand in white paint. I tried the handle; it turned.

A skinny man in dirty white was feeding dishes to a steaming dishwasher with a curved metal hood. I put a finger to my lips as I walked in and he looked up. I could see the back of the counter from this unaccustomed side and there was Jennifer with a coffee in front of her. I pulled a white apron on over my coat and took off my hat, winking at a waitress who began to give me a look. I went straight to Jennifer.

"Is he still there?"

"Benny!" Her eyes looked like she'd been rubbing them. Her hair was dirty and lank.

"Is he still out there?"

"I don't know. I'm scared to turn around."

I looked over the top of Jennifer's head at the passing figures on the street. Everybody appeared to be minding his own business. I felt a tug at my elbow. I looked over and it was the manager, a short man with a stubble of curly hair beginning and giving up soon after it left the shelter of his ears.

"What's going on?" he asked.

"Police work," I lied. "We'll be out of your way in a minute."

"I don't want no trouble," he protested, and I nodded that that was the way I saw it too. That was when the face looked in the window. It was a big enough face to cut off a large share of the light and the body under it reduced the view of the street to a tall narrow strip. I couldn't make out his features, because he stood in his own shadow. It didn't look as though he could see too well either, because he brought both hands up to shield his face.

"Listen, Jennifer. When I say the word, get up and come around the counter. Put some money by your saucer now, but don't do it too obviously." Then I thought better. "Never mind, let me." I dug out a dollar after moving away from Jennifer along the counter. I slipped it near her coffee cup on my return trip. The face was still pressed to the glass, hat pulled down over the eyes, standing about six one or two. Nobody you'd want to run into in the dark. Luke Handler: Bill Ashland's ticket to half a million bucks, unless my guess was wrong.

The shadow on the window shifted, then moved off.

"Now!" I rasped to Jennifer, who was up in an instant and on her way around the right end of the counter. I slipped off the apron and put it back on a peg, just in time to grab Jennifer's mittened hand as she caught up to me. "Out the back," I said and we went through a billow of steam from the dishwasher and a cry from the manager for an explanation.

There was a truck unloading pastel blue and pink cribs jamming the alley, but we were able to slip past. When we got to the entrance to St. Andrew Street, I held her back while I looked around the corner in the direction of the fish and chip store. I saw the guy's back walking slowly away from us. A second later, we were both cutting across the street toward the theatre. I brought out my wallet when we reached the box office, and the woman behind the glass smiled so that I could see where her molars used to be. Jennifer glanced toward the restaurant. I saw that two tickets would eat up all of a ten-dollar bill, so I put my wallet back and pulled the girl along the sidewalk away from the theatre. Next door sat St. Andrew Street Presbyterian Church. We went up the walk and through the modern doorway that spoiled the effect of the pointed front door. I liked a Presbyterian church better than the Lincoln; you didn't even have to buy candles.

Inside, there was a table with brochures fanned out and a noticeboard telling that the Boy Scouts were now meeting in the basement on Tuesday nights not Wednesday nights. Ahead the fading light came through tall pointed windows on each side of the nave, and the pulpit was caught in a beam that added extra authority. I led Jennifer down the nave to the middle, where I opened up one of the white box pews. We had a chance of hiding successfully here even if we'd been followed. Jennifer was clutching the back of the pew in front. I could feel her breathing next to me through my overcoat. I was a little out of breath myself.

"Okay," I said. "Tell me about it." She rolled her head so that it touched the back of the pew. A sign on the wall by the pulpit advertised the hymns to be sung, a series of numbers that could as well be lottery winners.

"He told me his name was Chandler or Handler," she said, putting a fuzzy black mitten in her mouth and tugging on it until it came off. Then she did the other one. She was wearing the familiar faded blue jeans and a sweater under her red nylon parka. "He wanted to talk to Rolf, but wouldn't believe me when I told him he'd been taken away." I nodded and she seemed to calm down a little. "He said he wanted to look around. He's so big, I couldn't do anything to stop him, so I just got away as soon as he was out of sight. Rolf left the keys to the Fiat. But he followed me into town. I saw him waiting for me outside the doctor's office, so I went out the back way. He followed me somehow from there to the General, then he saw me go to the restaurant. I don't think he cares whether I see him or not. I think he's working on my nerves." She rubbed a balled Kleenex into her red eyes and managed to do further damage.

"Why all the medical attention?" She suppressed a shy smile. Then she went blurry again, and started to cry.

"Rolf and I are going to . . . I just found out. The radiologist did an ultra-sound. He says it's going to be twins. And Rolf doesn't even know!" The word "know" was stretched so that it became part of the long sob that shook her. She wasn't happy about the news at all. I guess twins kind of put a cramp in lives built around a sleeping bag and a knapsack. I patted her shoulder and muttered "there, there" a few times. It had worked the last time.

"Jennifer, listen to me." I shook her gently until I got a bigger share of her attention. "I'm going to leave you here and I want you to stay for ten minues, then go back to the farm. It will be all right." She was looking at me with wide-open eyes, but her head was shaking like an albino trying to focus in bright light. I told her again, but she held on to my arm. I had to peel off her fingers one at a time. "Remember, ten minutes, then get back home." This time she nodded slowly, and I got up and left her. She was still nodding when I got up the nave. It had grown a few hundred feet since I'd come in.

From the front of the church I could see Handler standing on the sidewalk, looking up the street and down. I cut across

140

St. Andrew Street moving away from him. Then, when I was sure he wasn't watching me, I went up to him.

"Are you Luke Handler?"

"Who wants to know?"

"My name's Cooperman. I'm an investigator same as you are. Only I don't bother little girls."

"Yeah, but I hear you lose your clients in the bathtub."

"That beats finding them in the gutter. I want to talk to you."

"Who needs it?"

"Your boss talked to me. You could do worse."

"I doubt it."

"Let's get out of the draught," I suggested, and he walked me down St. Andrew Street to the Murray Hotel, into the noise and yellow smoke of the Gents' beverage room.

Handler found a red-topped pedestal table and retrieved the chairs that belonged to it from the neighbourhood. I took one from him, and sat down in it in my own way to show that in small things at least I was my own man. The waiter plunked down two draft beers between us, and Handler downed his without a second thought. I sipped at mine.

"Well," he said, daring me to tell him something he didn't already know.

"You're wasting your time on the girl," I said. "She's clean, and besides that she's the Crown Prosecutor's daughter."

"That tramp?" he grunted.

"That tramp has a line in the social register any day she wants it. Her old man is pretty thick with the Tories. He's got home numbers for the whole provincial cabinet, I'll bet. Without getting up, he could have your licence on his desk."

"Where did her boyfriend go?" He looked like it pained him to talk at all. A man of some pride. I thought of what Savas had said about him. The top portion of his heavy, brooding bulk was given over to springy, dirty blond hair that came down under his fedora in a widow's peak, about a half inch above his bushy eyebrows. The eyes were a washed-out blue that reminded me of tinted Kleenex. His large nose had been moved permanently to a new address on the right-hand side of his face. The chin looked hard, and the mouth didn't smile. He rested big hands on the table top. I didn't feel like messing with his powerful left, or his right for that matter.

"The Mounties picked him up for questioning." He chewed on that for a minute, then I added, "They'll let go soon. If he knows something, he's not likely to spill it. He's not the type to scare easily."

"Why the Horsemen?"

"Sounds like their kind of show," I said, sounding more British than I'd intended. "Who else have you bothered? Todd? I'll bet you haven't taken on Eddie Milano and his boys yet."

He sat there like a post with a knot in it, as close to a smile as he got. "What about Todd?" I asked, sensing something.

"Todd's been picked up."

"What!" I said, a little too loudly.

"Grabbed an old lady at the bus terminal, tried to take her grip. Nobody can figure it out."

"When did this happen?" He didn't answer, and I couldn't make him.

I'd pictured Todd as a cool customer, not someone who would try a trick like that and spoil his parole record. It didn't make sense. But then what did? The only thing I could believe in was Handler, sitting within poking distance, in a stained wash-and-wear shirt and a dirty necktie. I wasn't going to get any more answers from him.

"Listen," I said. "I hear that Johnny Rosa's car was just towed in to Steve's Garage out on Niagara Street. There may not be anything in it, but maybe you could let me know what you find out. I'd appreciate that."

"Check. There's room for a lot more co-operation in this racket." He scraped his chair away from the table, drank the last of his beer on his feet. "You'll be hearing from me," he said, and walked out of the beverage room with a broad grin.

TWENTY-THREE

he Warren farm was set in a valley where complicated glaciation had interrupted the regular blue line of the Niagara Escarpment. A stream cut a notch through the rich earth instead of cascading over the lip of a precipice, as the Niagara River itself did, spectacularly, seventeen miles to the east. It meandered around the gently descending hills, just then reddened by the last of the sun, to the lakeshore plain. The farms along Gillingham Creek were some of the most sought after in the whole Niagara district. Peaches, cherries, plums from these orchards were prized in the central markets of the great cities of North America, and rightly so. The abandoned Warren farm seemed a sin against the whole community, the conspicuous luxury of the very rich.

As I came up to it on the concession road, I could see vistas of neglected peach trees etched against the dun-coloured sky and the darkening blue of the hills, all returning to the wild condition of their ancestors. The fences were down in many places and no attempt had been made to mend them even with binder twine. I could see the wreckage of Pop's racing stable, a gray board and batten structure with a lantern and a bent weather-vane on top. In places the white wooden fence that enclosed an oval track appeared intact above the snow drifts, but mostly the wood had fallen away, or been carted off. The sign on the mail box read "Henry Angus Warren".

The house itself looked sound enough. I'd trade all the comforts of my hotel room for it without even looking through the glass in the many-paned windows. The eaves overhung the cut-stone walls by two feet on either side, and it rose three storeys as though it had been forced in on itself and up, just like Knudsen's place. The main impression was of stern respectability, especially in the failing light. It was as grave as the bearded faces I'd glanced at in the library while waiting for Muriel to show up. No wonder old Pop turned and returned to drink.

I was just manoeuvring the car to allow for a speedy withdrawal when I noticed an elderly man standing with his legs wide apart across the middle of the lane. If it was a boozy ghost of old Pop, I wondered why he was holding a twelve-gauge shotgun across his chest. I stopped the car, got out, and made a gesture with my hand going up to my hat that was aimed at his humane side. He didn't move. He stood up in a worn pair of twill trousers and a red wool jacket with leather patches on the pockets. His black hat had flaps to it which were like me, hanging loose.

"Afternoon!" I called, dropping the "good" so as to be taken for a friend from up the road rather than an enemy from the alien city. He didn't say anything. He didn't move.

"There's more snow predicted for the weekend," I said, scanning the horizon like a landowner. His grizzled chin didn't budge from the solid block of air it was leaning on.

"Are you Mr. Lyon?" My trump card, my ace in the hole, my last spit in the ocean.

"Who might you be?" His voice was a hunting knife.

"My name's Cooperman. I'm working for Mrs. Jarman. You can check. She knows I'm here." His face relaxed a notch.

"Get your tail over where I can see you better." Then, "What's your business?" He moved one leg, relaxing his stance so that he didn't look "on point" any more. I knew his next gesture would be to drop the gun and lean on it as though it were just a support for his infirmity all the while.

"Mrs. Jarman asked me to have a look in the barn for something. I guess you know Mrs. Jarman pretty well, Mr. Lyon? She speaks highly of you."

"I knowed them all." Here I thought he'd spit, but the weather was too dry for that, though he did lower the gun. "Her and her brother." Now Gloria's name worked like a laxative. "I knew the old gentleman and his lady too. I knowed them all one time and another. Her father came here the day afore he died. He'd had a warning, if you ask me. Came for his last look."

"Oh yes? What did he do?"

144

"We had a smoke and a drink together like in the old days, he slipped me a few dollars to get my Quebec heater fixed, and went over the stable the way he always did. Then he sort of wandered around for a while, looking at the house, then idled over to the barn. There was still some light, so he went in. Not that he stayed long. He was in there less than ten minutes. Before I'd gone more than twenty rods up the lane, he was back out and angry as a cat in a tizzy, red in the face like he was fixing to die of apoplexy. He got straight in his car, the chauffeur shrugs at me and off he drives, and I never saw him again until I saw him laid out."

"Did he bring anything out with him?"

"Nope."

"Are you sure?"

"Just a suitcase, that's all."

"And he took it into the car with him?"

"That's what I'm telling you."

"Did it look like it was full of something?"

"No, nothing. It was an empty suitcase."

"I see. Did Mr. Warren come up to the farm often?"

"Three times a year, regular as clockwork. I could almost set a bet going on it, although he never planned it that way. He just drifted in off the road, you know, to see how the old place was doing. Going to hell in a bucket, I told him, and he just laughed his sad laugh and said he hoped to put some time into the place before too long. He said that every time, and every time he believed it until he was out of sight. He used to wander over the place, kicking up old cow flaps, or dusting the horsehead tops of the rails in the stable, not saying anything. Did it for years."

"But this last time: was it the first time he went into the barn? Was it the first time you saw him get angry?"

"That's what I said, didn't I?"

"Well, if you don't mind, I'll have a look at the barn myself. Hope you don't mind, Mr. Lyon."

"No. You suit yourself. I just wanted to see what your business was on the property. If you want me, I'll be in the shack. Nice to meet you." He went off, holding the gun by its stock and letting the end of the barrel mark the badly plowed lane. He didn't look back.

The barn stood about fifty feet from the house and on the other side of the lane. It still looked solid, although two of the lightning rods had lost their china balls, and the line of the roof was no longer the shortest distance between two points. In the twilight it looked blueish and unpainted. I walked up the ramp leading to the huge double doors. Except for a few scraggly starlings, nothing was moving. I opened a door and let myself in. The empty barn was making a low moaning sound, like there was a high wind blowing outside. I guess that was only the sound a barn makes when you take away its pigs and cows. Inside, the boards of the walls were like wide black bars against the sky. I switched my flashlight on. The mows looked deserted even of mice and barn cats. The flashlight shifted the shadows so they leaned away from me, then crept up behind me. Halfway down the nave, or whatever you call the inside of a barn, I found a straw-covered stairway leading down. The moan of the barn was amplified under the floor. My eyes got used to the last remaining light that slanted in through knotholes and the few small windows. Hay dust fell from the ceiling every time I took a step from cow flap to horse manure. It was a big space down here, compressed by the space above the low ceiling and exaggerated by the vanished live-stock.

I made my way between the whitewashed pillars to the end below the big doors I'd come through. The wall, which was striped with droppings from a dozen generations of barn swallows, was made of wood. Pegs in it held a kerosene lantern, a few pieces of dead harness and a few coils of wire. Along the wall ran a workbench with a much-used vice at one end and a scattering of rusty tools, oily tools, bits of leather, pieces of tin at the other. A dusty gas mask grinned at me. I shone my flashlight on a calendar for the year 1945 which showed a girl in a women's auxiliary army uniform with her skirt caught in the door of a Jeep, leaving a lot of leg to be seen by the driver, an appreciative private.

I tried to pull one end of the bench away from the wall; nothing happened. I tried the other. The workbench glided back as I pulled, taking with it a portion of the wall behind. All I needed now was to catch the eyes behind the calendar moving. The bench stopped when it stood at right-angles to the wall. Behind it lay Pop's hole, a hole black enough for Calcutta. To get in I stepped through a doorway five feet high and three feet wide, and down one step to a packed earth floor. The beam of my flash pushed back the gloom to a wall of preserved jams about eight feet in front of me. On the other two walls I picked out shelves full of empty Gem jars, and in one corner I saw a few wooden cases which had held imported whisky. There were about a hundred neatly lined-up bottles against the back wall, a few broken sticks of furniture and a couple of wooden soft-drink cases to sit on. An oil lamp hung from the right spot, creasing my forehead when I blundered by it.

What caught my eye then was an open suitcase. In my flashlight beam it seemed to move against the far wall as I came closer. It was empty, of course. On the front, I could read a nearly worn-away sticker from the Hotel Byblos, St-Tropez. A small leather and plastic tag carried the names of Mr. and Mrs. George Warren. I suspect that if I'd torn the thing apart, I would have recovered a police tracking device in need of repair.

Except for a pile of clothes in the far corner, that seemed to be it. I should have left it at that, but, like my mother says, I never let well-enough alone. I shone my beam on the old clothes, which, the closer I got to them looked less and less like just old clothes. In the heap I recognized a hand and a couple of dark ankles. I went closer. On one knee, I turned it over. It was solid and cold. The bearded face in the harsh light of my failing flashlight stared up at me, a look of surprise frozen on its dead features. It was nobody I knew. That made it a little easier. He had taken two bullets in the chest, by the look of him. He'd grabbed himself and had gone down on his face. Small calibre weapon, I figured. It didn't knock him across the room, or tear him apart. But when I unbuttoned his coat I found one that could have. It was a .38 police special, oiled, loaded and ready for action. Some other time. Before easing him back on his face again, I tried going through the rest of his pockets. I found some keys, some papers and a wallet, nearly brand new, with a driver's licence made out to Giovanni Paulo Rosa. I had done what Muriel had paid me to do. I had found Johnny Rosa.

TWENTY-FOUR

I pulled into Black Horse Corners and fed coins to the phone. It took them at least ten minutes to locate Savas. I was feeling cold and weak as I stood in the draughty booth.

"Hello?"

"Savas? It's Cooperman."

"What have you got?"

"I've got Johnny Rosa. Cold."

"Where are you?" He sounded interested. But he didn't climb through the wire.

"I'm at Black Horse Corners, near . . ."

"I know where Black Horse Corners is, Benny. Stay calm. Light a cigarette and tell me all about it. Rosa's with you?" I tried to get out my cigarettes, but I felt like I was wearing mitts: my hands had become flukes. I got a half-crushed Player's lit and felt better for it. "No. He's down the road a piece. He's in the barn at the Warren farm between Effingham and St. John's, the third line, Swayze Township. There's a room under the ramp leading to the double doors. You open it by pulling one end of the workbench away from the wall, downstairs in the corral where the animals are milked. Am I making sense? Should I go over it again?"

"No, I got it. Now would you mind telling how Rosa got it?"

"Looked like he took two small calibre slugs in front. But I didn't stick around. The place is cold and dark, and he isn't going to get much stiffer."

"Okay, I'll get a couple of men on it right away. Is there anybody living on the place?"

"An old watchman named Lyon. The faithful family retainer with a twelve-gauge shotgun."

"Okay, Benny, how the hell did you find him? And don't tell me it was some kind of hunch."

"A frozen starling told me, Chris."

"Come clean or your name goes on this."

"Okay. I figured out that was the place where Johnny hid the ransom money after the kidnapping. He must have got shot when he went back to pick it up."

"But why the Warren place?"

"Well, for one thing it wasn't the Warren place at the time of the kidnapping. It belonged to an uncle, who wasn't working it because of a stroke. But the Warrens seem to be getting into this thing deeper and deeper. I'm going over to talk to a few of them when I hang up. I may try out a few theories on you later."

"Sure, as long as you're picking up the tab this time, Sherlock. Talk to you later." He was gone, and a woman with gold teeth at the ends of her smile was waiting to use the phone.

I was running late, so I drove grimly toward the Warren mansion. I had the radio turned up high to put a roof over my vagrant thoughts. I'd never approached the house from this direction, but the architect had been expecting me: it looked just as big from any angle. The leafless trees moved aside as I drove off the main road and up the lane. I drove under the *porte cochère* and parked the car around at the back, next to

Helen's Volvo. An antique Rolls Royce was sitting on the pavement in front of a multiple-car garage. Like a trainer giving a rub-down to a prize racehorse, the chauffeur was adding a little spit and polish to the gleaming front end. I was late, but this was too good to miss. I walked around, admiring.

"Nice piece of work that," I observed. The chauffeur stared at me from under his peak-cap, his matching livery stiffening.

"Takes a lot of upkeep, a car like this. You let it stand a few hours, and you can see the difference." I admired some more and fought down an instinct to kick the nearest tire.

"What sort of mileage do you get on her?"

"If you have to ask that, you can't afford to run her." He looked at a point near the silver lady radiator cap, and rubbed it with a chamois. He inspected the effect, and tried another caress. This time he seemed to approve the work and went on to repeat the process. I watched fascinated. In less than three minutes, the chauffeur had me wanting to take the chamois away from him to give the Rolls a few perfect rubs myself.

He was a small, neatly-put-together man, like a jockey's older brother. He wore shining leather greaves over his shins, and a yellow cigarette stub was held in his teeth with some skill when he talked.

"The day before he died, you drove George Warren to the farm, didn't you?" He stopped rubbing the car and straightened up, looking at me with not exactly suspicion, more like the sudden appearance of opportunity.

"Name's Cooperman. I'm working for Mrs. Jarman. You did drive him up there. Old Mr. Lyon told me."

"Why's that important? Mr. Warren's dead and buried."

"Maybe it isn't, but I won't know until I've got some answers." He took the cigarette butt from his teeth and flicked it away.

"I get paid for driving, not talking. You want information bad like you say, you must be willing to pay for it."

"Okay, I won't see you go short. Start talking." He bent over while lighting a new smoke, but kept his eyes on me. I thought

I'd prime the pump. "Mr. Warren went to the farm a few times a year, didn't he, just to wander around, look the place over?"

"That's right. I took him up there maybe every four months or so."

"Tell me about this last trip."

"It started like all the others. This time he was telling me about his father. The old gentleman was an alcoholic, he said, used to be a secret drinker. He asked me if I took a drink, and I told him I could take it or leave it alone. He got out, wandered around with his hands in his pockets, looked at a broken piece of machinery, walked up to the stable, and then went into the barn."

"Was he still wandering, or do you think he'd thought of something?"

"Don't know. I wasn't following all that close, if you know what I mean. I just saw him go up the ramp and disappear from view. He was gone maybe eight to ten minutes, and I was looking at the racing sheet, and then all of a sudden he comes running out of there like a bull's chasing him. I'd been with the family for quite a few years and I never saw him run before. He was holding an open suitcase, and he came running down to the car, looking like he was going to backfire. He didn't have to tell me that he wanted to leave pronto. He threw that suitcase in the back seat, and was on the car phone talking a mile a minute before we were back on the highway."

"Do you remember who he called?"

"Maybe if I tried real hard." I reached into my back pocket and brought my wallet into view.

"Try real hard," I suggested. He shot me a wolfish grin.

"It was Mr. Avery at the office. Thomas James Avery, his executive assistant at the head office of Archon. He was asking him to check up on some finances in a hurry. He said he wanted a report by nine that evening, which, I remember thinking, was hard on Mr. Avery, since it was past five when he called." I peeled two five-dollar bills from the three I had left in my wallet and let him have them. I had to get to the

151

bank in the morning, I reminded myself, and at the same time I thought that I could legitimately think of Mrs. Jarman as my client from now on.

"One last question: whose finances was he checking on?"

"Sorry. That's completely slipped my mind." His tongue was hanging out for more money. And I had three bucks between me and starvation.

"Look, my friend. I'm not playing games and asking questions to pass the time. I want that name and I want it now. You'll live longer, believe me. Unless you want to spend the rest of your life today, you better tell me everything. I've just seen one dead man an hour ago, and he thought he was as tough as he had to be to survive. I don't think you're in his league. Let's have it."

"Okay, okay. Don't get excited. Yeah, I remember now. Yeah, it was Mr. Jarman he wanted checked by Mr. Avery. Yeah, it was Mr. Jarman all right."

"Good. Now, when he got back here, what did the old man do?"

"He took the suitcase—he'd fastened it together again— and went into the house with it. He didn't say good night, or give me orders to put the car away, he just walked away like I wasn't there."

"Did you ever see the suitcase again?"

"Yeah, a couple of weeks after the old man's funeral, Miss Gloria gave me a lot of things to get rid of. The suitcase was there with a bunch of other stuff I took into town."

"You drive for Mr. Jarman now?"

"Yeah, and Miss Gloria when she wants me."

"Well, I'd keep this little talk under your cap, if I were you. You may be a valuable witness, so you'd better protect yourself so that you'll live to testify."

"I don't scare easy."

"Suit yourself." I grinned at him and went up to Helen's entrance. The chauffeur's eyes burned a .45 calibre hole in the back of my coat. I rang Helen's bell.

TWENTY-FIVE

S he was wearing a dress that was striped blue and white, but the effect was softer than stripes from any distance. Her eyes were smiling when she saw it was me, and she opened the door wider to let me pass. I remembered the yellow stairwell leading up to her apartment, but couldn't recall anything about the apartment itself. The main room, once I stood in it, was bright and high-ceilinged. I recognized two of Gloria's doll pictures on one wall, and another above a dark marble fireplace. Helen reached for my hands as soon as she came up to me fixing a firm kiss on my mouth. I was taken by surprise. I'd thought that all this closeness belonged to days and nights of getting shot at, but not just in cold blood and just for the fun of it. As she pulled away, her eyes were scanning mine like she was looking for a lost eyelash or something.

"I was wondering when you were going to get here. I was worried. The others are in the library waiting for you. Do you want a fast drink here before we go down? I've had one." I shook my head. I kept drink for emergencies, and meeting the Jarmans in their library didn't scare me as much as maybe it should have. She finished off a last swallow from an Old-Fashioned glass, fussed with her hair in front of the mirror for a second, then started laughing and pointing at my knees. I looked down and saw for the first time that my usually baggy knees were also dirty from the bad housekeeping in Pop's hole. I tried to dust them off with my hands.

"Could I try this in your bathroom?"

"Second door on your left, if you insist on not remembering." I found it and managed to transfer the stains to Helen's towels. Short of running them under the tap, I was helpless to figure out the next step. I put a comb through my hair while I was in there, and got rid of more of Pop's hole in the sink. In the medicine chest I could see that Helen plucked her eyebrows and took sleeping pills infrequently. She also went in for the same contact lens paraphernalia that Jennifer Bryant did. I hadn't even noticed.

When I came out, she gave me a thorough inspection, made me turn around and finally declared me fit to be seen. She took my hand and led me through the corridors to the front part of the house.

The library stood behind two cream-coloured doors which opened together. It was a big room, but made cosy by lots of books in tall shelves and the right sort of leather furniture to go with them. It was an interior decorator's library, with shelves of books that looked like they opened up into something, but here and there were corners that looked like they'd seen use. There's nothing worse than rich people with taste and a feeling for the first-rate. It seems unnatural. Gloria Jarman was on her feet as we came into the room and smiled as she walked toward me. "Mr. Cooperman, I'm so glad you were able to make it." She was trying on her mother's voice again, and I was falling back on tunnel vision to keep things straight.

Bob Jarman bounced up from his leather seat and crossed to me with his hand outstretched before the chair he'd jumped from got a chance to take a breath.

"Good to see you again, Cooperman."

"Nice to see you, Mr. Jarman."

"That's 'Bob', remember. Your name's Ben, isn't it?"

"Uh huh. Feel free."

"Can I fix you something?" I shook my head, but he headed for the bar trolley and freshened a drink for his wife and himself. He gave me a look, and I let him twist my arm into taking a Scotch with water. He told me it was a single malt. I guessed he saved doubles for the family.

"I wonder, Mrs. Jarman," I said, when I had burned my tongue on the Scotch—Jarman hated putting in the water, I could see that—"if you could tell me where you were around noon today. I know I asked you over the phone before. But it's become more important. I'll explain in a minute."

"At noon? You mean when I was supposed to be meeting Johnny Rosa?"

"That's right."

"Why, I was here. In my studio, I mean. I was working all day. Until just an hour ago, as a matter of fact."

"I know that a husband makes a weak witness, Ben, but I'll vouch for Gloria's being in her studio. I dropped in to see her just about that time. Why all the interest? And why on earth is Rosa still bothering Gloria?"

"Because of the money."

"The money? You mean the ransom money? I thought that was a scheme to sell newspapers. Surely . . . Look, Ben, the first time I met you, you said that you weren't going to re-open the kidnapping case. Nobody pressured you; that was your own idea. But now it sounds as though it's not that clear anymore. Could you explain?" He gave me that Steinway smile of his again; all eighty-eight teeth were bared but there was no warmth in it. It was like he'd learned humanity through a mail-order kit. Then he said: "How do you like that Scotch?" like he heard me thinking. I nodded my appreciation again, more vigorously this time, and Jarman turned his smile to his wife. She turned a well-composed face toward him. Her green eyes were very bright, set off by a red silk dress which did for her what Calvin Klein jeans never could."

"It would help, Mr., I mean Bob, if you could tell me a little about the ransom, how it was gathered, whether the notes were marked, what denominations, and so on."

"Of course. It's going back a long time, but I think I can remember most of it. George, Gloria's father, got the money. He was a director of the Upper Canadian Bank, you know, and he was able to raise the money after making a few frantic calls. It was a long weekend, you remember, and it was hard to find the right people at short notice. The original demand in the note had been for a million dollars in small bills. Not only is that a lot of money, Ben, it is a very heavy bundle to carry around. The police suggested that as long as we filled suitcases with the used bills they'd asked for, we wouldn't have to worry about haggling at the point of exchange. The suitcases were old ones belonging to George, ordinary Mark Cross, brown, with three clasps and straps. We were able to stuff in only two hundred and fifty thousand dollars into each. The police added a tracking device which I guess is now quite common, but was then an experimental idea. It was a small bug inside the lining of one of the pockets. Because it was the latest thing, just introduced from the States, and because time was not on our side, no exact record of the bills was taken. We didn't get serial numbers, because we were sure that the bug would prevent the money straying very far. That was a serious error. George, of course, had to repay that money himself." He paused to take a sip from his drink. Gloria Jarman crossed her legs, and I was once again distracted. The two of them looked so comfortable sitting opposite me. I had thought that Helen had followed me into the room, but she had stayed behind. I faced them without allies. They both smiled at me expectantly for my next question.

"I know a little about Mrs. Jarman's background before the kidnapping, Bob, but I know next to nothing about you. I suppose I should read the Wall Street and Bay Street papers more avidly."

"Well, let's see. I didn't come up the hard way. My family is an old one without being a very wealthy one. I can't remember a time when I wasn't interested in business. I follow some sports. I ride. I've joined the local hunt. I used to water ski. I like electronic gadgets. That about covers it. You know that I'm a director of Archon Corporation."

"Bob's going to be president, aren't you?" Gloria said with pride showing in her cheeks.

"In time. I'm a vice-president now, and with Gloria's family association with Archon and her block of shares added to my own, together we have more clout than any other share-holding group. Now may I freshen your drink?" He jumped up again as he asked, and was away to the trolley.

"You've been working on this Johnny Rosa business for some time, Ben?" he asked over his shoulder while pouring.

"Since the beginning of the week. A lot of people have been looking for him: his old partners in crime, the parole board, a couple of mobsters, as well as my late client."

"Yes, her search didn't do her very much good, did it?"

"Looks that way."

"And with so many people looking, Ben, may I ask what makes you think that you have the edge?" Jarman smiled this question at me, and I could see Gloria stiffen slightly in her chair.

"I can see why you might ask that, but as it happens, I'm the only one of the hunters who's had any luck so far. I've found Johnny Rosa."

TWENTY-SIX

As a sensation, what I said didn't make the casements rattle. No one dropped his glass, no guilty looks were exchanged. Gloria was the first to speak.

"Does that mean he will go back to prison?"

"He has violated his parole, dear. Society has to be protected." Jarman looked at me thoughtfully. "I thought you said a few minutes ago that you'd never met Mr. Rosa? Did I misunderstand you?"

"No. You heard right. I found Johnny Rosa, but he was in no condition to talk to me. He was dead." Both showed interest. It was like I was telling them the plot of a television program. I went on in a way that I thought might bring it all home to them. "Not only was he dead, but he was killed, murdered on the property of the family farm, Mrs. Jarman. I found him today in what you call Pop's hole."

"That's terrible. When did it happen? I mean, I'm truly

shocked. That awful man. But I don't understand how he came to be found at the farm?''

"You're sure that it's Rosa?" Jarman asked.

"Well, it's somebody wearing his wallet. I just came from there. The police will fill in the details when they've finished their investigation. They probably will bother you, as owners of the property. I doubt if you'll have to go out there.''

"I see. I suppose Mr. Lyon will be able to handle the authorities. Although I wouldn't mind driving out there if it will expedite matters. I haven't been there in two years. We really must do something about that place.''

"But why at our farm, Mr. Cooperman? Why does that man haunt us, even now that he's dead?''

"That's a good question. I hope I'll be able to answer it. Can you think of any other connection between Johnny Rosa and your family that I don't know about?'' Neither of them spoke. Jarman looked at his wife, and she returned his glance steadily and then looked at me.

"I can't think of a connection, Mr. Cooperman. I'm sorry.''

"Don't be sorry. Just hope that the cops don't find one.''

"Ben, do you think that my wife is withholding information?''

"Did I say that? Didn't mean to give that impression.''

"We don't generally withhold things from the authorities. Unlike some.'' He sighed this last part and let it hang in the air vaguely, under the green porcelain chandelier.

"Look, the way I see it, it's like sex,'' I said. "You can have carnal knowledge and you can have carnal hearsay. One's evidence, the other isn't, that's all.''

"Is there any other way in which we can help you right now, Ben? We are a bit pushed this evening and we have to put in an appearance at the University. The new theatre is opening tonight. Gloria's father endowed the building, so it's only proper that we should be there.''

"Don't let me hold you up.''

"Ah, but before I forget, we should do something to regularize your association with the family. I understand you

158

wouldn't accept a retainer earlier in the week." I didn't give him my life story, but I explained as quickly as I could about how I was still working for Muriel when Gloria first offered the money. I think I convinced him that I was as susceptible to money as the next man. He wrote me a cheque and I put it in my breast pocket with the telephone bill.

"Good," Jarman said, getting up and putting away his blue cheque book. "That puts it on a business-like basis."

"We should really run, now, Bob." Gloria said. "Unless you have any further questions, Mr. Cooperman?" She looked at me with her eyes wide open, hoping for a negative response, I figured.

"No, I'm through with asking questions, if I could have a word in private with you, Bob?"

"Sure. Gloria, I won't be a minute. I'll meet you at the car. We'll walk around the long way." Gloria got up and shook my hand, and swished out the double doors. I told her that I would keep in touch. Jarman led me through another hallway that looked like a display room in the museum, and into a large open court with a glass roof and a large swimming pool.

"I didn't want to ask you about Mrs. Jarman's brother in front of her, Mr. Jarman."

"I understand. He was a wild young man, and his loss has tended to shadow certain things about him."

"Like . . .?"

"Well, let's say he never realized his potential."

"You could have said that in front of your wife."

"That's right. You should have asked. He was a madman in many ways. He drank widely, deeply and indiscriminately."

"You know that he was acquainted with Johnny Rosa?"

"No. I can believe it, now that you say it, but I didn't know that they were acquainted. He knew lots of people just as bad."

"What do you know about the circumstances of his death?"

"What do you mean?"

"What started him drinking that last day?" Jarman had

stopped at the diving board and was busy refastening the neat black lace of his right shoe.

"Russ didn't drink because of any particularly stressful incident, he drank all the time. He and his father had stopped speaking to one another. He was also on the outs with the family because of Helen Blackwood. You know about that?"

"Yes."

"All of it?"

"Well, I could be wrong."

"Did you know that she was under age? That they were living together quite openly? That George thought it was all a plot against him, an attempt to heap discredit on the family name?"

"More or less."

"Well, I tried to talk sense into him several times, but I had no standing in those days. I was almost equally on the outs with George. I was a fortune-hunter to George, a cashless opportunist."

"He didn't like you."

"He didn't like anyone that Gloria liked. An interest in Gloria was automatically suspicious. I had been seeing her for over a year and not getting anywhere. Every time I met George, it was like meeting him for the first time. I couldn't build up any credit with him. He was always polite, of course. He knew that I was in business, and that I was ready to move up, but he wouldn't say the word. If it weren't for unforeseen circumstances, Gloria would still be meeting me on the sly. I've always been an out-front kind of person, Ben. I don't like hole-in-the-corner business."

"By 'unforeseen cirumstances' you mean the kidnapping?"

"Yes. During that crisis, I was able to be of service. I guess that George could see that I was worried about Gloria, that I felt responsible for not protecting her. I got to know that he was a man with a profound affection for his daughter, and that his suspicion of me was no more than I deserved. I was flattered that he let me come with him to the point where we exchanged the money. It was a long hot drive, and I had a large bump on my head. We talked frankly to one another. When the day was out, I think I had a better opinion of him and he had some sort of opinion of me, which was a modest improvement in my stock.''

"You left the money in suitcases behind a bush?''

"Yes, we got our instructions in a series of calls coming to pay telephones. We did a lot of waiting and a lot of driving. I don't want to admit to you the fantasies that went through my mind. I'm not a violent man, Ben, but I'm glad I didn't catch up to any of the kidnappers myself. I just wasn't rational.''

"I see. And the last time you saw the suitcases was when you put them behind that bush. How did the voice on the phone describe the place?''

"Oh, it was clear that they'd been over the ground very carefully. Everything was exactly where they said it was going to be.''

We started down the length of the pool. The underwater lights were making dancing shadows on the walls. "Is this the pool where Mr. Warren drowned?'' I asked.

"Yes. He used to swim about twenty lengths a morning. He was a good swimmer, but he was in his seventies. Black-wood said that he looked like he was resting on the bottom. He couldn't have suffered. I got to know him very well after I married Gloria. He was a truly wonderful human being. I mean that sincerely.''

"I'm sure you do,'' I said, worrying the corner of my mouth. "But you wouldn't describe Russ that way?''

"We got along, but then our paths didn't cross much. I didn't go to car races, knew nothing about rallies or fast cars, detested speed for its own sake, and, for his part, he showed no interest in business, hated the routine of office work, and simply disliked the notions of stocks, shares, corporate business and power. I think he respected me for liking his sister. That was really our only bond.'' We had by this time cleared the end of the pool and come out into a side hall leading to the parking lot. A coat and hat were waiting for Jarman here and he slipped into a pair of slim rubbers.

"Did you see Russ the day he died?''

"As a matter of fact, yes, I did. I'd been hanging around trying to see George about business, and Gloria about us, when I ran into him in the morning-room. He'd been drinking, but he took pity on my long face and brought me a much-needed drink. He gave me some advice about handling his father better, which I discounted seeing that he had failed to handle his father at all, and I tried to get him to ease off on the drinking. It was a touchy point, but as I had no particular axe to grind, I thought he might listen. Unfortunately, he didn't."

"How do you know for sure?"

"Russ drove his Lotus off the road at over a hundred miles an hour. He was drinking from a small bottle of whisky, a 'mickey' they call it. The bottle was driven right into his skull." I heard myself give a long low whistle through my teeth, and so felt more than usually awkward when he shook hands with me at his own threshold. He strode off toward his car, leaving me to find my own way back to Helen's apartment to retrieve my hat and coat.

Helen was waiting for me when I found my way through the loot of Europe to her door. I had wandered back the way I'd come, through the hall and along the long side of the pool. The green water was shimmering. I tried to imagine an experienced swimmer like George Warren drowning there with the array of life-saving equipment standing readily at hand. Helen had another drink going, and quickly got up to get me a fresh one. It was bad enough it being February without bringing *delirium tremens* into it. But she was a good hostess. What could I do?

"Here, drink this. How was it? How did you get along with Bob?" Her eyes were big because she was standing close. I wasn't used to people, especially girl-people, standing so close that I became conscious of my oral hygiene. I sat down on her blue couch listening to the ice hit the sides of the glass, and trying to make sense of the conversation in the library.

"Why are you dressed up?" I asked. Helen was still wearing the blue and white striped dress she had welcomed me in, and it still looked too festive for just Benny Cooperman. I realized that the world of the Warrens wasn't my world, but I expected to see a few familiar outlines at least. She was wearing a very fetching fragrance too, that made concentrating on the library conversation very difficult.

"Oh, it's just something old and comfortable that I like to wear. Don't you like it?"

"I like it fine. When I stand this close to you, I can see your contacts. It's a new skill I'm working on. Don't they bother you?"

"Not a bit. Greatest invention since strong drink. I was always misplacing my glasses, but I've had these for three years without a hitch. I can't really get along without them now, but I do sometimes take them out in the evening when I'm tired. If you look close, you can see a tiny dot on the right one." I stood close to her, but I couldn't see anything except a face I wanted to touch. "That's in case I get them mixed up," she said. I had to take a step backwards.

"Helen, was Gloria working in her studio at . . ."

"Oh, Benny! Stop asking questions for ten minutes. Stop those little wheels running around in your head. Forget the case for a while." She broke away from me and fell into the blue couch. I followed her, but to the neutral corner at the far end.

"Okay. It's forgotten. Do we still have anything to talk about?"

"That's aggressive and unfriendly. What's the matter? I sometimes think that you're afraid of me. Are you?"

"Is there something I should be afraid of?" She put her palms to her ears in mock horror.

"More questions! Don't you know that there's another way to talk? It's called conversation. Some people develop it to a sophisticated level. Why are you cramped into the corner of that couch like that? The Jarmans are away for the evening, and I'm not the babysitter. You should see your neck, Benny, the cords in it look like they're going to break." She got up and came around beside me. "Here," she said, "turn your back to me."

I thought of the bump on Jarman's head on the day of the kidnapping. I thought of the—what was it that Savas called it?

The ecchymoses, that was it—at the back of Muriel Falkirk's head. I turned my back, slowly, hoping that I would be able to recover enough after the blow to prevent a second. I was still under the impression that it wasn't sporting to hit a lady first. I could smell her perfume and hear the rustling of her dress as she planted one knee on the cushion beside me, and with her long clever fingers was able to seek out and rub away the stiffness in my back and shoulders. She had a real talent for it. I loosened my tie and took off my jacket. She was able to get closer to the deep tense centres then, and with a little more of her very welcome skill, the names of Muriel Falkirk and Johnny Rosa slipped out of my head, across the warm rug and out the window for the next two and a half hours during which I asked no questions.

TWENTY-SEVEN

It was very late when I turned the key in the lock of my hotel room. After the Warren place, the City House was feeling a little cramped. I felt like I wanted to go back to my seat at the movies. Life was nicer there. Here the dusty curtains, the pile of books on the chair, the laundry balled up with promises in the cupboard, the faint chemical smell that came from the sheets, even when they'd been changed, always got me thinking the things I didn't want to think about. I heard distorted voices of my parents coming at me from the notice on the door about loud noises after ten o'clock at night. I pulled my clothes off and threw myself in the shower for ten minutes. It didn't do any good. When I got the blacks there wasn't anything I could take to wipe them out. I tried doing the crossword puzzle in the TV guide that came with last Saturday's paper. But who the hell cared what a four-letter word for "oblique or slanting" was? I buried my head in the pillow and tried to pretend that I was going to get some sleep. The last few days had hammered at all my muscles so that I was twitching with weariness under the covers.

But I did finally get to sleep. I even had a dream. I was walking down the curved lane leading away from the Warren mansion to the road. I heard a noise and turned to see a big Rolls Royce coming down the lane after me. I tried to step aside to let it by, but the thick green hedges on both sides prevented me. The Rolls fitted the gap between hedges like a bullet fills the barrel of a gun. The Rolls wasn't speeding, but I was aware of its mass and its determination to sweep me out of its path. I started to run. The Rolls speeded up. I kept looking back over my shoulder, trying to see who was at the wheel, but I couldn't. The face was a blank. I ran faster and faster, the highway kept retreating. I could feel the heat from the radiator on my back as I ran. I could feel a scream starting down under my diaphragm. It rose and overwhelmed me. Then I was sitting up in bed wearing a pair of pajamas that had been sweated through. The horror of the dream began to disperse, and I was about to punch my pillow and try again, when I was suddenly aware that I had company. I could see two shadows at the foot of my bed. For a second I tried to put them into the context of the nightmare I'd just come out of. But they were real. I could see faces in the shadows, and I recognized the faces.

"Get dressed," Vito said.

"We ain't got all night," Frank added, crunching a Lifesaver between his back teeth.

"If you're going to finish me, why not do it here? I'm beat."

"Grab your socks, Cooperman," Vito added, "the boss wants words with you."

"You'll have to tell him about the telephone. It'll change his life." They didn't move around, although Vito looked with some disgust at some art on the wall. It was from a friend, what could I do? By the time I was fully awake I was in my trousers and zipped. Another minute and we were all trooping out of my room and down the hallway. Frank led the way with me in the middle and Vito bringing up the rear. It must have been about three in the morning, but I hadn't put my watch on. I didn't care about time anymore. I was too tired to care. I felt like my blood had been drained and sold to the highest bidder.

The smell of the papermill was heavy on the chilly air as we stepped out of the dark hotel and onto the deserted sidewalk. Even the flashing neon sign had called it a night. I scanned both sides of the street. For some people there might be a cop trying doors along King Street, but not for me. Frank opened the curb-side door of the blue Mustang and bent the seat forward. I got in. Vito followed. Frank went around and opened the door on the driver's side.

"Comfortable," I said.

"Save your wind," Vito suggested with an elbow in my ribs, not hard, but hard enough to discourage any further sallies of wit or conversation to lighten the road ahead.

Frank started the car, nearly flooding it, since it was hot and the night wasn't. He followed Lake Street out to the highway and turned toward Niagara Falls.

"Mind if I smoke?" I tried again, with my arm protecting my ribcage.

"If you have to," said Frank from the front, pushing in the car lighter. I carefully fished for my cigarettes in my coat pocket. Vito stiffened until I brought out the pack instead of what he was afraid of. He passed me the lighter when Frank waved it generally in our direction.

"You're killing yourself with those cigarettes, you know that?" Vito said.

"And what about us?" Frank said. "We don't smoke, but we gotta breathe in his fumes. We got just as much chance of hitting the Big C as he has."

"He's right, it isn't too considerate of your fellow passengers to smoke, pal." I offered to get out, but that didn't help. "You gotta understand," Vito continued, "that in public you don't act like you do at home. You see what I mean? Like when I go to show rooms to look at the antiques, I don't spit on nobody's old Persian rug, you get me? Same thing in elevators. You don't smoke. It ain't right."

"They should have 'smoking' and 'non-smoking' elevators," Frank suggested.

"What are you talking about? They already have *all* elevators as 'non-smoking'," Vito said, getting a little hot at his fellow hoodlum. "You want to turn the clock back? Talk when you know what you're talking about."

"Since when are you so perfect all of a sudden? Since we're on the subject, I don't much care for the way you mash up a roll of Lifesavers when you get offered one. You can louse up a new package faster than a kid of six."

"How about the way you're crunching them out loud?" Vito rejoined. "It gives me the pip the way you do that all the time."

"Well, at least I'm not spreading cancer cells all over the place."

"I'm nearly done. Smoking helps remind me I'm still alive. Otherwise I'd begin to doubt it. Why not roll down your window?" I tried to sound pleasant. But my voice sounded false to me. Neither of the boys evidently thought much of half-measures, and the windows remained closed.

It was only a few miles from Grantham to Niagara Falls. Frank came off the highway, rounded the curve between the international bridge and the big hotel, and took the next right, driving up a steep hill away from the Niagara gorge and through a canyon of tourist attractions smelling of hot popcorn and pizza even at this hour. A life-size figure of Blondin, the great French tightrope walker, straddled a wire stretched across the street, and the figure appeared to balance itself with a curving fifteen-foot pole. The signs were gaudy enough with the neon shut off. If you wanted to see it, here was the car that Archduke Ferdinand was driving in when an assassin turned

Sarajevo into a household word, the favourite car of Field-Marshal Erwin Rommel, or the trick model-T Ford Mack Sennett used in many of his one-reel comedies.

High on the hill overlooking the Falls stood a series of observation towers. Each was built with a revolving restaurant, bar and arcades for the small types. The newest of these the newspapers had taken to calling the "egg on a stick", for reasons that were obvious but which just the same angered the group who had it put there. I'd heard about these towers, but for some reason had never been lured up one before. This was the night.

Frank pulled into the empty parking lot behind the "egg on a stick". Nearby were the silhouettes of the older towers, all dark and deserted at this hour. Vito moved me outside. The air was sharp with the smell of chemicals, and loud with the sound of the Niagara, less than half a mile away. He opened a metal door in the back of the base of the tower, and we went into a storage area with cartons of popcorn containers, display signs, gas cylinders for the soft drinks stands and lockers for the staff. Another key in another door brought us to the elevator. Another key turned the lights on and opened the doors. It was one of those bubble elevators, with plastic windows on all but the side with the door. It was black outside except for the street lights, but they showed me how fast we were going up.

"You'd pay five bucks for this ride in daylight," Frank said. I wasn't impressed. I hadn't asked to come and my joints protested every step. After a few seconds I could see that part of the blackness outside was the Niagara. The coloured lights had been turned off several hours ago, but the Falls seemed to have a light of its own. If the light in the elevator itself were dimmer, it would have made a bigger impression. But just then I was preoccupied with other matters. I was so distracted that I tried to light a smoke. Vito gave me a dirty look, and Frank crunched a Lifesaver menacingly. The elevator stopped. We got out into a round, broadloom-covered observation room with glass walls.

"Downstairs is the outside deck, and upstairs is the revolving restaurant. You been here before?"

"No. I read somewhere never eat in a place more than a hundred feet off the ground especially if it's moving."

"Come on. Don't talk smart all the time. The way you smoke, your days are numbered."

"Without the cigarettes, they're numbered," Frank suggested.

"Go on. Don't scare him. The boss only wants to talk to him, right?"

"Skew!" I said.

"Watch the language. One thing about Vito and me is we don't tolerate bad language. Right, Vito?"

"Yeah, it makes a crummy impression. So watch it."

"Skew is a four-letter word for 'oblique or slanting'."

They didn't answer, they just pushed me through a flush metal door and up a narrow set of stairs. At the top was a door with a judas window in it, like in speakeasies in the movies. Vito pushed a buzzer; another buzzer opened the door. A shove from behind moved me into a large, dimly lit office. The light came from a desk lamp, one of those jointed metal things with springs. The desk was antique pine and enormous. The boss sat in front of the view I'd glimpsed from the elevator, only from here, with the subdued lighting, I could see the mist rising from the Falls and the dark line of the shore of Goat Island on the American side. The boss was a surprise. Somehow I'd assumed that Eddie Milano was a fiftyish hood, on the stocky side with a face that had escaped smallpox only to find worse. In fact, the boss was about my age, and looked down at me from about six inches nearer heaven. He had a broad boyish face under what could have been a crew-cut allowed to grow in. His suit was strictly ivy-league tweed, well-cut and from real sheep. He got up and came across to me with a hand extended in my direction. His clasp was warm and friendly without the bone-crushing pressure that suggests the reformed bedwetter. He threw a quarter of a glance at the boys, and they disappeared through the door.

"Thank you for coming Mr. Cooperman. I'm sorry about the hour, but it's easier to find busy people after midnight." He walked back toward his desk and brought a chair for me to sit in. It was a modern chair, but it didn't clash with the antiques that were scattered throughout the room. I tried to take them in as he returned to his own large executive swivel chair. I let my eyes close for half a second. It felt good. "I won't beat about the bush with you, Mr. Cooperman. I'm being drawn into the murder of Muriel Falkirk and I don't much like it. I didn't kill her, I don't know who did kill her, and I don't like the kind of inquiry the Regional Police have started. I'm not only worried for myself, but I have business associates, as you may know, and none of us can afford to be mixed up in a case like this." He spread his hands fanlike on the desk-top, to show the extent of his candour, I guess. He went on talking. "I understand that you were hired by Muriel a few days ago to try to find Johnny Rosa. No need to play games with me, Mr. Cooperman. Neither of us have time for that. Your client is dead, and yet you haven't abandoned your investigation. Why? Another thing: have you any idea who the real killer of Muriel Falkirk is? Was her death linked with Johnny's disappearance? If you can tell me about that, I may get some sleep tonight after all. And you too, incidentally." His eyes were actually twinkling. The idea of sleep at the end of this endless tunnel appealed to the optimist in me.

"Well, in answer to your first question, I didn't stop my investigation when Muriel was killed because she'd paid me more money than I'd earned at the time of her death. I owed her another couple of days digging. As far as knowing who murdered Muriel, I agree that you're a prime suspect. The only thing that saves you is the fact that I think you went to her apartment to see her the night she was killed."

"How do you know that?"

"She'd been drinking Crown Royal, your well-known favourite brand. She didn't offer any resistance to the killer. You were one of her oldest and dearest."

"But why does that save me?"

"Your activities are famous, Mr. Milano. You're the man who is always somewhere else. You're the man with the platinum alibi. So why would you drop in to kill Muriel when you could have it done expertly by professionals while you open the charity bazaar. Although you would hardly be able to use that in court, the cops aren't dummies. You've been on their hit parade for a few years, Mr. Milano. They can recognize your label."

"I see," he said, not unlike Bob Jarman.

"Before I can help you, Mr. Milano, I want to get a few things straight. They all bear on the ultimate question 'Who killed Muriel?' "

"Shoot." He leaned well back in his chair with hands behind his neck: for all the world, the posture of a relaxing man. Only it was after three in the morning on top of an overgrown barber's pole and Eddie Milano was not a leading member of the Chamber of Commerce. Hell, maybe he was.

"You and Muriel set up Johnny. You let her move in with him in order for her to find out where he put the ransom money . . ."

"I'm not going to admit to anything, Mr. Cooperman. You may interpret my occasional nods not as affirmation, but simply as a sign that I'm awake and following your argument."

"Fine. Okay. You and Muriel were going to split the take and throw Johnny to the Mounties or whoever else would take him. Muriel wasn't visiting some friend in Kingston the day Johnny got out, you sent her on purpose to meet him. They'd known one another down south, so it would be an easy job for a good-looking girl like Muriel to catch Johnny's attention. She was attractive enough to play that game on a man who hadn't been locked up for six years. With Johnny, she couldn't miss. They set up house together and you sat back and waited. Right?"

"Keep talking."

"Now comes the part that's not so pleasant. Muriel decides that if she has to pick between the two of you, she prefers Rosa. With Johnny, she can count on at least half of the money and if she plays her hand right she can do better. With you, half is the best deal she can make. Besides, with you, the prospects are limited, you being a family man. Not that she'd say you stiffed her, or treated her badly. She had no

171

regrets. I think I can say that for her. She was looking after her future, that's all.''

"It was a business arrangement. I get your drift, Mr. Cooperman. She'd seen me make lots of business arrangements.'' I had to hand it to him. I couldn't see any cracks in his face. It continued to nod and smile, like I was talking about sow-belly futures or something.

"Okay. That meant she had to get you off her back. She and Johnny concocted his disappearance. And knowing you, she was sure her life depended on bringing it off well. This was no time for the amateur hour. So, she filled up the closet with new clothes for Johnny to disappear without. She ditched her car with Johnny's blood on the seat, handy to the canal and the kinds of constructions the cops place upon things like that. The next step was the clincher. I think that this is the one that really took you in. She hired a private detective to find Johnny. Now, he wasn't from Pinkerton's or one of the big agencies, but he would do. You had Vito and Frank check me out; I was earning my money. If I was legitimate, then it followed that Muriel was: Johnny really did disappear the way she told you. Sorry I missed that scene. It must have been a very affecting end to the first act.''

"It sounds plausible. But it's just a yarn. Your wind is the only thing holding it together.''

"You think it will fall apart if you blow hard enough? You don't have that much breath. How do you explain Muriel dropping you for a guy on parole, working in a foundry? How do you explain the fact that you didn't send Vito and Frank to repossess the fur coat and other expensive objects? No, Muriel was a better actor than you were. Her show had some nice touches. I was almost taken in too. So don't think that you're the only one with egg yolk on your chin. I performed like a trained bear. I reported everything I discovered to my pals at the Regional Police, and they started looking for person or persons unknown who executed poor Johnny in classic gangland style.''

"So Johnny's not dead,'' he said, swinging his chair around so that I could see his fingers interlocking at the back of his neck. "Well, well. Your story is holding my attention very well, Mr. Cooperman, in spite of the hour. Go on, please."

"Something happened and the plan to double-cross you fell off the table. Johnny set out to pick up the money. That had to be part of the plot. But maybe it wasn't there. The double-crosser double-crossed. It was almost too perfect. He gets in touch with Muriel. I'm guessing, now. She gets in touch with you. Just a friendly call to see if she can detect you gloating from your end of the wire. She thinks you've been playing with her all the time, and that now there is no escape. She sees what a spot she's in. You don't understand any of this, but you don't like the way she sounds on the phone, so you make a mental note to drop in for a friendly chat. How'm I doing?" Eddie was still staring out into the black patch where the Falls were. When I stopped talking, he swivelled himself around to face me.

"Supposing I did get this call. Just supposing. And supposing I made this visit. And supposing I'd found that I'd been set up on a serving platter for the police. What would you do then?"

"What you did. I'd remove the single most incriminating piece of evidence. I'd slip the bottle of Crown Royal in my pocket and let myself out of the apartment without touching anything else."

"Then that would be a pretty good thing to do when you are faced with a shock like that?"

"Better than passing grade, I'd say. You forgot to take her glass. That was careless. But even with the bottle found on the scene, it wouldn't have meant a thing unless the cops had more concrete evidence."

"You're right. I wasn't being very rational. It surprised me. Just as the phone call had. You see she'd been stalling me for weeks. I kept checking with her to hear whether she'd heard from him, and she'd keep asking me what we were going to do now that he'd disappeared. I didn't swallow her story completely. I had my doubts, that's how you happened to meet Frank and Vito. But that last call. It was Muriel being

173

Muriel again. Muriel buttering me up, wheedling for information, whining, telling me how much I meant to her. She wanted to see me. Out of the blue. Then a hand went over the receiver so I couldn't hear, and the line went dead.

"That's when I decided to pay a call at the apartment. I walked in and found Muriel packed and ready to leave town, except for the fact that she was floating face down in the bathtub." I could see him shudder as that picture hit him again. I got a few splinters myself.

"I liked Muriel, Mr. Cooperman. I had a lot of respect for her. She was intelligent and amusing at the same time. She was fun to be with. She . . . well, you met her; perhaps you know what I mean. She was Muriel." He must have felt his image of a man of business beginning to slip, because he suddenly rescued it, recomposed his face with the old calm interest and sat listening aggressively from his chair. I tried a new line on him.

"Now, tell me why your boys took a shot at me the other night."

"What are you talking about? You mean Frank or Vito? Don't make me laugh. I'll be frank with you Mr. Cooperman, if I wanted you to be removed from the scene, it would be a simple matter for me to buy you dead. I don't like to do it, I pride myself on having called in these tidiers on very few occasions. That's why I'm sitting here. I've got a reputation and I've come by it as honestly as a man in my position can. Perhaps you read too many magazines or too much cheap fiction: in business I do what's necessary for business, nothing more, nothing less. I know that you may think it's unflattering of me to say it, but your life does not stand in the way of any of my objects."

"Is that why you brought me here in the middle of the night, because I was so unimportant?"

"I didn't say you were unimportant. I said you aren't in my way. There's a difference. About your being brought to me in the middle of the night, well, I apologize about that, but you can understand my position. I have colleagues, business associates, whom I'd like to leave uninformed until I choose to inform them; a simple matter of self-preservation. I hope that when you see your friends from the police you'll be as generous with your theories with them as you have been with me. There remain, Mr. Cooperman, only two further matters of interest: the whereabouts of Johnny Rosa and of the ransom money."

"If I told you where the money was, would you still want to find Johnny?"

"A good point. Yes, my main interest is in the money. It isn't as great an interest as it was a few months ago—business has been very good to me lately—but, yes, I would like to find that money. Johnny Rosa? To me he is a dangerous man. It is unlikely that the details of his supposed death will implicate me, but I would just as soon see that he stayed dead. It is one of those cases I described, Mr. Cooperman. I would be happy to see him permanently out of the way. Is that frank enough?"

"Sure. In that case I've got good news for you: I ran across Johnny's very dead body yesterday afternoon. He'd been shot with a small calibre gun at fairly close range. That's the good news, from your point of view, Mr. Milano. The bad news is that I found the body where the money should have been. It wasn't there, and I'm no closer to finding it than he is."

"I see. So Johnny Rosa can go on pretending that he is dead now that he is dead."

"That's right. I don't think the cops will revive him in order to involve Muriel in a conspiracy case and then kill him off again. Life's too short. They'll leave his story as simple as possible, since the complicated version ends up with the same corpse. Sorry about the money. You're not the only one who is going to be disappointed about that."

"You mean those associates of his? The lawyer, the hippy and the loudmouth? Don't make me laugh. If they see the money in their dreams, that's as close as they're going to get. Now, Mr. Cooperman, it's late, and I have some other work to do before I can go home. Whoever said that the weed of crime bears bitter fruit might have developed his metaphor more fully: he might have said that it needs constant attention, that it needs careful pruning, that it grows up amongst the most respectable of flowers, and that its fruit, while bitter to those most closely associated with its cultivation, has been found to be most palatable to those not directly involved in its care. Sorry, I shouldn't lecture you when you didn't come here on your own. That's unforgivable. Good night, Mr. Cooperman. The boys will see that you get back to your hotel safely.'' We shook hands, he smiled, I smiled and I saw him press a buzzer on the top of his large pine desk.

TWENTY-EIGHT

It was Friday, five days since Muriel Falkirk had walked up the dirty stairs to my office wanting me to find Johnny Rosa. I said I'd try. It only took four days. Unfortunately, she only lived two of them. Her menthol cigarette butts were still in the ashtray when I opened up the shop after letting myself sleep in. I'd have to clean them out one of these days, I promised myself, like I was promising to fix somebody's roof.

The place was gloomy and deserted except for the sound of patients limping up the stairs to Frank Bushmill's office. The limps never came my way. I don't know why I was feeling the Februaries so keenly that morning; I had a rich client, and I'd just evened the score for the dead one. I'd found the hiding place where the money was kept. I'd seen Eddie Milano in his office and lived to drink coffee in the morning. I'd even had a postcard from my mother saying that they were coming home because the weather had been disappointing. Disappointing! She should measure disappointment from here.

I still had a few little problems to figure out. I didn't know what kind of work Gloria Jarman wanted me to do, for instance. Unless she suspected that Bob was mixing it up with the typing pool. She didn't need a go-between between her and Johnny Rosa. I used to be a red-hot divorce investigator. Everybody forgets that. Well, maybe it amuses rich ladies to keep a detective on the staff. In case something goes missing, I could be sent out to trace it like a bloodhound. Also, if Eddie Milano wasn't the man behind those shots at Helen and me, who was? At least Eddie was a pro. I didn't like the idea of some amateur looking down a telescopic sight at me. I felt the same way about amateurs that Savas did, only usually when he talked about amateurs, he meant me. And there were a few other questions to be answered, like who killed Muriel, and where had the ransom money hopped to next. And there was old George Warren's death troubling me too.

The mid-morning speculations stopped with the ring of the telephone. It was Savas.

"They just finished cutting up Johnny. You want to hear about it?"

"Sure. Any surprises?"

"You were right about the gun: .32 calibre hand-gun. He died almost instantly from one shot in the heart and the other close enough to have paid him up just the same. He was dead five to seven hours when you found him. That makes the time of death an hour either side of noon. Surprises? Didn't see any in the report, unless you're surprised by some pinch marks on his bum. That interest you, Benny? I thought that that might be up your street."

"Where on his bum, Chris?"

"Just a sec: yeah, they were low on the left buttock, where it's just becoming the top of the thigh. Just red pinch marks. Are you going to make a high court case from this, Benny?"

"The rest of him was clean? Any idea of where he'd been?"

"Some mud on his boots, straw, manure, like he'd

177

walked through a barnyard to get to the barn. Brilliant, eh? That's all. Be talking to you." He hung up.

So Johnny Rosa was killed around the time of his appointment with Gloria Jarman. She said—and her husband confirmed—that she didn't keep it. Maybe, like a few people I keep running into, she wasn't telling the truth. I should check with Helen to see whether she left the house before noon. Gloria had also said that only she, Russ Warren and their grandfather knew about the hole. Well, Johnny Rosa knew about it and so did old George Warren. Little Gloria imagines the truth or invents it.

The pipes in the overheated office began to croak, like a swamp full of bullfrogs. My galoshes under the hall tree were the mothers of many waters. Outside the frost-cornered window, the one-way traffic was moving slowly up St. Andrew Street, puffing in the cold like an ageing track team. The office was a mess. It made me feel busy, and busy was the best feeling.

I could sit around all day just chewing over the case, but I put an end to reverie by calling Nelson Christie at the Correctional Services office. I got someone named Simpson, who put me on to Miss Wright, who at last, after my second explanation, turned me loose on her boss.

"Oh, it's you is it? Well, I hope you haven't telephoned to gloat over my being wrong about that bandit, Rosa. He may have been alive when I talked to you, but he's just as dead now, Mr. Cooperman, as I said he was then. I've just spoken with Staff-Sergeant Savas of Niagara Regional. He wanted to know . . . Well, never mind what he wanted. What do *you* want? That's more to the point."

"I hear that Ian Todd is back in your live box."

"I should have guessed you'd be on about that. Yes, I had him here for an hour or two yesterday. He's here now, as a matter of fact, talking to one of the parole officers. He's calmed down a good deal. The woman isn't going to press charges, confesses to being frightened and confused. Bit of racism there, I think, but it won't come to the surface."

"If I come down there, can you tell it to me slowly and in words I can understand?"

"Come here? Well, if you must, you must. I'll tell Miss Wright to expect you. Goodbye."

I didn't waste any time getting over there. The post office building looked just as solid as it had earlier in the week, and Miss Wright looked just as devoted to Nelson Christie. Through an open doorway, I saw Ian Todd sitting in an orange office chair with big wrists and hands hanging idle between his spread knees. He looked like he was studying the carpet. He didn't see me, but then he wouldn't have seen the Moscow Circus if it had tumbled in behind him. This was a chastened Ian Todd, an Ian Todd who wasn't going to tell anybody to "piss up a rope". Miss Wright cleared the way into Christie's office and there he was in the same combination of greens that didn't match.

"Well, that didn't take you long. Sit down." I pulled a chair up to the desk to advertise my interest. Christie took out three pipes and began playing with them one after another while he talked. It was the same ritual with each one. If he departed from the liturgy, he'd have to go out and buy three new ones. In and out with the pipe cleaners, examine the effect, test the draw, scrape away at the bowl with a pen knife, empty the contents into the waste basket, dust the residue from his lap, put pipe in tobacco pouch, repeat again from the beginning.

"Tell me what happened." He nodded, and picked up a report sheet.

"Mrs. Charles Rothwell was on her way to the bus terminal on Academy Street. She was going to Toronto. Her name is Susan. She's been married to Mr. Rothwell since 1962. Rothwell works for Hyland Newbury at the . . ."

"I'm not going to write it up, Mr. Christie. Just the essentials will do."

"What a careful listener would appreciate, Mr. Cooperman, is that we have a dependable, middle-class witness here. No axe to grind, no notion of who Todd was. As she got out of the taxi, the driver took her suitcase from the trunk and placed it on the sidewalk while she paid the man. Meanwhile, Todd came up, looked at the suitcase and picked it up. Mrs. Rothwell assumed that Todd was stealing it. She panicked and tried to pull it away from him. He started to question her. The taxi driver got involved. There was some pushing and shoving. Todd kept asking Mrs. Rothwell in a highly excited way where she got the suitcase. Racial slurs were exchanged. Constable Moodie, off-duty, seeing his sister off on the Hamilton bus, intervened. Todd was detained. Too upset to take the bus, Mrs. Rothwell called her husband, and a complaint was made. They've since withdrawn it. Todd has been seriously shaken by the whole experience. He has been warned, and after a lot of consultation, we've decided not to send him back. He doesn't know that yet, because it hasn't been approved. Apart from this, his record is clean. He's just been blown off course, that's all. He'll straighten up."

"What's his version?"

"He says he was coming from the terminal, had just arrived from the Falls. The suitcase looked like one he'd lost some years ago, and he was simply looking at it to see if it had marks he might recognize. He is sorry, but blames the woman for losing her head. Says he wasn't trying to steal her case."

"Where did she get the suitcase?"

"I say, you are thorough. She says it came from a shop called 'Ex-Toggery', where you can find superior second-hand items. It's not a flea-market by any means. She's had it for some weeks. If he'd tried to pop it he couldn't have made more than a few dollars. But that's never been his game. I'm treating it as a misunderstanding and that's how I'm going to represent it when it goes before the board. What else?" He packed away the last of his pipes in the oilskin pouch. Like himself, they were small and conservative.

"I'd like to talk to him."

"Help yourself. You might cheer him up. Now, get out of here, I've got serious things to attend to." I got up, and left him with three pipes ready for action as soon as someone fired the starting pistol.

Todd hadn't moved. I coughed politely.

"Well, Mr. Sugarman. Bad news travels fast."

"Cooperman. I'm sorry to see you in this mess." His shoulders heaved a shrug and his eyes joined in. "Mr. Christie said I could talk to you."

"I'm not going anywhere." He said that bitterly, a little melodramatically even.

"Not right now, maybe, but you haven't robbed a bank or held up a payroll. You'll walk out of here."

"Is that on the level?"

"All it needs is the rubber stamp. You know the law well enough to guess that on your own. I want to ask you some questions."

"Yeah, I remember."

"And you remembered that suitcase, didn't you?" Todd looked up, like I'd suddenly passed a mild current through the chair he was sitting in. "It was one of the ones that held the ransom, wasn't it, one of the two you and Rosa picked up? Only this time it didn't have its share of half a million, just a nightgown, a toothbrush, and a change of clothes."

"I couldn't be sure. It looked like it all right. I'd driven with it tucked between my knees for over sixty miles, and I had a lot of time in jail to remember every detail of the way it looked. That was as close as I've ever been to that kind of money. Funny how a well-dressed woman goes wild when somebody messes with her stuff. I thought she was going crazy."

"She's not pressing charges."

"Is that the truth?"

"I didn't tell you, but that's the way it is. By the way, thanks for that tip about the investigator Ashland hired. He caught up to me. You still figure it was Ashland that tripped the whole scam into the mud?"

"Still looks that way to me. When we called it off the first time, he must have boasted about it to his pals."

"What do you mean 'the first time'?"

"We were ready to go for the long weekend in July, but we pulled up short when the girl's brother got himself killed. Later on, I guess it was in August, Johnny said 'Let's aim for the Labour Day weekend.' "

I don't know what else Todd said, my head started buzzing then and didn't stop until I found myself out of there and back at my own desk. I tried jumping all the old names through all the old hoops and set up a few new hoops to watch the results. Some things had started looking like sense for the first time.

The thread of thought, such as it was, was snapped by the telephone. It was Jennifer Bryant.

"Mr. Cooperman? He's back! Rolf!" I could see her beaming down the whole length of the wire. "He walked in an hour ago. The RCMP had been questioning him about Johnny Rosa. I don't know what you did to get him out, but we both want to thank you from the bottom of my . . ."

"Jennifer, forget it. Listen, what are friends for? So he's all right? Glad to hear it. Tell me, Jennifer do you happen to have a cracked toilet seat?"

"I don't understand. Our toilet seat?"

"Yes, is it cracked? The plastic?"

"Yes, I guess it is. The place is falling apart, but we're only renting. But, Mr. Cooperman, I don't understand. Here I am telling you what a kind, wonderful thing you've done for us and all you can do is ask about the toilet. I don't know how to reach that."

"Cracked on the right side? As you face it?"

"What? Oh, yes, yes. Just a second, Rolf wants to thanks you himself."

"Never mind, Jennifer. I'm coming right out there. See you in about twenty minutes." I hung up and rescued the floor from my galoshes. It had already been whitened under the coat stand from the road salt I'd tracked in from the street. In a minute I had the phone with the answering service and was heading around behind the office to pick up the car. I was able to run most of the lights out to the west end of town.

A long line of kids from the Catholic school was walking along Pelham Road, puffing like a dragon as I passed them. Wind-breakers, rubber boots and wool tuques on a noonday excursion. The recent snow still covered the rusting heaps in the auto-wreckers' yards on the high bank of the Eleven Mile Creek. The real estate signs looked as forlorn in the frozen vineyards as the straggling tendrils of last year's vines and the sagging wires looked like they'd have rusted out by spring.

182

I put my car beside a rusty little Fiat half-way up the drive of the Sanderson place on the Louth Road. It was feeling a little warmer as I pulled myself up on the wooden porch, my eyes blinking in the bright reflections from the white winter surfaces. Jennifer let me in. She was still beaming.

"Oh, Mr. Cooperman, I'm so glad you came." She called out "Rolf!" and he came into the front room from the back of the house, looking long and tall and vague, with a bottle of beer in his hand.

"Hi," he said, "can I get you a beer?"

"I will," said Jennifer, and she left us alone in the nearly empty front room. The original brown wallpaper was peeling from three seams, the rug showed glimpses of dirty floor in important places and the old horsehair sofa looked like it had been rescued from the barn. I recognized the unmistakeable calling card of the barn swallow.

"Were they hard on you?" I asked.

"Naw. They gave me lots of time to think, that's all. They didn't even raise their voices at me when they asked their questions."

"Did you get an idea that they knew anything?"

"No, they were just hunting. They told me that Johnny's car had been found and that it had blood in it."

"But you knew that that was just window-dressing."

"I knew that . . .? What are you talking about?" His eyes were hard now, and the friendly welcome was going up in smoke.

"I'm talking about the fact that when Johnny Rosa disappeared, he came here, that he lived here with you until he left to pick up the money. He was probably here when I came the other night, or if not, he wasn't far away." Jennifer had come into the room with a beer for me in her hand, still beaming. But she saw Knudsen's changed expression, and slowly lost her lustre.

"What's the matter?" she asked, handing me the bottle. I couldn't understand drinking out of cold bottles in the winter.

"He thinks that Johnny was living here with us," he told her curtly.

"What does that matter now?" she asked.

"Shut up and leave us alone." Jennifer was wounded and crept away showing it.

"Where do you stand in all this? First you ask questions like all the others, then you help me, and now you're coming on like the riot police again. What's with you?"

"If you'd told me the truth at the start, your pal wouldn't be lying in the morgue with two bullet holes in him."

"I don't scare that easy. You're putting me on."

"Yeah, well, if you don't believe me, you'll be able to read about it in tonight's paper. Or you can phone the Regional Police and ask. They'll tell you that I found the body and that he was killed not in a car out by the canal a couple of weeks ago by the mob, but less than twenty-four hours ago in a barn on Gillingham Creek. Now you were with the Horsemen; if that's so, nobody's going to say you did it. But they might be very interested in hearing you talk all over again. So you'd better come clean with me. We've already wasted too much time."

"I told you all I know."

"Rolf." That was Jennifer from the doorway. "Tell him."

"You were listening!"

"Tell him everything. He knows anyway."

"She's right. I know that Johnny was here. When did he come, when did he go?" He whistled off-key between his teeth.

"He came right from Muriel's place, after he planted the car. I don't know the date. Just after he finished his last shift at the foundry. There's a cabin with a stove in it on the other side of the creek at the north end of the farm. He hid out there most of the time, but he came up to the house once a day or so for supplies, a meal and a bath. The last time I saw him was earlier the day I spoke to you. He said that now was the time to collect the money, since everybody was beginning to think that he was dead. He'd been busy trying to get a passport in a new name."

"Did you know that he was also splitting the money with Muriel?"

"We knew she was in for a cut, sure."

"Did you know he was double-crossing Eddie Milano with Muriel?"

"Eddie just got caught in his own trap. He was trying to steal the money from under Johnny's nose by using Muriel. Johnny was just too smart for Eddie and his whole organization, that's all."

"He's still as dead as if he'd told Eddie all about it. Don't let's split hairs."

"The plan was for Johnny to go and collect the money, then meet us back here."

"When?"

"The night you came. I expected him after you left. He didn't come. He didn't get in touch. We were going frantic when the Mounties came for me. I didn't think Johnny would try that kind of stuff, but I didn't know what to think. I just kept my mouth shut."

There was a noise outside: the slamming of a car door. Jennifer ran to the window. She looked at Knudsen.

"It's Daddy," she said, her eyes searching Knudsen's face for direction. He shrugged and finished the beer left in his bottle in one gulp.

"Had to happen, I guess." I never got it straight whether he meant that it was inevitable that Jennifer's father would catch up on them or that even smoothies like Johnny Rosa can't live for ever. Jennifer went to the door. Her face had taken on a flushed look that made her look like she'd eaten a little more red meat recently than was probably the case.

I wondered if she'd told Rolf about the twins. The man in the doorway filled it. His expensive overcoat covered an expensive suit. His muffler probably cost as much as my coat, and his hat looked like it had been placed on his head by the owner of the store. He was the sort of man who didn't know the meaning of the word wholesale.

"Jenny?" he said through the door.

"Coming, Daddy," she said, and opened the door for him. Knudsen hadn't moved. He stood there in his ragged denims and dirty sweat socks and probably felt naked after

185

discarding the empty bottle he'd been holding. Chet Bryant was doing his best to look less than his massive six-foot-six. His hat came off, he pretended that his neat little slip-on rubbers were going to damage the priceless sheet of plastic inside the front door, and he even smiled at me, whom he didn't know from a melting popsicle. Chet Bryant, the crown prosecutor, was used to dominating any stage. It was usually a courtroom, where his antics had been newspaper copy for ten years. He was like the spread-eagle district attorney on a television series, the one who always has it in for the young lawyers just getting started.

Rolf came forward, repeated a conventional welcome and helped the man with his coat. Bryant looked embarrassed about his clothes. He explained that he had to appear in court in an hour, and had just been passing. No one challenged him. Jennifer introduced me. It didn't mean anything.

"How are you getting on, Jenny? Your mother . . ."

"Just fine, Daddy. Everybody well?"

"Oh, yes. Yes. Your mother and I were wondering if, ah, you and Rolf might not drop over to the house on Sunday. Your mother thought that, maybe if . . ."

"Oh, I don't think that we . . ."

"This Sunday?" Rolf put in, adding his first contribution to the conversation since Bryant's arrival. "Are we doing anything special this Sunday, Jennifer?"

"Rolf! I think we should talk about this for a minute. Would you excuse us?" They went off into the kitchen together and in a moment we could both hear voices raised through the stout kitchen door. Bryant looked like he didn't like his part. The lines weren't right for him, and he didn't like the ending, but he was gamely playing on, on the understanding that there are no bad parts only bad actors.

"Are you from out here?" he asked, looking at the dark spaces in the patterned metal floor register.

"No, I'm from town. I should be getting back, actually." I shifted haunches, but got a look from Bryant which implored me to see him through this. "But I guess I can wait to say goodbye. I think," I said, "that you've come at a good time.

With a little give and take on both sides, I think you should be able to work this out. He's not a bad sort, you know, and he doesn't beat her."

"Thanks, Mr. . . .?"

"Cooperman. Just a friend of the family. I think that with the right start and a vacuum cleaner they might surprise you. He's made a bad mistake, Mr. Bryant, but he's no criminal. He doesn't have the head for it." I was beginning to sound like a sob-sister on televison or in the comics. I was glad when they came back. Both looked a little flushed, but they were both smiling.

"We'd love to come out on Sunday Daddy, is there anything we can bring?"

"Bring? No, I mean yes. Bring out some cider if you can find it. I've lost track of where to get it, being in the city. You might be able to lay hands on some. I've discovered that I have a thirst for good cider that must be thirty years old. Don't go to any trouble, now, Rolf. Just if you can find some easily."

"Sure, I'll see what I can do, Mr. Bryant."

"Chet. Call me Chet. Try it on." They were all grinning now, then Bryant left in a flurry of "See you Sundays".

I didn't stick around after that for longer than it took me to grab Knudsen by the arm and tell him that he'd better not blow this chance, because he probably wasn't going to get many more opportunities to break even. I told him that he wasn't bright enough to be a master criminal, so he'd better settle for what he had going for him. I told him to try to put Johnny Rosa out of his mind. So much for me and the lecture circuit. Rolf said that he'd try. I should leave the fairy god-mother role to somebody who can make it with the crinolines. If everything went well on Sunday, I might take the credit for letting Bryant know about the Sanderson place. I was meddling, I know, but I've been feeling a little unsteady in my ethics for about twenty years or so. And the itching on my healing buttock didn't help. I'd pinched it on the broken toilet seat the night I spent on Knudsen's couch. The desire to have a good scratch made me lose all perspective.

TWENTY-NINE

I grabbed a sandwich at the United on my way back to the office telling myself that in the long run a steady diet is better than the sort of Greek feast we had at Savas's cousin's cousin's place. Although, I must admit, I missed my mother's unique cooking. When she takes a chicken out of the soup pot and then roasts it, I get sensations along my backbone that make it feel like a xylophone. Well, at least I could look forward to her return from Miami in a few days. And in a couple of weeks it wouldn't even be February any more.

Once back at the office, I put in a call to Thomas Avery, old George Warren's executive assistant, only to discover that he was now a vice-president who didn't come into the office except for board meetings. The young man I was talking to led me to believe that the board met every time there was a total eclipse. I fought him to get Avery's home number, but he told me they don't give out that kind of information. He wasn't impressed when I told him that I was Manfred B. Curtis from the *Wall Street Journal*. He even shared a little homily with me about rules that are set up for the public applying equally to the press. I should have told him I'd order a general audit if he didn't give me the number, but then I would have had to have been John Watson from the Taxation Branch. I think I do the Taxation Branch pretty well.

I phoned Savas with my problem and he told me to get lost. Pete Staziak was out, so I came down to the only resource man left on my list: Barney Reynolds, of the *Beacon*. It took me two calls to locate him in the beverage room at the Harding House. I could hardly hear him above the din.

"Yeah?"

"It's Benny Cooperman."

"Benny? How are you?"

"In the pink, Barney. How's the boy?"

"They got me doing obits and weddings again. Like I was summer relief. Bastards!"

"What happened?"

"Foster must have recognized my anonymous note in the suggestion box about firing everybody with a college degree. I thought he'd go for it, but he's one of these drop-out snobs, you know what I mean? He didn't finish high school but he's taken in by these guys with their journalism degrees. Bastards!"

Barney had been with the *Beacon* when it still ran on coal oil, or at least I kidded him about his length of tenure. He once told me, in his beer, that he had seen three city editors die in office. For a while, they gave the chair to him, but his habits of life did not repay a position of administrative responsibility.

"Barney, I need your help."

"Name it."

"George Warren had an assistant named Thomas James Avery."

"Yeah, I remember. Another old school tie."

"Do you know where to reach him? They made him a vice-president when the old man died, sort of a pay-off for services rendered, I guess. Do you know where he hangs out?"

"Try the Mallet Club. They'd know. That's my best shot away from the office." Barney kept a ready reference file written down one wall by his office phone. If you could read it, it would show you how to phone anywhere in the world through a network of direct lines and government and business switchboards. His crowning achievement came during a revolution in a certain South American state (a series of illnesses and holidays made him the *Beacon*'s man in San Hermano) where the rising military dictator promised him an interview and ended up stealing his tape recorder. I tried to think of a way to warn Barney about the RCMP, but I remembered that he owed me for the time he needed a secret place for an exclusive interview and I lent him my room at the hotel. The interview went on all night, and in the morning I had to clean up the room, throwing out two empty bottles of Seagram's VO, and half a pair of panties.

I thanked Barney and listened to him go on about how they'd cut to ribbons a nice human interest piece he'd done on Johnny Rosa. "I bet they'd rather have the stupid copy written by the computers. Bastards!'' I hung up and slipped into my coat.

The Mallet Club stood in the best-looking old building in Grantham, right at the end of King Street. It was one of those clubs that had never rejoiced to the happy sounds of a bar mitzvah. Nor had any of its members ever attended one. Nor had any of the bartenders, stewards or waiters. At least, that's what my father told me. And he was right about Henry Ford.

I walked in behind a man in a black homberg with a white scarf neatly tucked into his dark overcoat.

"Good afternoon, Mr. Macaulay,'' said the butler, or whatever he was. "Nice to see the cold easing off.''

"Afternoon, Gerald. Spring can't come too fast for me. Next year we'll definitely go south.'' Gerald busily took Mr. Macaulay's things all the while examining me minutely.

"May I help you, sir?'' he said brightly, but with a warning in his voice.

"Yes, I'm trying to find an old friend, Tom Avery. I've just arrived in town, and I was hoping to catch him before I have to catch my plane. Plane was re-routed here because of the weather. Don't know why. I do hope I can find Avery. It will be the only thing to go right since this beastly day started.'' Both Gerald and Mr. Macaulay eyed me suspiciously. I thought I'd pronounced all the words flawlessly.

"You are a friend of Mr. Avery's, young man?'' Mr. Macaulay asked.

"Yes, sir. I'd hate missing him. But, I suppose it can't be helped. Pity.'' They were quiet for a moment, and then Mr. Macaulay said: "You'll find him in the Private Patients' Pavilion at the General Hospital. He'll be cheered up seeing you. Give some of the rest of us a chance to catch our breath.'' He seemed to like what he'd said, so he repeated it. Gerald and I laughed politely. I thanked them both and bowed my way out of the halls I might never tread again. On my way down the steps, I passed Dr. Adelstein. He opened the door and walked in to a greeting by Gerald. The door closed and I missed the rest.

Rooms in the Private Patients' Pavilion had been built for more gracious living and dying than was currently going on.

The original wooden doors had been taken out and replaced with wider ones that sat in a white metal frame. The life-support systems and all the other plumbing that had been added over the years as an afterthought were plainly not the idea of the original architect, who must have believed that patients would get well from being wheeled on and off the screened-in balconies. I had no trouble locating Tom Avery. I found out from the nursing station that Mr. Avery was a pet, a favourite with all the nurses. Pretending I was his brother from New York, I discovered that he had been admitted with complications arising from adenocarcinoma in the head of his pancreas. When I asked what his chances were, the nurse smiled brightly, which was her way of shaking her head slowly in the negative.

He hardly made a bump in the high bed. He looked dead already, only his eyelids flickered when I stood in the light at the foot of the bed.

"Mr. Avery? How are you? I'm a friend of Gloria Jarman. She and Bob send their very best. Is there anything they can do for you? Just name it, they said. Anything."

He looked at me from behind his purplish skin that had burned up every ounce of fat. I don't know whether he believed me or not. I don't think he cared. A gray stubble caught the light on his trembling chin. I didn't like looking at him, but I couldn't see how to look away.

"You know Gloria?" His voice was a whisper. I had to move closer to him and the tubes running in and out of him. I didn't like the smell. He continued in a spider-web croak: "How do you know her?"

"I work for her. I'm a private detective. I'm trying to find out who killed her father. I'm pretty sure now that it was murder."

He didn't answer for a minute. Then: "You think George was killed? Why? You have proof? That's serious." He couldn't talk for long, and each burst of speech came with his normal exhaling of spent air.

"He called you late on the afternoon before he died, right?"

"You know that?"

"Yes. And that he asked you to check on Jarman's holdings and finances and wanted to hear from you before morning. He needed the information by nine that night, he said."

"It's a long time ago."

"Yes, but you remember it like yesterday, don't you?"

"Are you doing this for Gloria?" His blinking eyes lay deep in his skull and they held me with the strength of a hospital orderly.

"She's paying me. But maybe it's not Gloria I'm doing this for. I don't like to see people pushed around and murdered because it suits them. If George Warren was murdered, I want to find out about it. Other people you don't know have been killed too. It's time the killing stopped, Mr. Avery. I know that you'd like to help it stop."

"You ever write speeches? That used to be half my job. Trying to make them talk English and not get the company sued."

"What did you find out about Jarman? Did you talk to Mr. Warren that night?"

"I found out that over the years since Mr. Jarman joined Archon Corporation, he had slowly but steadily been increasing his holdings. He was never a poor man, but to start with he wasn't stock rich. But we know that he became stock wealthy over a short time. What I told George that night was that Jarman's had become the largest block of stock apart from his own. He got control of small groups of shares whenever they came up. He did it quietly and without trumpets and drums. Together with Gloria's share—she was a lovely girl. I remember—"

"I know, Mr. Avery. This is important."

"Together they were bigger than George. And George hadn't seen it happen. Nobody saw it happen, because he kept what they call a low profile, did it through small companies that were owned by other companies, where Jarman's name was registered as R. Hallam Jarman. Pretty feeble, eh? But he must have thought he wouldn't be found out. Well, George did. But getting rich isn't a crime yet, is it? Jarman's always had a nose for money, for the drift of the market. Uncanny man. George couldn't stand Jarman when he was on the make. Old George saw him coming. But after the kidnapping, he went soft on Jarman, took him in, let him marry Gloria. It was Russ's death too. They didn't get on, but he thought the world of his son, thought he was the salt of the earth, but never would have said it to the lad's face where it might have done some good."

Just then, a nurse came in. She looked at me with friendly suspicion, and announced that she was doing a routine check for vital signs. Avery made a joke about giving her a cigar if she found any. Then he asked the girl: "Was your mother May Ingram?" The nurse nodded with surprise. Avery tried to put her at ease by adding, "I know your whole family. You've got the Ingram look. What's your name?" I took that as a cue to leave, but before I'd cleared the door, Avery called after me: "Remember me to Gloria. I always was fond of her. Tell her that when I get out of here I'm going to come up and look at her pictures. Might even buy one. Tell her that." Then he chuckled like he'd made a big joke. "When I get out of here," he repeated, in case I'd missed it. I joined him in his joke. I guess it's what they call having the last laugh.

THIRTY

On a piece of paper in front of me, I wrote down the names of all the people I'd run into since Muriel Falkirk found her way to my front door. I'd met most of the owners of the names, but a few, like old George Warren and Johnny Rosa, had escaped me. In prying open a foam plastic container of coffee, which I'd brought back to the office more for comfort than taste, I managed to spill an ounce or two on top of my faded green desk blotter. In trying to prevent a flood I got most of it on the names I was working on. The coffee did in the ink and names began running into names in a very thought-provoking way. Could Muriel Falkirk have had an affair with old George Warren? Could Tom Avery have anything to do with Bill Ashland? Gloria's name suffered worst. The ink from it began to dissolve the names of people she'd never met, people she might not even know existed.

There was a tap at the door. My heart sank; it sounded like Muriel coming back to haunt me. I hadn't heard any steps coming up the stairs, but I put that down to my absorption in my list and its lake of drowned names.

"Come in," I shouted in a friendly voice, although I thought it came out sounding sharp and unwelcoming, the proper way to welcome a ghost. But it wasn't Muriel either alive or dead; it was Helen Blackwood, bundled up in a beige coat, camelhair and very nicely cut. Her cheeks were bright from the cold street and the steep climb. I came around the desk and gave her a peck on her icy cheek before she got the door closed.

"Am I disturbing you?" she asked, smiling.

"I just spilled some coffee, but otherwise everything's under control. What brings you to the city?"

"You. I just wanted to see where you work." She shucked the coat and came out in a slate gray dress, wool by the look of it, with a Liberty scarf tied at the throat. Her eyes began taking in the centre of operations while I piled her coat above mine on the coat rack. I could see that she was having difficulty getting on to my system: in it the items with the earliest dates are found toward the bottom of any pile. Recent items are invariably on top. She drew a long dust-probing finger along a pile of files near the window.

"It's not very big, is it?"

"I'm out a lot. It's big enough. I keep the details in my head," I added. She nodded, and began to look restless after a visit of less than five minutes. I felt ashamed that my life should exhaust interest after so short a time, and was relieved when Frank Bushmill poked his head through the door. He was about to poke it back after seeing that I had company, but I called him in and introduced them.

"Frank's always shoving good books my way. Trying to improve my mind."

"Nothing's the matter with your mind, Benny. I sometimes think, Miss, that Benny sprang fully-formed from the brow of Dr. Seuss." He cocked his head impishly like the bog man he was. "It's only pretending to learning that gets you in trouble in this world. At Trinity I once met a woman who claimed to have read *Ben Hur* in the original Latin. Now can you beat that?" We both smiled. It was the kind of thing Frank was always saying, and I was always smiling at. One day, it would all be revealed to me. "Well, my children, I must be leaving. Just looked in on Benny to see that he was still alive. He does the same service for me. Miss Blackwood, pleasure to have met you." And he was gone.

With the two of us in the office, it felt smaller than it had the day the whole Abromovich family congregated in front of my desk, all twelve of them and all talking at once. I had a hard time looking at Helen without putting my arms around her. Every time she moved, my heart skipped a couple of beats. I went over to her and held her close.

"What's the matter?" I asked, and her eyes ducked mine.

"I just wish this whole thing was cleared up. I hate it. I hate it." Her arms around me were strong, and she added emphasis to her words through them.

"Let's go get some coffee," I suggested. Not a prize-winning offer, but apart from slipping the Yale lock closed and making a pallet of dead files, it was the best suggestion I could make.

"Why not come back to the apartment? You look all tense and knotted." I accepted and we took her car. I settled deep into the passenger seat and tried not to concentrate on her driving. She did it well, moving the Volvo up the hairpin turns leading to the pillar-marked lane. From time to time she spared me a glance from the road and smiled.

We went in through the back way. It was clean and bright, with the last of the afternoon light making a pattern of rectangles across Gloria's doll picture hanging above the marble fireplace. Helen helped me out of my coat and took my jacket.

"Would you prefer a drink to coffee?"

"Coffee still sounds fine. But have a drink yourself."

"You need to unwind, that's what you need."

"My father used to go to the steambaths on Saturday night. He unwound on a regular weekly basis. Me? I never take the time."

"Well you should. You're like most men. You don't look after yourself." I heard the coffee grinder making a high-pitched electric hum for about fifteen seconds and then a minute or so later the kettle came to a boil. She brought me a cup of strong coffee and sat at the edge of the couch I'd fallen into. She had a drink in one hand and pulled the hem of her skirt down with the other. "I know what we should do," she said with some excitement. "We should wash some of the city off us in the pool. I can borrow you a suit from Bob. He won't mind."

"I don't know. I'm not much of a swimmer," I said.

"It'll do you a world of good. Excuse me, I'll just get that suit. I think that you and Bob will wear the same size."

"Yeah, if I bring a friend."

"Go on. He's not that big. I'll be right back." She disappeared into the rest of the house, and I remembered that I wanted to talk to Chris Savas about something. I put in the call while she was away, and sipped the coffee. She was back in less

196

than three minutes with two bathing suits, both too big, but belted, so I might be able to manage something.

Helen excused herself and retreated into the bedroom, her hands already reaching behind her to unhook her dress before the door closed. She left me no other play. I pulled off my pants and tried on both pairs of trunks. The second felt like they would stay up as long as I kept my knees well apart. I folded my pants, underwear and shirt in a neat ball and placed them on the couch. Helen came out in a very trim bright red Speedo and a yellow terrycloth beach coat. She was carrying two towels that looked brand new and another beach robe of brown corduroy for me.

"See if these fit," she said, and handed me a pair of Japanese thongs. I slipped them on and felt the skin between my first two toes protest. Feet hated change and so did I. Helen was frowning at me. Then she frowned at a bathing cap and portable radio both of which she stowed in a vinyl beachbag.

"Sorry," she smiled. "I always look cross without my lenses. You look like a fuzzy teddybear."

"With his woolly knees knocking," I said with some impatience. She gathered her bag and towels, then led the way through what looked like an empty house.

"Not so fast," I cautioned. "I'm not as anxious to get into the water as you are. This isn't Miami, you know."

"It's heated, silly. Come on. You'll soon forget it's February out there." She opened the door leading to the pool and turned on the lights, which were controlled from a box near the door. The lights from above danced on the surface, while those that were mounted at the bottom or on the sides added green-blue tints to the water and turned the tile walls to shimmering marble.

"Which is the shallow end?" I asked.

"The far end. Why not take the tube from the bench, then you can use the whole pool. Can't you really swim very well?"

"I'm good for a few strokes, then I lose my wind. I'll be fine in the shallow end." We left our things on a bench half-

197

way along the length of the pool. The radio started in with rock music. Helen made a spectacular dive off the board with hardly a splash on entering the water. I stood at the edge listening to the loud report of the springboard die away and not quite believing that the water was heated. To me, February is February and Grantham in February is no place to be found in swimming trunks. She came to the surface just in front of me, her skin shiny in the water.

"Come on," she taunted. I nodded and tried the water with a brave toe. It seemed safe to the toe, so I threw myself in, coughed and held on to the side. The water was refreshing without being tooth-rattling. I climbed out, shook myself off and plunged in again with one hand gripping my nose and the other lifted above my head, while my feet appeared to be peddling a bicycle as they disappeared from sight. It was a classical leap, and I gave myself seven out of ten for its near faultless execution. If this was the shallow end, the deep end must be five fathoms. Again I came up close to the edge and held on. When I looked up, Bob Jarman, drink in hand, was smiling down at me.

"Hi, Benny! Unwinding at the end of a hard week? Hello, Helen. Have you seen Gloria?" Helen was climbing up the ladder near the diving board.

"Hello, Bob. She's gone into town looking for some Number Seven brushes. She'll be back for cocktails at five-thirty." She went off the board again and, surfacing, continued to my end of the pool on her back. She continued doing lengths until I became tired watching. I took the rubber tube and began paddling across. When we passed one another, Helen gave me a smile. I was too busy to return it. She did two lengths to each of my widths. Finally, she climbed out and took off her cap, shaking water and hair most becomingly as she did so. "I'll be back in a minute," she called, taking her yellow beach robe with her through the door.

"How's the investigation going?" Jarman asked above the racket of the radio. He was standing over me at the edge of the pool, his expression masked by the freakish lighting in the room. "I see from the evening paper that it was Johnny Rosa you found all right. I'm glad they were able to keep the family name out of it." I held the rubber tube around me. The outside light coming in the windows seemed over-bright, and when I looked into it the rest of the room looked like a darkened den. "I'd hate to see the family name dragged into something unnecessary, wouldn't you, Ben? It's a reasonable approach, don't you agree?"

I agreed with him, and he kept standing there, looking bigger and darker as the time wore on.

"Helen tells me that you're not much of a swimmer, Ben."

"I make out," I said, noticing for the first time that the pressure in the tube I was using had been decreasing gradually and that a fine string of bubbles was escaping the tube, bursting without a sound when they reached the surface.

"She should have warned you about that tube. It has a leak." He sounded like he was shouting now. And the light on the water was making me feel a little giddy. I tried lying back on the tube, but the lights above me danced about the ceiling. I felt as though I was wearing lead weights on my feet. I tried to paddle toward the edge, but something prevented me. I couldn't get close to the edge. I tried the opposite edge, my nose getting closer to the waterline with every stroke, but everywhere I saw Bob Jarman's brown shoes and I couldn't get close to pull myself out.

"You've done a lot of digging, Benny. I guess you think that you are getting close to the end. In a way you are close to the end, if not the end of the investigation. Just the end of your contribution to it."

"Help me out," I called. My vision was completely off the rails now. It was the coffee, of course. Nothing too strong, just enough to disorient me. I felt the last of the air go out of the tube. I floundered with my arms and kicked with my feet. "Help me out!" I called again. I tried moving over to the opposite edge, but again I saw the brown shoes and I couldn't reach the other end. I could hear Jarman's voice talking to me out there somewhere in the echoing shadows. He was laughing at me. I couldn't make out what he was saying anymore. I went under the water and came up coughing. I could still hear him, above the music and above my cries for help. I was floundering, sputtering and coughing. Then I felt something slip over my head. It didn't confine me closely, but it played tricks with my vision, or what was left of it. It made the water turn from greenish-blue to milky white. I could feel it pulling me down under the water. I tried to grab whatever it was, but there was nothing I could grip. My head went under. I couldn't see any more. The pressure holding me under didn't let up, however hard I fought against it. My lungs were beginning to ache. I stopped trying to get up, and went down as far as I could go. When I came up, I was free of the white. I caught my breath, and heard a pounding at the door. The brown shoes had gone from the edge of the pool. I heard voices above the radio music. I heard the door splinter. In a second I saw or felt, I couldn't be sure which, hands reaching for me. This time the shoes on the tiles were black, regulation issue.

THIRTY-ONE

It was about half an hour after I'd nearly drowned in the Warren pool that I became aware of where I was and what was going on. I was still wearing Jarman's bathing suit and brown robe. There was a blanket rolled around me and I felt warm and comfortable despite the shivering that I couldn't control. I had to keep my jaw tense or I would have lost a few

200

teeth. The coffee was still on my breath with its unpleasant aftertaste. I was looking up at a ceiling I'd seen before. The green lamps told me it was the library at the Warren place. Better than the bottom of the pool, I thought. There were faces in the room too. Nearest was Helen Blackwood. A bit further off, Chris Savas and two or three policemen in uniform. I seemed to be holding the centre of the stage, and I was sure that I would forget my lines. I decided not to ask "Where am I?"; I asked the time instead. That's how I knew that half an hour of unconsciousness separated me from the swimming pool.

"He's coming around," I heard her say. And then to me she said: "Can you speak? Are you okay?" Her eyes were wide with worry, real worry. I was beginning to feel better. The shivering began to subside a little.

"Th-there was something in the coffee," I said, and "He held me under with a net."

"Don't worry about it now," she said. Savas stuck his big face into the picture frame.

"You held on there pretty good, Ben." He grinned, and I could only think of Mr. McCammus's rules about the use of *good* and *well* but didn't feel strong enough just then to carry the point. It was good to see Savas and I felt better for seeing the policemen in the background.

"Where's Bob Jarman?" I asked. Helen looked at Savas. Savas's meaty face was crowding hers out again.

"Jarman heard us at the door and went out the back. He got into the Rolls and tried to make a run for it down the mountain. He was going too fast for the switchbacks. He made two of them, but missed the third, went through the railing. Must have been doing sixty. Jesus. Took a drop of nearly fifty feet. Not very pretty. He's not expected to live. Mrs. Jarman is with him at the General." I nodded and tried to show that I understood. Helen handed me a mug with something hot in it. I liked the warmth on my hands, but I looked at her eyes for a few seconds before letting her help lift the mug up to my lips. She tried to smile, but failed. She couldn't look me in the eye. I didn't blame her. She was still in her bathing suit, with the terrycloth robe tightly belted at the waist. I sipped coffee. It had something in it: it was whiskey.

"Are you feeling strong enough to tell us what happened, Ben?" Savas asked. I nodded, and he pulled a chair closer. I took a long swallow. I would have felt better wearing my trousers.

"You sure you don't want me to go through this downtown?"

"Just sketch it in for me. We can go into the fine print when you're up to it."

"Fine," I said. "Fine."

I tried to collect my thoughts. It wasn't any good. I knew that I'd have to start jabbering. Once my mouth was running, I could idle along for a few minutes, then let out the clutch slowly and engage my mind.

"To begin with, you have to go back before the kidnapping. Take a look at what everybody was doing. Old George Warren was a tycoon with big bucks, power to burn and a complicated family situation. His wife had run off to the Riviera. His son was mad about speed, cars and young girls, and hated the sight of a panelled office with matching desk-set. His daughter was good-looking and bait for every fortune-hunter in North America. Jarman was a fortune-hunter with the drawbacks of being a local one. He hardly rated with the American, British and European sharpsters ringing the doorbell: smoking jackets and tennis togs in the back seat of their rented cars and an overdraft at the bank. They were easy for an old hand like George to spot. But he slipped up on Jarman, because the kidnapping threw sand in those shrewd eyes." The cops over by the window had stopped whispering and were looking my way.

"Jarman met Gloria and saw in her not only an heiress but also a stepping-stone to power in business. That was heaven to a man like that, but with George on the watch he couldn't get anywhere. To make matters worse, Gloria liked the guy. That was the worst thing that could happen. George had to use both hands to keep them apart.

"Who else is there? Yes: Johnny Rosa, a young man on

the fringe of the rackets, a man with daring and cunning up to a point, but not a mastermind. At this point he is hanging around a dive called the Kit Kat Klub, where he loses some money to people like my old man, and meets people like Rolf Knudsen, a dullish hippie with a taste for pot and beer, and Ian Todd, a lawyer with no clients but a willingness to try his hand at anything. They lead him to Bill Ashland. He doesn't have dreams as big as Bob Jarman's, but they're bigger than retiring from a time-clock job at sixty-five with a gold watch or a barometer for his trouble. They all live in or regularly visit the Norton Apartments where Johnny Rosa can find them when he wants them.

"At the same time, watching from afar we have Eddie Milano, who is just getting a foothold in the diversified side of the rackets. Down in Florida Muriel Falkirk is getting her education in double dealing in the numbers racket.

"Now, who is the string that ties this strangely assorted bundle together?" The more I talked, the less I shivered. "The only one who knew Johnny Rosa, Jarman, Gloria and old George Warren: his son, Russ. Russ, who didn't give a damn for gray flannel suits, but loved his sister so deeply it may have raised a few eyebrows. They'd shared an idyllic childhood at the family farm with games that excluded outsiders and focussed on the hideaway called Pop's hole. But kids grow up, and neither Gloria nor Russ were getting what they wanted out of life. We'll let a psychiatrist tell us what Russ wanted. It was clear to Russ what his sister wanted. She wanted Jarman. But Jarman wasn't to be had in the ordinary way. Daddy didn't like the cut of Jarman's ready-to-wear shirts or his off-the-rack suits. Maybe it went deeper than that. He didn't like a snake when he saw one.

"When I went to see Nelson Christie at the parole board early this week, he told me that none of the kidnappers were bright enough to have planned the elaborate plot to snatch Gloria. He said they weren't officer material, none of them could have made corporal in his book, although he granted them motive and practical abilities. But they needed a leader. If the leader wasn't Johnny Rosa, then who was it?

"Would Gloria arrange her own kidnapping so that Jarman could play Prince Charming on a white horse? It might work, but Gloria lacked the contacts that would make it practical. Jarman? He had everything to gain, but he would attract the full blast of a police investigation. Still, when it was all over, Jarman had benefitted handsomely: he was now a strong suitor for the girl and he had the old man falling all over him with thanks. The engagement was announced. Jarman went into the business. Marriage bells sounded. Nice for Gloria, nice for Jarman. But Jarman isn't the mastermind." My throat was getting a bit dry, and I'd just got started.

"The perfect brain for this job was Russ Warren. Certainly he would have applauded the results. There was the winning over of George to acceptance of Jarman. There was a loud continuing news story, which was a source of embarrassment to news-shy George. There was the exchange of a large sum of money, a further annoyance to his father. Yes, if Russ Warren had been alive at the time of the kidnapping, I'd say that he would have been the brains behind it.

"I'd been thinking that, when I remembered something Ian Todd told me. He said something about how Ashland had blabbed when it was called off *the first time*. So, it had been planned in detail long before that Labour Day weekend. If it had been planned for the Canada Day weekend on the first of July, we have to put Russ Warren back in the cast of characters. He could have worked out the details with Johnny Rosa in the spring. He knew about Pop's hole, and the snatch took place in territory he knew like he knew the gears of a Lotus. He knew all about the cottage at Dittrick Lake. He had driven the route dozens of times. He took Johnny Rosa over it inch by inch. Ian Todd was able to help with a few details about contacting the family. With his knowledge of legal and police procedure, it made an excellent plan perfect. Gloria wasn't told, and none of the other conspirators knew about Russ Warren's role. Only Johnny Rosa. The plan would have been executed on schedule except for one thing. Russ Warren was killed in a car crash just a few days before the long weekend. Johnny called it off. He probably intended to abandon the scheme permanently at first, but after a while he could see that a plan that would work on the first of July weekend would work just as well on the Labour Day weekend. Just as many cars would be on the road from the cottage country and it would be just as hard for the police to catch the kidnappers during the crucial time when they had the money in their possession.

"So, the brain that planned the whole scam had died weeks before it went forward without him. To his credit, it worked just the way he planned it, and nobody got hurt. The invisible flaw was the fact that after the first cancellation, Ashland had done a little bragging. He couldn't know that Johnny was going to dust off Russ Warren's blueprint in a few weeks. So Ashland was the spoiler. They were rounded up, questioned and tried. Johnny Rosa, as the apparent mastermind, drew the longest sentence. When he got out, on a parole which finally came, even for someone as little repentant as Johnny Rosa, there were lots of people waiting for him.

"We know about most of them. We know that Eddie Milano and Muriel Falkirk had a foolproof plan to get their hands on the missing ransom money. We know that Ashland and Todd and Knudsen in their varying ways were waiting to be given their cut. After all, they'd earned it. Johnny knew too that he was still being watched closely not only by the parole board but by the Horsemen. He knew that was the price of parole. He thought he knew how to handle everybody. He established a routine: solid foundry worker by day and loving lover by night. He thought he would be able to hypnotize all the Johnny Rosa-watchers by the humdrumness of his reformed life. He dropped no hint that out there hidden in Pop's hole were two suitcases full of unmarked ten- and twenty-dollar bills. Johnny played a cool hand, and when it suited him to make his move, he had worked it so that he would at the same time shake off Muriel's partner in crime, Eddie Milano. Johnny and Muriel had become more than just partners. Muriel was someone he finally cared about.

"You know how they worked the disappearing act, how I was brought into the case in order to help establish that

Johnny Rosa was dead. In reality, he went to live in a cabin at the back of the Knudsen place. When he was sure that all the fish were biting on the phoney bait, he made his move. He went back to Pop's hole. But, instead of finding the money under the cobwebs of six years, all he found was a lot of Pop's empty bottles.

"That nearly stopped him. It shook him more than anything ever had or would again. He was frustrated, confused, and, most of all, angry. Angry at Muriel, because it had to be Muriel who'd leaked the news. Todd, Ashland and Knudsen were in the clear because they didn't know anything, and the money couldn't have been found by accident. It had to be Muriel. She'd added another cross to the double-cross they'd planned to pull on Eddie Milano. She had to be working with Milano again. He called Muriel and gave her the news, then went around to the apartment. With that beard, he didn't have to worry about being spotted easily. When he let himself in quietly, Muriel was on the phone talking to Eddie, asking to see him. It confirmed all his fears. She'd made a sap of him, cheated him of the ransom money he'd spent six years paying for. Muriel and Eddie'd dished him completely. So he killed her. She should have got away as soon as she'd heard the loot was gone. She could have been out of there in less than a minute.

"When Johnny finally left Muriel's place, a bottle of Crown Royal was sitting, like a calling card, where it couldn't be missed. I know that Eddie had heard from Muriel. According to him, she was all over him like a tent after weeks of putting him off. That's why he paid that visit, saw Muriel in the tub, beyond double and triple crosses. Now she only needed one. Milano took the bottle and backed away from there.

"Then Johnny had a whole night to think it over. He wasn't the sort to lick his wounds on the run. He went through it all step by step, until 'It had to be Muriel' gave way to 'Who else could it have been?' If she and Eddie had snatched the money, why had Muriel waited for his call? Why was she caught on the phone? If she'd known from Eddie that the money'd been picked up, she would have beat it fast.

206

"But who else could have known? Pop's hole had been Russ Warren's idea and he was dead. But Russ could have blabbed before he killed himself in that sportscar. It was an odd idea, but it led over the body of Muriel Falkirk to new and more promising territory. It might even lead him straight to the money. Whom could Russ have told? His father? Not bloody likely. His sister? Possibly. Jarman? Well, now: Jarman was the big benefactor, wasn't he? Maybe Russ Warren couldn't keep it from him at the end. Maybe he told him all about it just before he took that final mad drive in his Lotus. We'll never know now. But see how it works out. Jarman and Gloria look like the only people Russ could have spoken to. So Johnny calls them both to see what happens, giving them a time for the meeting and warning them to come alone. Since Gloria was innocent, she reported her call to me.

"Now if Jarman did have guilty knowledge, but was innocent of any wrongdoing, he could have told me that he'd had a similar call. But he said nothing. So he kept the noon appointment and confronted Johnny Rosa. Rosa was expecting a businessman, who might be willing to pay for his silence. By now, he'd probably given up any idea of getting all of the money. But the possibilities of blackmail were attractive. He even brought along a gun with him, just to provide the scene with all necessary props. He didn't expect that Jarman hadn't come to talk. Jarman let his .32 calibre piece talk for him. With Rosa dead, Jarman was safe. He had known since he first visited Pop's hole that Rosa would eventually find the money missing." I took another gulp of coffee. It was getting cold in my hands. Helen took it from me and refilled it from a stainless steel thermos that looked like it had gone A.W.O.L. from a boardroom. I shifted around, still feeling damp and cold, and sat up a little. She shoved a pillow under my back.

"When I realized that Johnny had been killed around the time of that noon appointment with Gloria, I quizzed her about where she was at the time. That's when Jarman came running to his wife's side confirming that she was in her studio painting. Sounds like the chivalrous thing to do, except when you consider that in giving his wife an alibi he also gave himself one. Gloria would never have suspected his motives in vouching for her like that. That was her blind side." I seemed to be holding my audience, so I took a breath and kept on talking.

"Jarman hadn't waited for Johnny to get out of prison. He had pocketed the money as soon as the coast was clear, leaving behind the suitcases, which he knew would be recognized. According to Tom Avery, George Warren's executive assistant, Jarman began to buy up shares in devious ways soon after the kidnapping. He must have invested part of the money at high interest, bought gold low and watched it soar, or some such thing. It can be checked. Avery did a fast check for George Warren the night before he drowned and found that there were a number of small companies controlled by Jarman using variations of his name. While Johnny Rosa and his pals were sewing mailbags, Jarman was making his fortune. By the time George Warren died, even before his estate made Gloria a very powerful woman, Jarman held enough shares of Archon to debate any of George's decisions without even calling for his wife's shares. Together, they could have moved George to a broom closet.

"What triggered George's fast check on Jarman was one of George's idle wanders through the farm he lived on as a boy. According to several sources, he went up there a few times a year just to look over the place, usually concentrating on the stable where his father used to keep his thoroughbreds. Gloria maintains that only she, Russ and old Pop knew about the hiding place. She was wrong. George knew that his father drank, and he knew where he did it. He'd been talking to the chauffeur about his father's problems with alcohol, so it isn't odd that his rambles around the old place finally took in the barn. Behind the false wall he found the suitcases. He recognized them at once, rushed out in a rage and called Avery to check up on Jarman. George was nobody's fool. He felt sure that it had to be Jarman, as soon as it was clear that the kidnapping was an inside job. He confronted Jarman with the suitcase he'd carried from the barn. He threatened exposure. Jarman, who was only a thief up to this time, decided that

208

George had to be eliminated, the way you take a dead company off the exchange." I was running out of breath, and I'd spread my few facts as thinly as I dared. There was only a little way to go.

"Jarman knew about George's early morning swims. He knew that his breath was short and heart weak. He wasn't taking much of a chance with both doors locked and that nylon net in his hands. It's a very efficient way to get rid of trouble. It took real imagination to see that the net could be used to hold the old man under water until he was dead. That was first kill for Jarman. But he knew that there might be more. By today he was a seasoned killer."

"At least he didn't kill Muriel," Savas said, pulling at his chin in an unnecessary way. It was getting dark in the library. One of the cops by the curtains turned on the overhead lights. "There are still a few loose ends to be accounted for, Benny. If you're feeling up to it, after you get your pants on, we can take a proper statement downtown." I agreed and tried to get up from the couch. Helen was holding my elbow. Savas supervised without actually getting close. When we were half-way to the door, the phone rang. Savas took it, grunted and hung up. "That was the hospital," he said. "Jarman's dead. Mrs. Jarman's in shock and is being kept under a close watch at the hospital for the night. I guess that's all the damage we can do here."

THIRTY-TWO

As soon as we got back to Helen's apartment, she closed the door and leant back against it.

"I'd better change," I said lamely, unwrapping myself from the blanket I'd been wearing. Helen came into the room like a kid looking for the bathroom in the middle of the night.

"Benny, you didn't tell them about me. You left me out completely. You know that I've been unwillingly mixed up in all this." I tried to remember where I'd put my trousers. She stood in front of me with the colour drained from her face.

"Well, let's say you aren't blameless. Did you see where I put my stuff?" I asked.

"Be still for a moment. Benny, I hope you're sure of what you're doing. And I promise I'll try to make it up to you. I will. When you know the circumstances . . ."

"It was Jarman, right? You had Jarman twisting your arm. What could you do?"

"Benny, it was terrible. But we can get clear of it now. Did you hear what that policeman said? He's dead. He can never spoil anything again, not for either of us."

"He put you up to the Valium in my coffee this afternoon. He made you play up to me."

"Yes, at first. That was his plan. But when I met you . . ."

"Sure. A little play-acting in a good cause."

"Yes, at the beginning. I admit it. But now, everything is changed."

"You aren't just whistling Dixie. You were the link between Johnny Rosa and Russ."

"That doesn't matter. Not now."

"Yes it does. I want to hear the truth for once."

"Benny, Benny! Stop. I can't bear any more questions. It's all like a nightmare. I need your help."

"It's a nightmare all right. You didn't plan this ending, did you? Jarman's dead. That wasn't in the script until a few minutes ago. So you're ad libbing a last scene, and it looks a little desperate, Helen."

"No, no. Benny, I love you!" She was shouting through violent sobs which wracked her shoulders and practically shook off the yellow robe.

"First of all there are some things that you'd better tell me. The shooting in the parking lot; that was Jarman, wasn't it?" She nodded her red moist face and tried to talk but couldn't. "Thought that a little excitement might get us better acquainted? Well, it worked fine. You had me up here and tucked up in bed before the rifle cooled off. Yeah, I'd say that was a success. But today, that was below your form. I laid it on a bit strong about my bad swimming. I'm no Tarzan, but I can stay afloat. I guess that helped me fight that drug, the diazepam you hit me with in the coffee." She kept shaking her head, as though I was putting the wrong construction on all of these facts, as though they would add up differently if I let her do the adding. I couldn't stop myself now that I'd started in.

"Jarman was low. We know that. But you were in it with him right from the beginning. You were there that night when Russ laid it all out for you. It was natural for you to be there; you were Russ's girl and Russ was really flying with his plan. You must have been bug-eyed listening. Russ told how it would get him even with his old man, how it would get Jarman to Gloria's bed in a way that the family would approve. There was something for everybody in the scheme. Well, not quite everybody. He'd forgotten about you, hadn't he? But you knew a good thing when you heard it. If there was money going to be passed around, you were sure that you'd get your share."

"That's a lie! I loved Russ. I only went along with it because it was Russ's scheme. But when Bob started telling how the money could be made to grow, how it could be turned into power, it made Russ's plan look like a boy's prank. We'd all been drinking. I must have said something. Russ thought that I was siding with Bob against him. I can't remember the

211

words. I held my hands over my ears. Russ slapped me. Bob pulled him away. I heard the Lotus screech away from the house. I loved Russ. I didn't want him to die!''

"But after he was dead, you pointed out to Jarman how valuable it would be to him to have you working for Gloria. I'm sure that you paid him for suggesting you countless times. After all, in those days, before the kidnapping, Jarman's stock was at an all-time low at the Warren house. He needed a friend at court. So you cooked up a story, something pathetic, something with a smatch of scandal in it. What was it?''

"Stop it! Stop it! You make everything sound so filthy. I loved Russ, I've told you and told you. I wanted his child, but the family wouldn't let me. Gloria was wonderful. We both loved Russ . . .''

"So that was it. An abortion. And so you were installed as a permanent fixture, with a life of comfortable ease leading to who knows what. And then you had your little brainwave, didn't you?''

"What are you talking about?'' She'd stopped crying now. Her faced was livid with hate. We stood in the middle of the room shouting at one another, our robes come undone and flapping about as we leaned like a couple of prizefighters into the battle.

"You'd kept up with Johnny Rosa from high on the hill. You hated to give something away for nothing, so you told him your idea. You convinced your old pal that the plan was as good as ever; you showed him how it would make him rich. Johnny was always easy for you to handle, wasn't he? But then, you never found men difficult. And Johnny liked the idea of you and all that money. So he went ahead on the Labour Day weekend.''

"I only suggested it. I had nothing to do with any part of it. I was here, I wasn't even at the cottage. Why would I want to hurt Gloria? I loved her. She'd been so good to me.''

"You knew she'd live through it. Don't lie any more. There've been too many lies.''

"I didn't have anything to do with it. It was all Johnny!''

"You told Jarman, didn't you, so he'd be ready?''

"I had to. Bob wasn't going to go to the lake. I had to tell him. He was getting depressed, not getting anywhere with Mr. Warren. I had to tell him."

"Then you knew that he'd picked up the money as soon as the dust settled after the kidnapping. You watched him make it grow the way he said he would. You watched him make his way from an outsider into the heart of the family, even closer than you to the old man and to Gloria. You're lucky he didn't kill you. But that's before he discovered how easy it is to kill anyone in the way."

"You bastard, you twist everything. It wasn't like that. Bob loved me. He would do anything for me. Gloria was dear and kind, but she wasn't a woman. Bob and I understood each other."

"I'll bet. I'll bet. Gloria went on with her dream-like pictures, those strange dolls with the knowing faces that knew what she couldn't admit even to herself."

"Oh, shut up. You sound like a soap opera. It was a practical arrangement. It worked for all of us, even if Gloria didn't know anything about it. Why are you tormenting me? Why are you punishing me?" I ignored that, and kept hitting her with more questions.

"Then George Warren found the suitcase in Pop's hole. You hadn't expected that. George must have sailed into the house shouting at the top of his voice. Did you calm him? Did you try your talents on him?"

"You're disgusting."

"Nevertheless. You took the fight out of him, kept him from making any more phone calls. Perhaps you made him a nice bedtime posset with Valium in it, and then prepared some coffee for him before his daily swim. Jarman did the dirty work, of course. You didn't even have to watch that. But I'll bet you were up most of the night stiffening Jarman to do the job. I'll bet you painted a grim picture of failure. Prison, ruin, separation from you.

"Then Johnny came looking for the money and found nothing. In killing Muriel he got rid of a supposed swindler, but it didn't take him to the money, so he got in touch with you very soon after leaving Muriel dead. What did you do? Play for time? Plead ignorance? No. I'll bet you suggested the noon meeting approach. That would give you time to figure out what to do. Johnny was never very strong in the thinking department, so you gave him a plan. By bringing Gloria into it, you were taking a chance, but it kept Johnny from the answer to the big question. And you needed to keep Johnny dangling in the dark until you could get to Jarman. Did you tell Johnny that Jarman was a pushover for a soft touch? Did you tell him that if Jarman had the money, he would cough it up if Johnny raised his voice a little? You didn't tell him about Jarman's gun.''

''Stop it! I won't hear any more. Sending Bob with a gun just evened the sides. Johnny grew up in a tougher league than Bob. Johnny had all the advantages.''

She was running down, and so was I. Sweat was pouring down my chin, and I could see that her forehead was shining. I caught my breath and called: ''Have you got enough, Savas? I'm about played out. I still haven't had a chance to get my pants on.'' Chris Savas appeared through the door with another cop in uniform. He nodded at Helen's open mouth, and asked her to get dressed and come down to the station with him. He could have cautioned her right there and then, but I guess he was saving it for some reason. A rather slight police matron pushed by me into the bedroom. The closed door kept the noise down to a dull roar. I took the temporary absence of women for a cue and finally climbed out of Jarman's bathing suit. My own clothes felt better, but I was still feeling far from good.

''I'll need a ride out of here,'' I said. Savas agreed. Neither of us looked at each other. The battle continued in the bedroom. Between us we felt like two cents. I couldn't even look one of Gloria's doll pictures in the eye. In about five minutes, the door opened and the matron pushed Helen back into the room, dressed again in the gray dress she'd worn earlier in the day. The Liberty scarf somehow got left behind.

THIRTY-THREE

We were back in the café run by Chris's cousin's cousin. The room had been cleared and all the tables had been pushed together. Pete was seated opposite me. Chris was next to him. Between us lay the cold wreckage of a whole roast lamb. The bottles of ouzo were scattered here and there and the bouzouki music was loud on the record player. I'd had about four full helpings of lamb and roast potatoes with eggplant and spinach. The rest of the table was filled with Chris's cousins, uncles and aunts. The owner and chef, Antonaki, wouldn't believe that by now I didn't speak Greek. By the time I was ready to fall asleep in my place, I'd mastered my first Greek words since "eureka". The toast was "yahsoo", and I'd learned to describe my feeling of well-fed completeness as "thavma". Short of that, things were "oréo" or "endaxi". Every time I used one of the words, somebody laughed. I didn't care so much about that. I was wrestling with a larger problem. It was the ouzo. It should be illegal for hard liquor to taste like candy. Ouzo hit me like a binge of licorice. I was fine so long as I didn't try to get up.

"Yahsoo!" called Savas, across the table, his face bright with sweat and drink.

"Yahsoo, yourself," I countered. Pete looked like he was going to fall asleep. I tried another roast potato. It was cooked all the way through. My mother's potatoes always manage to trap a belt of mealiness between an envelope of leather and an uncooked core. This was a surprising change.

"This was cooked thieves' style, Benny," Chris had told me when the lamb came trembling and fragrant to the table an hour earlier.

"Where do the thieves come into it?"

"In the old days, thieves on the run started a fire in a brick oven before daybreak, then they'd clear out the embers, add the food, and let it cook in smokeless safety for the rest of the day."

215

"You seem to know a lot about it for a cop," I said.

"In Cyprus, my family didn't always run to cops. As a matter of fact," he said, drawing himself up to his full height, "I was named after a very great painter." I didn't see how that followed exactly, but I didn't dispute it.

"Tell me, Benny," Pete intoned, leaning across the carcass on the big white platter, "what would you have done if Chris and I'd been out on business when you called for help?"

"I guess I'd have drowned. Don't remind me while I'm eating."

"And you were right about listening at the girl's door. We didn't need an amplifier, that's for sure." Chris was chewing on a rib. Somebody called "yahsas". There was friendly grease on Savas's face. I was feeling full of goodwill and answered "yahsas" back to the other end of the table. Let there be grease on the faces of friends.

"I still can't figure out how you knew that Johnny Rosa'd been holed up at Knudsen's place all that time." I pretended that I didn't hear him. One of Chris's cousins was giving me the eye. Chris'd told me she was a graphic illustrator. She had nice teeth when she smiled.

We all sat silently for a minute, then we all started talking at once. It was an awkward moment, then Pete took the floor while we went back to starting at our plates.

"Ashland's going to be spending the weekend in the cooler." I looked up, mildly interested. "He and that ex-cop Handler had a dust-up on St. Andrew Street last night. Right across from your office. They were coming out of the Russell House just after closing time. Ashland tried to put Handler through a plate-glass window. Handler's in the General, and there's somebody waiting outside his room who wants to examine his licence."

"Couldn't happen to a nicer couple of fellows," I said.

"Benny, what about Rosa's hiding place?" Pete was on his familiar track again. I ignored him by stuffing my face until he tried a different line.

"And how was it you first suspected Helen Blackwood, Benny?" I pushed my empty plate away from me and looked

216

at the red stubble catching the light on Pete's chin. No wonder he kept a second razor in his desk drawer.

"When George Warren drowned," I said, "Helen Blackwood jumped into the pool fully clothed and pulled the body up from the bottom and hauled it to the tile deck, just as you would expect of a trusted old family retainer. She did mouth-to-mouth, she had to be dragged away from the old man. She should have been given a medal, mentioned in dispatches, all that. Only a funny thing happened when she jumped into the pool. She didn't lose her contact lenses. She had to have her eyes open to bring up the body, so why didn't she lose them? She told me that she'd had them for three years 'without a hitch'. She didn't lose them because she wasn't wearing them. And she wasn't wearing them because she knew ahead of time that she was going to have an unscheduled morning swim."

"Well, I'll be damned," said Savas.

"I'll go along with that," added Pete. I shrugged, since I was only shooting from the lip as usual.

"That's why she mixed up the mail that morning. She couldn't see straight."

"But what about Rosa?" Staziak wasn't going to let go. "You keep dodging my question. How did you know he was with Knudsen all that time?" Chris looked over at me like I was going to give him a lesson in the fine art of detection at a private party, and for nothing.

"It's a question of sensitivity," I said, and left it at that.

Since last Friday, I haven't been to the office more than a half dozen times. There was a card from my mother telling me that the family would be back from Florida on Wednesday. She said that property values in Miami were continuing to soar. The prices of condos read like telephone numbers. She reminded me about watering the plants, which set off a chain-reaction which included Vito, Frank and Eddie Milano. My cousin, Melvyn, sent me his best regards.

Gloria Jarman didn't get much for her money. Of course, for her there would be no more worries about money. She was in a state of shock about Bob and Helen for a while. I was sorry about her losing the two people closest to her. It seemed like a dirty trick. I got a late-night telephone call from her last night. She'd been drinking, but she said that she's just been invited to show some pictures at the Venice Biennale, which brought a note of excitement to her voice. She tried to give me expense money to pay for the bullet holes in the Olds, but I told her that that happened before I was on the payroll. I didn't argue about the cheque she mailed. It will keep me out of trouble for a few weeks if I stay away from the card tables. Neither could I stop her giving me one of those crazy paintings of hers, one of those dolls with a cracked head and a Victorian smock. I've got it over at the hotel, but I haven't had the nerve to hang it yet.

Frank Bushmill keeps asking about my girl. I guess he doesn't read the papers. I try to avoid meeting him coming up the stairs and I've stopped looking in on him before I go home. Chris and Pete also keep trying to keep me in touch with what's going on, but sometimes I don't bother to answer the phone. I've been watching a lot of television either at the hotel or over at my parents' condominium. I can turn the sound up louder there. It may be good for the plants. Don't ask me what I've been watching. Another couple of weeks' television should do it, and then I won't have the Februaries any more. Bill Hall, the barber, tells me that the month really is going to end and that the almanac promises an early spring.